True Royals

Book #4 In The Ironborn Saga
by Andrew Cavanagh
© 2024 all rights reserved

Chapter 1
A Long Voyage

'Reporting to the navy office already,' said Sergeant Zander. 'I hoped we'd get a bit more time on leave.'

'Orders I got were quite clear,' said Cedric. 'Begin preparations for a long voyage and report to the admiral at noon today.'

As Cedric and the marines left the Auld Faithful and walked along the docks, Crutch noticed quite a few men chatting with the captains of merchant ships.

'Who are they?' said Crutch.

'Most likely maritime agents,' said Cedric. 'I had one talk to me just yesterday. They arrange deals for ships bringing in cargo to get the best price. At present, there seems to be someone offering a premium for ships bringing in food.'

'That's not too surprising,' said Sergeant Zander. 'War puts pressure on the supply of food, and the battle in Papageenar can't have helped the production of food there.'

They walked down King's Way through the city. Crutch noted the increased number of young soldiers present. New recruits, most likely. There were also wagons headed for the army barracks. With Teevilgrad in chaos, it was likely Ironbay's army planned to attack.

They walked until they came to the navy office.

'Well, here we are,' said Crutch.

'You must be getting used to seeing the admiral by now,' said Zander. 'Seeing Abagail so much.'

'It's not something you ever get used to,' said Crutch.

Corporal Markham escorted them through the navy office building to the admiral's room. They stood waiting outside the large double wooden doors, flanked by two guards in full navy dress.

'Been here before,' said Zander.

'It's like waiting for your own execution,' said Quicksilver.

Memories of Zanithburg with Sergeant Zander and Quicksilver on the gallows, nooses around their necks, flooded back into Crutch's mind. Quicksilver was still missing an ear after being interrogated there.

'What kind of impossible suicide mission are they sending us on this time?' said Crutch.

'A long voyage does not sound promising,' said Cedric.

'If the past is anything to go by, it'll be something deadly,' said Quicksilver.

'You might get to burn things,' said Crutch.

Quicksilver smiled. 'Well, at least that's something to look forward to.'

'Enter,' came the admiral's voice from inside the room.

The two guards opened the large wooden doors and there was Admiral Hastings sitting behind a large wooden desk.

'Come in,' said Admiral Hastings. 'No need to look so worried. This is not what you think.'

Cedric and the marines marched in and stood at attention in front of the admiral.

'At ease, men,' said the admiral. 'I'm sure you're wondering why you're here.'

'We are,' said Cedric.

'I have good news for you. My daughter Abagail seems to think that I've been trying to send you all to your early deaths with your last missions. I'd like to clear that up before we begin.'

'Can I speak?' said Sergeant Zander.

'You can all speak freely today, sergeant.'

'Thank you, admiral,' said Sergeant Zander. 'On our last two missions, we were sent with a hundred and fifty men to fight three thousand Estovians in the jungles of Papageenar. Then we were sent inside the capital of Estovia to retrieve the most valuable military asset Emperor Solokov had. It feels very much like someone is trying to get us killed.'

The admiral frowned. 'You should know that neither of those missions originated in the navy office, and they certainly didn't come from me.'

'With respect, the orders came from you, admiral,' said Cedric.

'That's just the chain of command at work. I'd never send my best ship with my best squad of marines to die.'

'Can you tell us who gave the orders?' said Cedric.

'Not specifically who, but as you can surmise, if the orders did not come from me, there is only one higher authority in Ironbay and its territories.'

'The palace,' said Cedric.

'Precisely.'

'Do you know why?'

'Hard to say,' said the admiral. 'It could be that you turned to a life of piracy. His majesty is not too fond of pirates.'

'We've already explained more than once how we were forced into piracy,' said Cedric.

'Yes, you have,' said the admiral. 'It doesn't reflect on you well that quite a number of pirates who were captured are still calling you the king of pirates, Cedric.'

'Do I need to explain that again?' said Cedric.

'No, you don't,' said the admiral. 'In any case, it appears your troubles with the palace are behind you. They're sending you on a nice, safe mission to Yavenland.'

'Yavenland? That's a three-week voyage each way,' said Sergeant Zander.

'Through heavy seas with highly unpredictable weather,' said Cedric.

'Well, yes, there is that,' said the admiral. 'But when you get there, there won't be any fighting, no hiding behind enemy lines.'

'What do you want us to do?' said Cedric.

'Word has got to the palace that there's a young man there claiming to be the rightful king. All you have to do is find this man and escort him safely back to Ironbay.'

'I suppose this rightful king has an army of followers?' said Sergeant Zander.

'No. Nothing like that,' said the admiral. 'I believe he's there with just a single companion. Not violent, as far as we know.'

'Why do you need us? Why not send a regular navy warship?' said Sergeant Zander.

'A couple of reasons. First, Yavenland is neutral territory. It could be seen as an act of war sending a fully armed warship there. The Auld Faithful is not currently armed which makes it perfect for the mission.'

'Unless the Estovians see the ship that carried away their glowstone,' said Sergeant Zander. 'Then we'll all be back in a prison in Zanithburg or Teevilgrad.'

'Yes, I have authorised a new paint job and some cosmetic changes.'

'It still doesn't seem to warrant sending my marines,' said Cedric.

'That's where this mission gets a little more interesting. Apparently, the palace is not sure exactly where the man claiming to be the rightful king is. Spies say he is constantly on the move. There are temples and places of worship all over Yavenland, in the city and in the jungle.'

'So you want us to find someone hiding in the jungle?' said Sergeant Zander.

'Hopefully it won't come to that,' said the admiral. 'But if that's what's required, then yes.'

'Wonderful,' said Longshot. 'We can never get too much of the bloody jungle.'

The admiral ignored Longshot's sarcasm. 'I hope you can see that I've gone out of my way to insist to the palace that there will be no more suicide missions for you and your ship. Corporal Crutch, perhaps you could convey that to Abagail next time you're together.'

'I will,' said Crutch. 'Thank you, admiral.'

'Thank you, admiral,' said Cedric.

The marines and Cedric left the navy office with more questions than when they arrived.

'Do you really think whoever is trying to kill us has changed their minds?' said Longshot.

'I very much doubt it,' said Cedric. 'The only way that could happen is if the reason they want us dead no longer exists.'

'And we don't know what the reason is,' said Sergeant Zander.

'Unless he's straight out lying, the admiral's not behind trying to get us killed,' said Crutch.

'Straight out lying is always a possibility,' said Cedric. 'You don't become an admiral without learning to play the game of diplomacy and deceit.'

'That's comforting,' said Sergeant Zander.

'Do you really think this will be a nice, safe mission?' said Crutch.

'Not to Yavenland,' said Cedric. 'Yavenland is one of the most remote islands on the map. It's neutral because neither Ironbay nor Estovia are interested in its main produce.'

'Which is?'

'Fish. The mainland is surrounded by reefs. It takes weeks to get there, then you have to get through those reefs to dock. They do export some dried fish, but not enough to be of any major interest to Ironbay. We already have fish.'

'So we have weeks of sailing ahead of us,' said Crutch.

'I haven't told you the worst part yet.'

'What's that?'

'Being so far from any mainland, the ocean is treacherous. Storms blow through there regularly, and there's nothing to slow them down. Get some serious damage to your mast or hull, and you could be adrift for weeks before you can land on a desert island and make repairs.'

'Sounds delightful,' said Sergeant Zander.

'And the ocean is full of sharks and other creatures.'

'It just gets better and better,' said Longshot.

'Sailing to Yavenland is not a voyage,' said Cedric. 'It's an ordeal.'

'I can hardly wait,' said Crutch.

Chapter 2
End Of The Naked Lady

Cedric was at the bow of the Auld Faithful with an axe hacking at the naked lady figure head. Crutch watched, smiling as Cedric took the head off with a final huge blow, his face sweating. The naked lady's head bounced off the hull, then into the water, floating on its side, bobbing up and down, its eye staring back at Cedric as if in silent accusation.

'I can't tell you how much I've wanted to get that abomination off my ship,' said Cedric.

'Can we get the rest off now and start the new figure head?' said the carpenter, who'd watched while Cedric did his chopping.

'Just one more thing,' said Cedric. He leant over the rail and chopped off the two breasts of the figure head. 'Much better. It's all yours.'

'I hope these changes work,' said Crutch. 'I really don't want to end up back in an Estovian prison.'

'That makes two of us,' said Cedric. 'I still have horrible memories of the cuisine we endured in Zanithburg.'

'You mean the cockroaches?' said Crutch.

'And the rat parts.'

'They're more tasty cooked,' said Crutch.

'I'd rather we didn't talk about it.'

Sergeant Zander joined them on the deck. 'Jasper says there's nothing special we need to know about this fake king. She did tell me Yavenland is a melting pot for every crazy cult in the Endless Seas.'

'Where do they all come from?' said Crutch.

'Jasper says missionaries have been landing there for centuries. They're the only people crazy enough to make the trip and stay for more than the time it takes to restock a ship and sail off.'

'When she says crazy, how crazy are we talking?' said Crutch.

'When I was in Yavenland, there was a cult that worshipped those tiny killifish,' said Cedric. 'Once a week, they sacrificed thirteen seagulls to their god, then ate their feathers and their arses.'

'They must be really nuts,' said Crutch. 'Seagull feathers are terrible. Even cooked.'

'Jasper says our biggest threat is likely to be Estovians,' said Sergeant Zander. 'They come and go freely from Yavenland. They may not be too friendly towards any Ironborn they encounter.'

Their conversation was interrupted when Cedric went to speak to a man asking for him at the rail of the Auld Faithful. Crutch listened in when he noticed Cedric losing his usual calm.

'We won't be coming back with any cargo of value,' said Cedric. 'Certainly no food.'

'So you can't tell me where you're going?' said the man.

'Certainly not,' said Cedric. 'And if you ask again or come here again, I'll have you arrested as a spy. I'm very much considering doing that now.'

'No need for that,' said the man. 'I'm just representing a trader looking to secure some goods.'

'Then I've told you what you need to know,' said Cedric.

Crutch and the marines watched the upper window of the building, waiting for a candle to be lit.

'There it is,' whispered Quicksilver. 'Just a little flame, but even the smallest flame has so much promise.'

'Are we going through the window again?' whispered Longshot.

'No, we're not,' whispered Sergeant Zander. 'We're trained in the art of espionage now. We'll be knocking on his front door.'

They made their way up the stairs to the first floor of the building. Crutch knocked softly on the door.

'I told you I'll pay your rent on Friday,' yelled Caleb from inside.

Crutch knocked again.

'For pity's sake.' Caleb opened the door. His eyes went wide with fear and his lips trembled. 'I told you everything I know.'

Crutch and the marines pushed their way through the door. Quicksilver closed it behind them. Boulder stood towering over Caleb. Caleb backed into the wall.

'What is that smell?' said Sergeant Zander.

Crutch looked down and saw liquid dripping down from Caleb's crotch to the leg of his pants.

'He's pissed himself,' said Longshot.

'That really stinks,' said Sergeant Zander. 'What have you been drinking?'

'There's no point asking me more questions. I don't know nothing more,' said Caleb.

'We're inclined to believe you,' said Sergeant Zander. 'Which is why we want your help.'

'Help?'

'Yes. And we're going to pay you for it. One nice, shiny gold sovereign.' Sergeant Zander pulled a gold sovereign out of his pocket and held it in front of Caleb's face.

'I'm not falling for that trick. You lure me down a dark alley with the promise of a sovereign, then you stick a knife in my back.'

'If we wanted to do that, this little room of yours is more than dark enough,' said Sergeant Zander.

'We really do want your help,' said Crutch. 'The gold sovereign's yours if you do what we want.'

'I won't kill anyone for you,' said Caleb.

'No killing,' said Sergeant Zander. 'Just want you to point someone out.'

Chapter 3
Distinguished Gentlemen

Caleb and the marines stood outside The Distinguished Gentleman's Club. Before they left Caleb's room, Sergeant Zander had them all change into disguises he'd brought with him. Now they looked like a comical parody of nobility.

'This is where all those fancy palace staff and nobles go to drink,' said Sergeant Zander.

'How'd you find that out?' said Crutch.

'I've been doing a little espionage,' said Sergeant Zander proudly.

'Sarge and I hid in a privy near the palace for a couple of nights and watched the comings and goings,' said Longshot.

'Two of you crammed into a shitter. That must have been pleasant,' said Crutch.

'Worst two nights of my life,' said Longshot.

'But worth it,' said Sergeant Zander.

'So you say Sarge,' said Longshot, looking unconvinced.

'Are we going inside?' said Crutch.

'We are,' said Sergeant Zander. 'Let me do the talking.'

This will be interesting, thought Crutch. And it was.

'Good evening, my good man,' said Sergeant Zander. 'Me and my noble companions would like a table in your fine establishment.'

The concierge looked them up and down, sniffed, and his head jerked back like someone had punched him in the face.

'I'm afraid we don't have any tables available, sir. We're quite full.'

'You don't understand,' said Sergeant Zander. 'We're nobles. From the nobility. We've got titles and everything.'

'Titles?'

'Yes. I am Lord Zanderith, the third, Count of the Dumiky Isles and holder of the order of the red box.'

'Count of the Dumic…'

'Dumiky Isles,' said Sergeant Zander.

'Yes, I don't believe I've heard of them. Or the order of the red box.'

'That's because they're secret,' said Sergeant Zander. 'But I'm sure you've heard of Lord Boulderdash here.'

'Lord Boulderdash?' said the concierge, looking up at Boulder. 'The name doesn't ring a bell.'

'I'm a lord,' said Boulder.

'Yes, I can see that,' said the concierge, looking from Boulder's body bulging out of the suit that was four sizes two small all the way down to his filthy bare feet. 'As I said, I'm afraid the club is quite full at present.'

Crutch leaned in to the concierge and said quietly, 'We'll sit quietly in a dark corner where no one will notice us, and we'll keep to ourselves.' He slipped the concierge two gold sovereigns.

'Right this way,' said the concierge leading them inside.

'I knew our disguises and fancy titles would work,' whispered Sergeant Zander.

'Yes, well done, Sarge,' whispered Crutch. 'Did you think of maybe getting Boulder a suit that fit him a little better?'

'I did, but these suits are expensive.'

The concierge sat them in a dark corner at the back of the club. From where they sat, they could see anyone who came in.

'Your waiter will be along presently,' said the concierge.

'All you have to do is point out the man who told you to rat us out,' whispered Sergeant Zander.

'I can do that,' whispered Caleb, still trembling with fear and stinking from pissing himself earlier, even after a change of clothes.

'Now who'd like something to drink?' said Sergeant Zander. 'First round's on me.'

The marines cheered.

'Not so loud,' whispered Crutch as all the heads in the club turned towards them.

A waiter came to their table, looking at them like he was assessing a turd that had just got stuck on the bottom of his shoe.

'How may I help you, gentlemen?'

'Just in time,' said Sergeant Zander. 'How much is your honeysap rum, premium?'

'It is not customary for our guests to ask the price of our fare,' said the waiter.

'I don't need the price of a fare,' said Sergeant Zander. 'Just your rum.'

'Of course, sir,' said the waiter. 'Honeysap premium rum is ten sovereigns.'

'Ten sovereigns?' said Sergeant Zander. 'Is that for the whole bottle?'

'Ten sovereigns for one glass of rum, sir.'

'How much for third grade?' said Sergeant Zander.

'Five sovereigns.'

'I could sail to Honeysap Grove and get it myself for that. How much is your cheapest beer?'

'Cheapest?' said the waiter, spitting out the word like it was a rotten piece of meat stuck in his mouth.

'Yes. How much is your cheapest beer?'

'That would be one sovereign a glass,' said the waiter.

'Bring me three beers then.'

'And will your other three acquaintances be drinking too?' said the waiter.

'We'll share the three beers,' said Sergeant Zander.

'Share?'

'Yes, we'll share. You know. Take turns drinking from the same mugs.'

'Very well,' said the waiter, sniffing, then walking off as if he needed to escape the stench of a septic pit.

Crutch noticed one of the gentlemen in the club listened to every word they said. Once the waiter left, the gentleman made his way to their table.

'I am Lord Burnley. Could I sit at your table?'

'Well, we're kind of busy,' said Sergeant Zander.

'Nonsense,' said Lord Burnley, who pulled up one of the ornate wooden chairs and sat down next to Crutch. The lord rubbed at his palm, then showed it to Crutch under the table. Crutch saw the tattoo of a faded heart with the name Rosee written below it.

'Jasper?' whispered Crutch. Jasper nodded.

Crutch turned to Sergeant Zander. 'This is Jasper.'

Sergeant Zander looked at Jasper for a long moment. 'Jasper?' whispered Sergeant Zander.

Jasper nodded, his face scowling. 'What are you idiots doing here?'

'Looking for the person who's trying to kill us,' whispered Sergeant Zander.

'Do you have any idea how out of place you look?' whispered Jasper. 'You could have come in here carrying a big sign with 'bilge scum' painted on it, singing a bawdy sailor's shanty at the top of your lungs, and been more discrete.'

'Singing a shanty,' whispered Sergeant Zander. 'Why didn't I think of that? I've heard nobles like their bawdy songs.'

'You really have no idea, do you?' whispered Jasper.

'I thought we did alright on our disguises,' whispered Sergeant Zander.

'Disguises? You're not even wearing shoes.'

'Might have missed a few minor details,' whispered Sergeant Zander.

'Did you have anything to do with this farce Crutch?' whispered Jasper.

'It was all me,' whispered Sergeant Zander. 'I wanted to show you I could pull off a clandestine mission so you'd be proud of me.'

Jasper giggled. First softly, then he started laughing out loud, head back, hand on stomach laughter that drew the attention of all the tables around them. When he got himself together, he looked at Sergeant Zander.

'Did you come up with names for yourselves?' 'whispered Jasper.

'I'm Lord Zanderith the third,' said Sergeant Zander. 'Count of the Dumiky Isles and holder of the order of the red box.'

'Yes,' said Jasper, forcing down a laugh. 'Any others?'

'And this is Lord Boulderdash.'

Jasper exploded with laughter. Tears ran down his face.

'Oh, Zandy, you are so adorably inept at this kind of thing, it's comical.'

'There he is,' said Caleb.

'Don't point at him,' whispered Jasper.

'Seems I'm not quite as inept as you thought,' whispered Sergeant Zander.

Jasper raised his eyebrows.

'Who is that?' whispered Crutch.

'That,' whispered Jasper, 'is the assistant to the king's chief counsel.'

'Why does he want us dead?' whispered Longshot.

'Could be him, but more likely it'd be the king's chief counsel,' whispered Jasper. 'His assistant is just his trained monkey. In any case, you've got what you came for. Let me see if I can clean up the mess you made. Follow me.'

Jasper took them to the concierge at the front of The Distinguished Gentleman's Club.

'Edgar, my good man. My friends here have played the most delightful practical joke on me,' said Jasper. 'Thank you for letting them in.' Jasper slipped Edgar several gold sovereigns.

'My pleasure, Lord Burnley,' said the concierge. 'I guessed from the look of them and the *smell* of them that they were on some kind of caper.'

'Indeed, they were,' said Jasper. 'Most I've laughed in years.'

When they got outside, Jasper took Sergeant Zander aside. Crutch and the marines could still hear them talking.

'Get out of these clothes as soon as you can and make sure you're not followed,' said Jasper. 'If someone is trying to kill you, you don't want to make it easy for them.'

'We will,' said Sergeant Zander.

'How long until you ship out to Yavenland?' said Jasper.

'We sail tomorrow,' said Sergeant Zander.

'Would you like to come around tonight, Zandy?'

'Will you be…?'

'Yes, I will,' said Jasper.

'I'd love to.'

'See you later then, Zandy,' said Jasper as he walked off.

'So nice to see you happy with someone,' said Longshot.

'Even if it is a man,' said Quicksilver.

'Laugh it up, boys. I'm a full-on nancy boy now. Does that make you happy?'

'We're not judging you,' said Longshot.

'Love is love,' said Boulder.

Crutch smiled. Jasper must have explained to Sergeant Zander why keeping her disguise as a man was so important in Ironbay. Part of that disguise would mean any of Jasper's lovers would have to pretend to like men.

It might go against every fibre of his being for Sergeant Zander to do it, but it seemed it was a burden he would willingly endure for Jasper's safety. Love is love.

Chapter 4
We're Always Saying Goodbye

With preparations for the voyage, Cedric and the marines didn't have a chance to discuss why the king's chief counsel might want them dead. The following day, they loaded on the final supplies, then it was time to leave.

The families of the crew had gathered on the docks in front of the Auld Faithful to say their last farewells before they sailed.

'We're on the docks with a hundred people saying goodbye,' said Crutch. 'I'm fairly certain you don't need to worry about Abagail's safety.'

'The admiral was quite particular that I should make sure his daughter doesn't go on board the Auld Faithful,' said Corporal Levi.

Crutch stared at the corporal for a few seconds.

'I'll go wait for Abagail over there next to those fishing nets,' said Corporal Levi.

'Thank you,' said Crutch.

Abagail looked at Crutch with those ocean blue eyes.

'It feels like we're always saying goodbye.'

'At least I'm not going to war or into enemy territory this time,' said Crutch.

'No, but Yavenland is a long, long way from Ironbay,' said Abagail.

'I'll miss you every second I'm away from you,' said Crutch.

'I'll miss you too. So much.' A tear slid down her cheek. 'I'm sorry. I promised myself I wouldn't cry.'

'It's okay,' said Crutch. 'I feel like crying too.'

'That'd be quite a sight, Ironbay's Iron Cross winner crying his eyes out,' said Abagail, wiping away a tear with a handkerchief.

'It wouldn't be the first time I've cried over missing you,' said Crutch.

'Really?' said Abagail.

'Really.'

Abagail pulled in close to Crutch and hugged him. 'Stay safe.'

'I'll try,' said Crutch.

'No, you won't,' said Abagail. 'Come back alive, at least.'

'I'm good at that.'

'Yes, you are,' said Abagail. 'You really are.' She gave him the best smile she could.

Crutch put his hand on her cheek. 'I'd go through anything to get back to you.'

The crew were nervous about the voyage to Yavenland. That night in the galley, after leaving Ironbay, the sailors started sharing stories they heard.

'I heard the storms can last for days, and there are reefs a good lookout can't see in broad daylight, let alone in a storm,' said one deckhand.

'Plenty of ships never make it there or never make it back,' said another.

'It's not just the weather,' said another sailor. 'There are foul beasts in the oceans. Things that are born from evil.'

'That's just superstitious nonsense,' said Sergeant Zander.

'Maybe nonsense, maybe not. I had a friend who saw the shadow wraith.'

'The shadow wraith is just a bedtime story made to scare children into behaving themselves,' said Sergeant Zander.

'He swears he saw it,' said the sailor. 'Killed two of his friends. Left 'em like empty shells, the life sucked out of 'em, their dead faces stuck like they was screaming.'

'I've heard that children's tale too,' said Sergeant Zander.

'True enough. But my friend's not the type to make up stories.'

Other crew members told stories of the perils of the voyage to Yavenland. Crutch put most of it down to the crew being anxious about the trip, but he did remember Cedric had told him there were sharks and other creatures in the ocean. Cedric wasn't the type to make up stories, either.

Cedric gave Crutch a book to read called Pilgrimage to Yavenland.

'It's the only book I've got about the island,' said Cedric. You might get some useful insights from it.

Cedric also gave Crutch lessons on how to captain and steer a ship. When the wind and the sea were gentle, Cedric put Crutch in command for the first time.

Crutch held onto the wheel and looked ahead. This was much harder than Cedric or Captain Featherstone had made it look. He kept the movements of a couple of dozen crewmen in his head, the bearing of the ship, watched for patches of wind on the water, checked the sails for trim, and scanned the water ahead for hazards.

'How do you keep it all in your head?' said Crutch.

'Practice,' said Cedric. 'After a while, it becomes second nature. Also, you have to know your crew and put people in charge of tasks you know they can handle. That gives you less problems to worry about.'

The crew of the Auld Faithful were trained, disciplined, and solid. Crutch tried to imagine what it must be like to captain a ship where the crew were a disorganised rabble. It didn't bear thinking about. The captain would go insane.

Crutch had an hour at the helm before Cedric took command back. By then, Crutch's head was spinning with the effort.

Chapter 5
Raft On The Water

When he was back below deck, Crutch heard the lookout blow his whistle.

'Raft on the water, captain. There's someone on it.'

Crutch and the marines came on deck and saw the raft bobbing in the waves. A bedraggled looking sailor was lashed with rope to a raft made of the wood from a ship's deck. Some poor souls had met their end in this vast ocean, and this sailor was likely the only one left alive.

The sailor lay on his side, groaning. The Auld Faithful crew yelled at him, but he didn't stir or acknowledge them.

'Marines, can you get him aboard?' said Cedric.

'We can and we will,' said Sergeant Zander.

'Show some caution,' said Cedric. 'You don't know what's in the water.'

'Will do, captain.'

The waves were big enough that Sergeant Zander and Crutch both tied ropes around themselves as the crew threw out the climbing ropes.

'Can you bring us close, captain?' yelled Sergeant Zander.

'Yes sergeant.'

'Okay, Crutch,' said Sergeant Zander. 'We'll get as close as we can, then you and I will try to jump to the raft. We might have to swim. Once we're on, we'll hang on tight, and the crew can drag us back. Then I'll untie, and we can use my rope to haul this sailor up the side.'

'Got it,' said Crutch.

They both climbed down the side of the hull. When the raft was five yards out, Cedric said, 'That's as close as I can get. Any closer, and the waves will throw the ship into the raft.'

'Thank you, captain,' yelled Sergeant Zander.

Sergeant Zander went first, jumping as far as he could. He took a huge leap and landed in the water, two yards from the raft. He swam the rest of the way and clambered on, being careful not to tip the raft over.

Crutch leapt as far as he could, but with the waves and the movement of the ship, he was still four yards from the raft. When he hit the water and came up swimming, he saw something that sent a chill down his spine.

'Shark!' yelled the lookout.

Crutch felt for his walking cane and realised he'd left it on the deck of the Auld Faithful along with his dagger. That seemed perfectly reasonable at the time. Why would you need a walking cane or a weapon to swim to a raft and haul it back?

Sergeant Zander clung onto the raft with both hands and yelled, 'Haul me in!'

Crutch swam for the raft at full speed. He could see the fin of the shark coming towards him over the water to the right, and the raft in front of him. Then the fin disappeared.

Crutch was almost to the raft when he saw a huge shape under him coming up fast. He hadn't counted on the raft moving towards him with such speed, and when he got to it, the wooden boards on the side of the raft smacked him in the face. The shape got bigger, and it was so close he could see the shark's mouth open, ready to bite him in half.

Sergeant Zander clung to the raft with one hand and grabbed Crutch's arm with the other. Their arms clasped, and with a desperate heave, Sergeant Zander hauled Crutch on to the raft. The shark came right behind him and hit the bottom of the raft, lifting up its side and rolling all three of them off the other side and into the water.

'Haul them in now!' yelled Cedric.

Sergeant Zander grabbed the sailor under both arms as he was dragged back towards the ship. Crutch was behind him, looking down, looking around. Where did the shark go?

Then he saw it coming across the water, its mouth open again. Crutch could see Boulder on the deck hauling in the line tied to his waist, but the shark moved faster than Boulder could pull him in.

As the shark got to him, Crutch used his good leg and kicked its eye, pushing himself sideways. The shark reacted to being kicked in the eye, giving up its attack, but its momentum kept it going forward. As it closed its mouth, it bit through Crutch's rope, then went down under the surface of the water.

Sergeant Zander and the man from the raft were out of Crutch's reach in seconds. He was stuck between the raft and the ship with at least one shark in the water, probably more. Crutch could hope that kicking the shark in the eye had put it off attacking him, but he knew that was unlikely.

Crutch started swimming for the Auld Faithful with everything he had. Sergeant Zander was still in the water, holding on to the climbing ropes with one hand and the sailor from the raft with the other. Longshot and Quicksilver climbed down to help lift the sailor up onto the deck.

Crutch swam over a wave and saw that the ship was only four yards away. Out of the corner of his eye, he saw the shark coming from his right, heading straight for him. He swam at full speed, his lungs burning with the effort, but he knew he couldn't make it. The shark surfaced, its mouth wide open. Crutch could see its jagged teeth just a foot away.

Then he saw Boulder leaping off the railing, a spear out in front of him, held in both his hands. The spear went straight through the top of the shark's head, the sheer force of it pushing the head of the spear through its bottom jaw.

Boulder pulled up the spear and thrust it down into the shark's head again, blood ballooning into the water from the wound.

'More sharks!' yelled the lookout.

They'd be coming for the blood, thought Crutch. Boulder was in the water now, and the shark flopped to its side with Boulder still hanging on to the spear in its head.

'Get to the ship,' yelled Crutch. He could see fins in the water, at least four, maybe more, and he knew in just a few seconds there'd be sharks here biting at anything they found.

Boulder and Crutch swam for the Auld Faithful and clambered up the climbing ropes. When Crutch was halfway up, he saw a shark coming straight for him. It launched itself out of the water, jaws open wide. Sergeant Zander and Longshot above him grabbed his arms and pulled him over the rail, and the shark snapped its jaws shut, just missing his feet.

The sailor lay there on the deck, groaning.

'He's not big on conversation,' said Sergeant Zander. 'Hasn't said a word since I got to him. Just that groan.'

'Get him to the sick bay,' said Doc. 'Hopefully he'll pick up after a day or two of beer and rations.'

Crutch went down to the sick bay a few hours later to check on the sailor. He saw Doc watching over him. The sailor still made that low groan.

'Any improvement?'

'I'm afraid not,' said Doc.

'Do you think he'll get better?' said Crutch.

'I hope so. I'd hate to think you risked your lives for nothing.'

Chapter 6
A Strange Death

'You're on your back chained to a sacrificial altar,' said Sergeant Zander. 'The cult leader is leaning over you with one of those long curvy daggers they use to sacrifice people with. What do you do?'

It was an hour before dawn, and, as always, Crutch trained with the marines. Today's session seemed to be based around all the stories Sergeant Zander had heard or read in works of fiction about religious sects and cults. Still, Sergeant Zander's training sessions had a strange way of turning out to be very useful in the field.

'I tell him his god has given me a message for him,' said Longshot.

'Right,' said Sergeant Zander.

'Then I whisper it real soft.'

'Right.'

'Then, when he gets his ear close to hear what I'm saying, I headbutt him,' said Longshot.

'Brilliant,' said Sergeant Zander. 'Doesn't get you off the altar, but at least you're giving him a broken nose as a memento of your death. What about you, Quicksilver?'

'As they're catching me to take me to the altar, I get a little ball of bluefire and hide it in my hand like this so they can't see it. Then, when they least expect it, I set it off with my finger.'

'I'm not sure how setting your hand and your arm on fire is going to help you,' said Sergeant Zander.

'If I used a bigger ball of bluefire, it would make a much bigger fire.'

'So you set your whole body on fire?'

'Well yes.'

'How does setting your whole body on fire help you?'

'Well, I haven't quite worked through the details yet,' said Quicksilver. 'You just sprung this on us now.'

'Marines think on their feet and come up with solutions on the spot,' said Sergeant Zander. 'You don't have a few hours to think things through when some crazed cult leader has his knife hovering over you about to plunge it into your chest and use your blood as an aperitif. Boulder, do you have any ideas?'

'Pull out the chains,' said Boulder.

'Nice work, Boulder. At least one of us will be getting out of this alive. Crutch?'

'I think Longshot has the best idea,' said Crutch. 'Pretending their god has spoken to you and you have some kind of message might buy you some time. You'd have to pay close attention to the language they use and try to get into their heads.'

'That could work,' said Sergeant Zander.

'But it would make much more sense to stop them from chaining you to the altar in the first place,' said Crutch. 'At some point, they have to untie you or take off your shackles to get you chained to that altar. And how did they catch you in the first place? Where were they holding you? Should have been all kinds of opportunities to get away long before you ended up lying on your back, waiting for the dagger to fall.'

'Good,' said Sergeant Zander. 'Exactly the solution I hoped for. So today we work on how to get away from a group that's taken you captive.'

'Can I use bluefire?' said Quicksilver.

'You can,' said Sergeant Zander. 'As much as you want.'

'Nice,' said Quicksilver.

Their training was interrupted when the ship's bell began ringing.

Cedric appeared on the deck. 'What is it?'

'Someone's died, captain,' said the deckhand who rang the bell.

'Was he killed?' said Cedric.

'Hard to say, captain. Something's not right about it, that's for sure.'

'Show me,' said Cedric.

Crutch and the marines followed Cedric below to the crew's quarters. He was there in a hammock, a young deckhand with his mouth and his eyes wide open as if he was screaming, but no sound was coming out. His skin was pale and grey.

Doc inspected the deckhand.

'What is it?' said Cedric. 'Not the pox?'

'No, definitely not the pox,' said Cedric, checking his palms and behind his ears. 'I've never seen anything like this. I'll have to check my Medica Compendia.'

'I want this room scrubbed with vinegar,' said Cedric. And no one is to come back in here until the body's removed.'

'I'd like to thoroughly inspect the body if I could,' said Doc.

'How long do you need?' said Cedric.

'Perhaps an hour.'

'You can have an hour, but not a minute more.'

'Thank you captain,' said Doc.

'When Doc is finished, I want this man buried at sea. Assume he's infectious and observe all the protocols,' said Cedric.

The burial was a sad affair. Cedric and two men wore cloth masks over their faces while Cedric said a few words over the body. The rest of the crew stood on the other side of the deck near the rail, paying their respects from a distance as the two deckhands slid the body over the side into the water.

Deckhands, with buckets and vinegar, scrubbed the plank the body had been on and the deck around it.

Sergeant Zander and Crutch went to check on the sailor they'd saved from the raft again. He was right there in the sick bay where Crutch had seen him the last time, lying on his side and groaning.

'Doesn't look like he's improved any,' said Sergeant Zander.

'I'm afraid not,' said Doc. 'Maybe a bit more colour in his cheeks this morning, but that's faded since. I've tried, but I can't get him to eat or drink.'

'So you don't think he's going to make it?' said Crutch.

'Not unless he gets some food and liquids down. By the look of his body, he should be dead already. I'm not sure how he's holding on.'

'What about the deckhand who died today?' said Sergeant Zander.

'I've checked all my textbooks, and I can't find anything like it,' said Doc. 'A perfectly healthy young man dies in the night without a mark on him.'

'Could he have choked to death?'

'Nothing in his throat and no marks on his neck either, if that's what you're thinking.'

'I don't know what to think,' said Sergeant Zander.

Chapter 7
When Death Calls Again

That night, Crutch woke to screaming coming from the crew's quarters. He and the marines ran to find Niklas, one of the deckhands, standing at the hammock of Zak, another deckhand.

'He's not breathing!'

Cedric entered the crew quarters. 'Please stop that screaming and shouting. Keep your head together, Niklas.'

'Sorry, captain,' said Niklas.

'Has anyone called the ship's doctor?' said Cedric.

'I'll get him,' said Sergeant Zander.

Crutch looked at Zak in the hammock. It was the same as the man last night. Eyes and mouth wide open, as if he was screaming.

Doc came in and inspected the body, shaking his head. Doc checked the hands, the feet, and turned him over, looking for any kind of sign.

'Anything?' said Cedric.

'Same as the last time,' said Doc. 'Nothing. Just like the last man. There's not a mark on him. This man shouldn't be dead.'

'But he is,' said Cedric.

Cedric ordered the same precautions: scrubbing of the crew quarters with vinegar, and burial at sea. After the morning meal, Doc inspected the entire crew one by one, looking for anything, any kind of sign of what had killed two healthy men.

'I can't find anything,' he said to Cedric after he'd finished.

The crew were restless, with rumours spreading.

'Could be the curse of the black mariner,' said one deckhand.

'I reckon it's that sailor from the raft,' said another. 'All this trouble started after he got on board.'

'Don't think he can be doing much just lying there in the sick bay moaning.'

'Maybe he brought a curse with him.'

'The curse might have brought on of them shadow wraiths.'

'That's it, alright. The curse of the black mariner.'

That night, none of the crew wanted to go to sleep in case they were the next to be taken. Eventually, Cedric ordered them out of the galley and into their hammocks.

'I can't have men staying up all night,' said Cedric. 'They'll be falling out of the rigging and off the side of the ship from exhaustion.'

Crutch fell asleep easily enough. He was in a hammock surrounded by his friends. Sure beat trying to sleep in an alley in Ironbay.

Crutch woke with his mouth open. He tried to draw in air, but it was as if the breath was sucked from his lungs. As his eyes focused, he could see something over him. Some kind of man or beast. It was black as the darkest night, its red eyes glowing with malevolence.

The thing's mouth was on him, open and dragging the very life from him through Cruth's mouth and his eyes. Crutch tried to yell, to scream, but nothing would come out. He moved his hand to his belt to get his dagger. It was an agony trying to move.

Crutch got his hand to the dagger and brought it up, fighting some unseen force as if something had his arm and pushed back against him. He pushed the dagger into the face of the dark beast, right into those red eyes, but Crutch's dagger and his hand passed straight through it. He forced his hand down lower and tried stabbing at the beast's body, but Crutch's hand and his dagger passed straight through the body like it was a dark black mist.

Crutch tried to think. His mind moved slow as molasses and was filled with fear, but he had to push that fear down and force himself to get his brains to work.

What was this thing?

He looked at its whole body. It was like a man, but bigger without legs. The bottom half of its body kept going out the cabin door, as far as he could see. If he followed that body, would it lead him to some way out of this nightmare? It was all he had.

He rolled out of his hammock and dropped to the floor with a painful thud. He tried pounding on the floor with his fist, but no one stirred. It was like the beast had the whole crew in the thralls of some deep slumber, and no amount of noise would wake them.

Crutch was on his own.

He crawled to the open cabin door, the beast staying on him like a giant leech sucking the breath and the life from him. Crutch tried to breathe, but no breath would come. With every second that passed, he got weaker.

He kept crawling, all the time looking at the black face and red eyes of the beast right in front of him, drawing from him, killing him. Crutch followed the bottom half of the body down the corridor, past the door to the crew quarters. Inch by inch, Crutch forced his body to move, with every inch an agony that got more laboured and difficult the longer that beast was on him.

He followed that black trail right to the sick bay. It came out of the man they'd saved from the raft. He still lay there, still groaning. But now the groan was much louder. It was like the sailor was screaming at the top of his lungs, right into his ear.

Crutch crawled closer, his lungs empty, burning, every muscle in his body screaming for relief. He pushed against the crippling fatigue, and got onto his knees next to the moaning sailor.

He could see the beast now; see it was part of the moaning sailor. The beast came out of the sailor, and the sailor was the beast.

With the last ounce of strength left in his body, Crutch raised his dagger and plunged it into the moaning sailor's chest. The moaning changed to a high-pitched shrieking like fingernails down a blackboard that went on and on. Crutch's ears rang with the awful sound.

The black beast disappeared into the sailor's mouth, shrieking as it went. Crutch felt his eyes go dim, then he fell, everything fading to black.

Chapter 8
Black As Tar

'Are you okay, Crutch? Please be okay.'

Crutch came to and focused his eyes. Doc and Boulder kneeled over him. The rest of the crew, including Cedric, were further back. Crutch's mind was foggy. He tried to get his thoughts together, then he remembered.

'The beast! Is it still here?' He sat up and looked at the hammock in the sick bay. There was the groaning man on his back with Crutch's dagger in his chest, blood dripping to the floor.

'What beast?' said Cedric.

'There was a black beast. It tried to suck the life out of me. It must have been what killed the other deckhands.'

'He's still delirious,' said Doc.

'I'm not delirious,' said Crutch, getting to his feet, still unsteady, with Boulder holding him under one arm.

'You should take it easy,' said Doc.

'Let me see it,' said Crutch, walking towards the sailor the beast had disappeared into. He got within arm's length and prodded it. Nothing. Then he got closer and looked at its face. The sailor had his mouth and eyes open wide as if he was screaming.

Crutch grabbed the body with both shoulders and shook it. Nothing. 'I think it's dead.'

'He's dead alright,' said Doc. 'A dagger through the heart will do that.'

'You don't understand,' said Crutch. 'A huge black beast made of some kind of mist came out of this man. It tried to suck the life out of me.'

'So you killed him?' said Cedric.

'Yes. No. I killed the beast.'

'Alright,' said Cedric. 'Everyone leave me alone with Doc and Crutch.'

'I'm glad you're alright,' said Boulder before leaving with the rest of the crew.

'What do you make of this Doc?' said Cedric.

'Hallucinations maybe. That can happen if you get some bad ham.'

'It's not hallucinations,' said Crutch. 'I know what happened to me.'

'Well, he seems convinced,' said Cedric. 'And Crutch has never lied to me.'

'I don't know how this man was still alive, so I'm not surprised he's dead,' said Doc. 'But the manner of his death is a concern.'

'We'll bury him at sea and hope this is the last of the deaths. Crutch, I'll speak to you later, when you've had a chance to think things through. You don't seem hurt. I'm glad of that.'

Doc leaned over the body of the man from the raft. He looked closely at the dagger in his heart and slowly slid it out. The blood on it was black as tar.

Cedric and the marines gathered in the galley. Cedric wanted to know exactly what happened.

'It was like a thick mist but black,' said Crutch. 'In the shape of a man.'

'Why didn't you yell for help?' said Sergeant Zander.

'I tried,' said Crutch. 'But that thing had a hold of my mind. It had a hold of everyone's mind. When I fell to the floor, nobody woke. I tried pounding on the deck with my fist, but all of you slept right through it.'

'Sounds like some kind of evil curse,' said Longshot.

'Did you try setting it on fire?' said Quicksilver.

'I was in the marines quarters below deck,' said Crutch. 'And I didn't have any bluefire.'

'That's why one of those things could never get me,' said Quicksilver. 'I always carry some bluefire with me.'

'We'd be stuck on the ocean in the burned-out hulk of a ship,' said Sergeant Zander, 'but at least you'd be safe.'

'I'm not sure how safe,' said Crutch. 'It was a mist. Mists don't burn.'

'You never know if something will burn unless you try it,' said Quicksilver.

'So how did you kill this spirit?' said Cedric.

'I crawled to the man we saved from the raft. He was screaming at the top of his lungs with the black thing coming out of him.'

'So you stabbed him?' said Cedric.

'Yes. And the thing went back into him, screaming as it went.'

'How do we know it's dead?' said Sergeant Zander.

'We don't,' said Cedric. 'But the man it went into, we just put over the side. Let's hope that's the end of it.'

Chapter 9
Without Killing?

An hour before dawn, the marines gathered on deck for their training. Crutch felt a little worse for wear, and Sergeant Zander told him he could sit out if he wanted, but Crutch hated missing training. It was the lesson that you missed that might get you killed.

'Yavenland is neutral but not lawless,' said Sergeant Zander. If we get into trouble, we can't leave a pile of dead bodies behind us. That will get us and the Auld Faithful in trouble that might be hard to get out of.

'So today we train disabling an opponent without killing him. Anyone have any ideas?'

'Set him on fire,' said Quicksilver.

'Disable an opponent *without* killing *or* maiming him,' said Sergeant Zander.

'Does that mean cutting one of his legs off is out?' said Longshot.

'Yes, it does.'

'Set his house on fire,' said Quicksilver.

'Creative,' said Sergeant Zander, 'but destruction of property can get us thrown in jail or executed in Yavenland too.'

'What sort of crazy laws will they come up with next?' said Quicksilver.

'Anyone have any other ideas?'

'Burn his… '

'Anyone apart from Quicksilver.'

Crutch tried to think hard, but disabling someone without killing them? All their training was based around killing someone as quickly and efficiently as they could. Not killing someone was a weird idea. Not injuring them at all was just crazy.

'You can grab them by the neck,' said Boulder.

'Good work, Boulder.'

Boulder smiled. 'If they have a weapon or they struggle too much, you just shake them a little bit.'

'Very good. Anyone else?'

Crutch, Quicksilver, and Longshot stood there, shaking their heads. They had nothing.

'Then we have some training to do. First choke holds.'

'Oh, choke holds,' said Longshot. 'I know how to do those.'

'Yes,' said Sergeant Zander. 'But the secret is, you let go of them when they pass out before you kill them.'

'Before you kill them?' said Longshot, struggling to grasp the concept.

'Yes. You just hold them, then you let them go after they go limp.'

'But then they'll get up again.'

'Exactly,' said Sergeant Zander. 'But it'll take them a few minutes before they come to. In that time, they'll be immobilised.'

'Wow,' said Longshot. 'Who would've thought.'

'Can you use your dagger too?' said Quicksilver.

'I did mention we're trying *not* to kill our opponent.'

'Oh yeh.'

'So that's the first thing you can use,' said Sergeant Zander. 'Choke holds. Now what do you do if someone threatens you with a knife or tries to stab you and you don't want to hurt them?'

'Sorry, Sarge, that doesn't make sense,' said Longshot.

'Yes, I know,' said Sergeant Zander, 'but just hypothetically.'

'Chop his arm off,' said Quicksilver.

Good idea, thought Crutch. He can't stab you if his dagger arm isn't attached to his body.

'We're trying not to maim him,' said Sergeant Zander.

'Can we kick him in the crotch?' said Crutch.

'We can,' said Sergeant Zander. 'Nice one, Crutch.'

'Then jump on top of him, grab his head, and slam it into the ground four or five times,' said Crutch.

'That would do some serious damage,' said Sergeant Zander. 'So no, you can't do that.'

'But the guy just pulled a knife on me.'

'They'll still throw you in jail,' said Sergeant Zander.

'I told you the laws were crazy,' said Quicksilver.

'What you can do,' said Sergeant Zander, 'is grab him just above the elbow here.' Sergeant Zander grabbed Quicksilver's arm and pressed hard. Quicksilver yelped, dropped to his knees, pulled out a dagger with his other arm, and held it to Sergeant Zander's groin.

'Keep pressing there, Sarge, and you'll be talking in a high, squeaky voice the rest of your life.'

Sergeant Zander grabbed Quicksilver's dagger hand in the same spot and pressed hard. Quicksilver yelped again and dropped the dagger.

'That's the pressure point right there,' said Sergeant Zander. 'Press hard enough, and your opponent will be too busy screaming to fight you.'

'I believe you!' yelled Quicksilver. 'Just stop. For pity's sake, stop!'

Sergeant Zander let Quicksilver go. 'There are other pressure points on your body too. Today we'll practice our choke holds and pressure points.'

'To stop someone trying to kill us without hurting them?' said Longshot.

'Exactly.'

'Doesn't this sound like a really bad idea to you?'

Chapter 10
The Storm

Cedric had warned them that the worst storms would likely hit in the stretch of the Endless Seas they now passed through. Crutch heard the thunder rumbling and saw the storm coming before it got to them. A wide front of heavy rain that he could hear advanced towards them at speed.

'Furl the sails,' said Cedric. 'Leave me just enough to sail with.'

The deckhands moved on the rigging with speed, not wanting to get caught when the storm they could see coming hit them.

When it did hit, the world exploded in driving rain and a wind that howled through the rigging and battered the Auld Faithful, blowing her down almost to her side with a combination of fierce gusts of wind and huge waves. Most of the deckhands retreated below, closing the hatches as they went.

Crutch and the marines stayed, lashing themselves with ropes to anything sturdy on deck to avoid being washed overboard. Cedric lashed himself to the wheel of the ship, standing there peering through the driving rain the best he could as the Auld Faithful was tossed like a cork on the ocean.

The waves were bigger than anything Crutch had ever seen. It was like sailing up a mountain, crashing through the top of the wave, then surfing down from the summit to the trough of the wave on the other side.

Cedric struggled to keep the Auld Faithful pointed into the waves, his arms straining with the effort. If a wave this huge caught them broadside, it would capsize the ship in an instant, then the ship would be smashed to pieces by the waves that came after it.

'What can we do to help?' yelled Crutch.

'Make me a sea anchor,' yelled Cedric. 'Do you know how to do that?'

The marines did. They went down the hatch, water pouring through behind them as they climbed down into the hold. They found a sail and ropes and tied the ends with the help of the crew below.

'Roll up the sail before we go back on deck,' said Sergeant Zander. 'Up there, we'll never hold the sail in those winds.'

They rolled up the sail and tied a rope around it so it couldn't be blown open, then the marines hauled it up the ladder onto the deck, each of them carrying a few feet of it. Sergeant Zander used a highwayman's hitch, a knot that would allow him to release the rope when he needed to unroll the sail.

When Crutch came up onto the deck, the wind blew him off his feet. He scrabbled across the deck, never letting go of the sail. A wave crashed over the deck, and in seconds the marines all clung to the rail, the rolled-up sail against them.

'Get to the stern,' yelled Sergeant Zander as the wave subsided.

They went as quick as they could, staggering across the deck as the ship pitched and rolled in the heavy seas. As they moved, Crutch clung on to anything he could find near him with one hand, holding the sail under his arm in the other.

Another wave hit, and Quicksilver was tossed across the deck, barely keeping hold of the sail as he smashed into the rail. Longshot pulled at the sail to help him get back to his feet. Somehow, they got to the stern without being washed overboard.

They each took the lines tied to the sail and secured them to the stern. Then they slid the still-rolled sail over the stern. It blew off into the water, with Sergeant Zander hanging on to the line that kept it from blowing open. He pulled on the line with a yank, releasing the highwayman's hitch and the sail blew open.

The next wave crashed over it, and it was underwater, dragging behind the ship. The Auld Faithful still moved fast, rocking and pitching in the waves, but it had slowed.

'Good work,' yelled Cedric. 'Now get yourselves secured.'

The marines didn't have to be told twice. Crutch and the marines each tied themselves near the bridge so they could help Cedric when he needed it.

Crutch looked up the main mast. The lookout up there pitched and rolled with the storm. He had tied his legs and his waist to the mast. Crutch tried to imagine how much worse it must be up there.

Waves crashed over the deck, leaving Crutch gasping for air, and the driving rain stung his face. Somehow, Cedric kept the Auld Faithful upright. When Crutch thought the storm would never end, the wind stopped and the sea calmed down to steady waves.

'We're in the eye of the storm,' said Cedric. 'You marines should arm yourselves.'

Crutch stayed on deck while the other marines went below to retrieve their weapons. Crutch already had his walking cane and his dagger.

As Boulder came back on deck with his axe, other deckhands came up, taking this opportunity to check lines and anything else shaken loose or damaged by the storm.

'Something in the water dead ahead,' yelled the lookout.

Cedric turned immediately to avoid whatever it was.

'What is it?' said Crutch, trying to get a fix on what was in the water.

'Monsters follow the storms out here looking for easy prey,' said Cedric.

Crutch could see it now. Like an octopus, but bigger. Much bigger. He could just make out tentacles in the water and the top of its head.

'Stay away from the rails!' yelled Cedric.

But he was too late. One of the tentacles came over the rail at the bow and coiled around a deckhand, dragging him overboard as he screamed.

Longshot came out of a hatch and already had his bow up, shooting at the sea monster's head. His first arrow bounced off its thick hide. Crutch and the marines ran towards the monster. Boulder hacked at one of its tentacles with his axe.

The monster was now half on the bow and half in the water, it's huge tentacles feeling across the deck, looking for more victims. Crutch could see its massive mouth open just off the rail.

Quicksilver was the closest and pulled out a ball of bluefire. He was about to throw when one of the monster's tentacles smacked his arm and hurled the bluefire into the ocean. Another tentacle wrapped around Quicksilver's waist and began dragging him over the side.

Boulder hacked at the tentacle that held Quicksilver, drawing blood in a huge gash, but the monster didn't stop. Crutch could see the deckhand the monster had already snatched, shaken violently in the water, drowned and lifeless, the air crushed from him with the force of the tentacles, and his body broken with the brutality of its shaking.

'Get its eyes!' yelled Sergeant Zander as Boulder hacked at the monster's tentacles.

Crutch leaned over the rail, stabbing at the monster's eyes with the blade of his walking cane. But the monster was just beyond range. He climbed over the rail and hung out so he could reach further, cane in one hand clinging on to the rail with his other arm.

Crutch saw the tentacles around Quicksilver, then saw another deckhand snatched off the deck. The sea monster lifted Quicksilver and moved him towards its open mouth. It planned on making a meal of him right here. Its tentacle was now out of Boulder's reach, so he began hacking at any tentacles he could reach.

Quicksilver was a foot from the monster's open mouth when he pulled out two balls of bluefire and threw them into the hole.

A blast of blue fire came out of its mouth, and it slid off the bow of the Auld Faithful taking Quicksilver and the deckhand with it in its tentacles. Crutch jumped into the water after it and swam for Quicksilver, who disappeared under the surface.

CHAPTER 11
RIDING THE STORM

Crutch grabbed Quicksilver's hand and went under the water with him. With his other hand, Crutch cut at the suckers holding Quicksilver's body to the monster. They sank fast. Crutch felt the pressure on his ears and his chest as they went deeper into the ocean.

He cut and sawed through the suckers on the tentacle going around Quicksilver's waist. Crutch went as fast as he could, but he had to be careful not to cut into Quicksilver. He was almost out of breath and starting to feel dizzy when Quicksilver finally came free.

Crutch slid his walking cane into his belt as they swam for the surface. They broke the surface of the water, and Crutch took in a mouthful of salt water as a wave broke over him. He coughed hard and tried to focus his eyes, disoriented. Where was the Auld Faithful?

Quicksilver grabbed him under the shoulder. 'This way, Crutch,' he said.

From the deck, Crutch could hear Cedric yelling.

'We're nearly through the eye of the storm. Get those men out of the water!'

The crew threw out two lines for Crutch and Quicksilver. Crutch clung onto a rope with his hands and legs as he was hauled on board. He could hear the storm coming as the crew helped him over the rail.

The first waves hit, and driving rain stung Crutch's face. Quicksilver was still in the water. A big wave lifted him up and smashed him into the hull at the bow. The crew hauled him in and got him over the rail just as another wave crashed over the bow and washed them all to the rail on the other side.

'Get below decks or tie yourselves on,' yelled Cedric. 'And get those hatches closed.'

Crutch lashed himself to the deck near Cedric at the wheel. For some reason, he felt safer when he was close to Cedric, as if just having him in sight might save him if the Auld Faithful was ripped apart in the waves.

Crutch knew that made no sense. He'd drown just as surely with or without Cedric nearby, but your thoughts are a strange thing. They go where they're not supposed to and can hide when you need them most.

'Reef ahead,' yelled the lookout.

'Any clear water?' yelled Cedric.

'There's a narrow channel to starboard,' yelled the lookout.

Cedric steered the Auld Faithful to starboard. Crutch could see him peering through the rain, looking for the reef and the channel. Crutch looked too, his eyes and his face stinging from the force of the rain, like needles jabbing into him over and over.

The way the waves broke, they couldn't change direction to avoid the reef. That would make it impossible to navigate the waves.

Crutch saw the reef first. He could hear the waves breaking over it, and see the spray flying ten yards in the air. Then he saw the channel and pointed to it.

'I see it,' said Cedric.

The Auld Faithful pitched and rocked from side to side, and its bow crashed through the waves as it went. The waves weren't as high as in the first half of the storm, but going through a channel between two reefs, they wouldn't need to be. One wave broadside at the wrong time or one miscalculation from Cedric, and they'd be slammed onto the reef, and the Auld Faithful would be ripped to pieces.

The chance of them surviving on the longboats or the wreckage of the ship in this storm was nonexistent. Their only hope was to rely on Cedric to get them through.

As they got closer, Crutch could see their chances of getting through that channel were terrible. The waves ran at enough of an angle to the channel that they moved from one side of the reef then broke on the other.

And the channel was no more than thirty yards across. It would take a true feat of helmsmanship to get them through.

'Can we turn back?' yelled Crutch.

'There's no turning back,' said Cedric, his eyes fixed on the reef and the channel. 'This would be a good time to say your prayers.'

No matter how bad things got Cedric had never told Crutch to pray before. He wished he had time to pray, but they came down a huge wave, and they were on the reef before Crutch had an opportunity.

As they came down the wave and the water was sucked ahead of them, Crutch could see the reef on both sides of the Auld Faithful. The ocean floor must be just a yard or two beneath the ship's hull.

The wave pushed the Auld Faithful towards the reef on the starboard side. Cedric steered the ship to port, so it headed in that direction but was washed to starboard by the wave at the same time.

Crutch had seen people sail a dinghy this way, usually just before they were swamped by a wave or capsized. He'd never imagined you could do it on a ship.

If the wave caught the Auld Faithful full force, they'd be thrown over and smashed onto the reef. If Cedric went too far to port or the wave pushed the ship too far to starboard, that would end with them smashed on the reef too. At this speed, almost broadside in the trough of the wave they were on, there was no margin for error. Cedric had to sail perfectly.

Crutch watched the reef rushing by on both sides of the ship, praying they wouldn't hit, and wincing with every sound that suggested they might have. He heard the wave beside them crash over the reef with tremendous force. Cedric kept his head moving, first to the wave, then to the reef off the port side, then to the reef off the starboard side.

The Auld Faithful surfed through the trough of the wave for what must have been a few seconds but felt like an hour. Then the lookout called out, 'We're through, captain!'

A deckhand on the bridge looked at Cedric and said, 'That's the greatest piece of sailing I've ever seen.'

Cedric nodded, still scanning the huge waves ahead and around them.

'We're not through this storm yet.'

Cedric stayed at the wheel for the next two hours, riding the Auld Faithful through the swell. There were no more reefs or rocks to avoid. When the storm and the swells eased, Cedric untied himself from the wheel and handed over comman to his first mate.

'Well done, captain,' said the first mate.

The deckhands lined his path to the hatch, making a line one each side. As he walked past, his arms and legs trembling with fatigue, each of them stood at attention and saluted.

'Thank you, men,' said Cedric.

'No other captain could have got us through that,' said one deckhand.

'The way he took us across the bottom of that wave through that reef. I've never seen anything like it,' said another.

Great helmsmanship aside, Crutch hoped he'd never see anything like it again.

Chapter 12
The City Of Temples

There were no more huge storms on their voyage. They'd used up their fresh provisions, and the crew now ate mainly hard tack, beans, and yams. There was still plenty of rum, even if it was watered down. Cedric had made sure they had plenty of food for the voyage.

'Never get tired of these beans,' said Longshot as the marines ate in the galley.

'I'll be glad when we reach dry land,' said Sergeant Zander. 'Cedric wasn't exaggerating when he said this voyage would be an ordeal.'

'If we do our job well, we'll be doing all this again, just going the other way,' said Longshot.

'That's something to look forward to,' said Quicksilver.

Before they got to the harbour of Zuren in Yavenland, Cedric had to navigate the Auld Faithful through the reefs around the mainland.

'I can see why they have so many fish,' said Sergeant Zander. 'The reefs are full of them.'

'The reefs also provide natural protection for the harbour,' said Cedric. 'Imagine trying to sail a fleet in here to invade or put Zuren under siege.'

'You'd have to take the ships in one at a time,' said Crutch.

'Yes, and the welcome you got would not be friendly,' said Cedric.

Crutch looked at the line of ballistas on the docks of Zuren and around the bay.

'Zuren's gunners train every day against moving targets in the bay,' said Cedric. 'I've heard they never miss.'

Off in the distance, Crutch could see small islands dotted around the mainland of Zuren. On one island was a ship. It was so far away, he couldn't make out what type. Going towards the small island was a sailing skiff.

'What's that island over there with the ship?' said Crutch.

'If you sail a warship to Yavenland, they don't let you in the harbour. You have to anchor off one of those small islands. Then you get to Zuren on one of those skiffs.'

'How do they load their cargo on and off the ships?' said Crutch.

'The same way.'

'That can't be easy.'

'It's damned inconvenient. That's why warships avoid using the port if they can. Yavenland has stayed neutral, partly because there's nothing here of value to Estovia or Ironbay, and partly because they have a combination of natural and planned defences.'

'Who sails the skiffs to load and unload cargo?' said Crutch.

'The Yavenlanders. They're masters at sailing small boats. Also masters of using them to sabotage large ships.'

'Really?' said Sergeant Zander.

'They can sail and row those skiffs in the pitch black of night and sabotage a ship to make it unsailable,' said Cedric.

'So they have specially trained sailors for that?' said Sergeant Zander.

'Every Yavenlander over the age of fourteen is trained for that,' said Cedric. 'They take their defence very seriously.'

'I'm looking forward to meeting some of these Yavenlanders,' said Sergeant Zander. 'Might pick up a few new tricks.'

'They might not be what you expect,' said Cedric.

'Why is that?'

'All Yavenlanders are trained sailors and saboteurs, but many won't kill or harm others. They take their religions and their gods very seriously here in Zuren.'

'So they can destroy a ship, but they won't stab you in the guts?' said Sergeant Zander.

'Some will, many won't,' said Cedric.

As they sailed to the docks, Crutch could see the roofs of the city and men and women in robes milling around in the streets off the docks.

'Zuren, the City of Temples,' said Cedric.

And there were temples. Crutch could see them everywhere, dotted among the other buildings. He could see at least four nestled in between the warehouses on the docks.

'You can't take weapons into the city of Zuren,' said Cedric. Only Yavenlanders are armed.'

'You heard Cedric,' said Sergeant Zander. 'Leave your weapons behind.'

'Do we have to?' said Longshot, taking his bow off his shoulder.

'If they catch you in the city with a weapon, they'll throw you in a dungeon cell overnight then give you a whipping the next morning,' said Cedric.

'How many lashes?' said Longshot.

'Leave your weapons behind,' said Sergeant Zander. 'That's an order. And that includes your bluefire Quicksilver.'

'Bluefire's not a weapon,' said Quicksilver.

'Hundreds of dead Estovians would disagree with that.'

No one was happy about going into a city they didn't know unarmed. Crutch had his cane, and he kept a dagger hidden under his belt and shirt too.

'Time to find this king,' said Sergeant Zander as they made their way down the gangplank onto the docks.

'Where should we start?' said Crutch.

They looked around at the mass of people. Sailors loading ships, pilgrims in robes, and then there were Yavenlanders. You could tell who they were immediately. Just regular clothes, and most of them openly carried weapons.

'Let's start by talking to a local,' said Sergeant Zander.

They saw a tall, muscular woman carrying a longsword in a sheath on her belt, along with four daggers.

'Let me do the talking,' said Longshot.

'Okay,' said Sergeant Zander.

The marines walked up to the woman. Longshot smiled.

'I love your weapons,' he said.

The woman smiled. 'You can never have too many daggers.'

'I'm Longshot. We're from the Ironbay royal marines.'

'I'm Captain Sophia Kellar. I've heard of the Ironbay marines.' She looked Longshot up and down, then her eyes locked onto his. 'Are the legends true or just made up crap?'

'They're true,' said Longshot. 'Is it true all you Yavenlanders train from the age of fourteen?'

'We do,' said Sophia. 'Can't kill shit unless you practice.'

'I've heard you can sail a skiff in the dark,' said Longshot.

'We can,' said Sophia. 'It's not as hard as it sounds. Most of the time, you're just sitting on your arse.'

'Can you use that sword?'

'Does a monkey shit from the trees?' said Sophia.

'I'm gonna guess yes on that,' said Longshot.

Sophia Laughed. 'What's your name, Ironborn marine?'

'They call me Longshot.'

'So you're good with a bow?'

'Yes, and some other things.'

'I bet you are. I can shoot a bow, but my accuracy is crap past two hundred yards,' said Sophia.

'Longshot shot a man inside a building through the eye once at five hundred yards. In the dark,' said Sergeant Zander.

'Five hundred and fifty,' said Longshot. 'But he was smoking a pipe, so that gave me something to aim at.'

'What a load of crap,' said Sophia. 'Do all you Ironborn marines make up shit stories?' said Sophia.

'I have to admit it does sound like a story, but Longshot can do anything with a bow,' said Sergeant Zander.

'You might be good,' said Sophia, 'but a five hundred and fifty yard shot sounds ridiculous. I'm not one of your silly Ironborn girls.'

'No, you're not,' said Longshot, still looking directly into her eyes.

'I've noticed that men who make big claims are trying to distract attention from their tiny cocks,' said Sophia.

'I'm not doing that,' said Longshot.

'Well, at least you're willing to admit you have a tiny cock,' said Sophia. 'That's something.'

'No,' said Longshot. 'It's not...'

Sophia laughed. 'I'm just messing with you, Longshot. If you come up to our training range here in Zuren,' said Sophia, 'we'll see exactly how good you are.'

'I'd love to,' said Longshot. 'Maybe you could teach me how you sail in the dark.'

'If you can teach me how to shoot a bow over three hundred yards, I'll teach you how to sail in the dark,' said Sophia. 'But I'm not holding my breath.'

'We're hoping you could give us some directions,' said Sergeant Zander.

'Do I look like a guide?' said Sophia.

'Well no,' said Sergeant Zander. 'But you are a local.'

'Okay,' said Sophia. 'I'll play your game. What are you looking for?'

'The biggest temple in Yavenland?' said Sergeant Zander. 'A temple with a following big enough for a king.'

'The biggest following isn't in a temple; it's in a tent.'

'A tent?'

'An old circus tent. It's right at the edge of the city.'

'And the man who leads it, is he a king?'

'To the idiot pilgrims who follow him, he is,' said Sophia.

'Sounds good,' said Sergeant Zander. 'Where is it, and how do we get there?'

'If you go now, you should make their next service. Just go down the main street here, all the way to the end, and you'll see the tent. You can't miss it. Unless you're blind or stupid.'

'Thank you,' said Sergeant Zander.

'I'll see you again soon, Longshot,' said Sophia. 'Then you can show me how full of shit you are.'

'I will,' said Longshot. 'I mean, I won't.'

Sophia laughed, moving into the crowd.

'I think I'm in love,' said Longshot as they walked off.

Chapter 13
Do You Want To Be Healed?

When they got to the end of the main street in Yavenland, they saw why Sophia told them they couldn't miss it. The tent was massive. More than high enough to hold elephants and big enough to hold hundreds of people.

'Looks like our king has already got himself a good following,' said Sergeant Zander.

They could hear singing coming from inside the tent. When they got to the entrance, people each side smiled and welcomed them.

'Welcome to the home of eternal wealth,' said one.

'Our prayers are with you,' said another.

'Thank you,' said Sergeant Zander. 'Can you tell me who your king is here?'

'That would be Father Jeremiah. He leads the faithful.'

'Sounds promising,' said Sergeant Zander as they sat down on a seat made from wooden planks.

A group of women stood on a large stage set up at the rear of the tent, singing harmonies. Crutch couldn't make out all the words, but they seemed to be singing about joining the wealth of the eternal or something along those lines. The words didn't really make sense.

'I like their singing,' said Boulder. 'It sounds pretty.'

A man came onto the stage, and applause rose from the audience.

'Welcome to the home of eternal wealth,' he said, and the pilgrims in the tent started clapping and cheering.

'They're easy to please,' said Crutch.

'Here is the man you've all been waiting to hear. The king of eternal wealth, Father Jeremiah!'

'The king,' said Sergeant Zander. 'Haven't been in Yavenland a day, and it looks like our search is already over.'

A man came onto the stage wearing a robe covered in what looked like gems, or at least coloured glass made to look like gems. He had gold rings with jewels on every finger and a gold chain around his neck.

'Brothers and sisters,' he said. 'Are you tired of poverty? Are you tired of scrabbling in the dirt for morsels to eat? Do you want to give up the chains of your present and walk to a future of wealth and prosperity?'

The pilgrims in the room cheered and yelled, 'Yes!' to everything Father Jeremiah said.

'Do you want to be healed of your afflictions?' said Father Jeremiah. 'Do you want to say goodbye to your pain and welcome in a life of glorious health?'

That sounded pretty good to Crutch.

'Do you think he could heal my leg?' said Crutch.

'Maybe,' said Sergeant Zander. 'There might be all kinds of magic here that you would never find in Ironbay.'

'The secret to life and wealth is giving,' said Father Jeremiah. 'What you give comes back to you ten times over, a hundred times over. Now listen to me, brothers and sisters. This is the greatest secret to wealth. You must give and give and give until it hurts. Then you must give some more.'

The followers of Brother Jeremiah passed wooden buckets down each row of seats.

'Remember, giving is the secret of life and wealth,' said Father Jeremiah. 'There is no bigger secret.'

When the bucket got to Sergeant Zander, he looked in it, looked up, and said, 'There's coins in here.'

The other marines looked in the bucket. It was a third full of coins. Mostly coppers, some pieces of silver, and a scattering of gold coins.

'I was poor, my brothers,' said Father Jeremiah. 'But once I started giving away the few coppers I did have, it came back to me multiplied.'

'Sounds like King Jeremiah is giving us this money,' said Crutch. 'Maybe he's trying to make his subjects happy.'

'Sounds good to me,' said Quicksilver, taking a handful of coins and stuffing them in his pocket.

All the marines took a handful, smiling and laughing as they did.

'Feel the joy of giving,' said Father Jeremiah.

'Oh, we do,' said Sergeant Zander. 'We really do.'

There were a few coins left at the bottom of the bucket.

'Leave some for the other people,' said Crutch.

They passed the bucket on, and the next people in line looked down into it and looked back at the marines, frowning. The marines smiled and waved back at them.

'I like this king,' said Boulder. 'He gives you pretty coins.'

'I like him too,' said Crutch. In Ironbay, the best you got begging on the street was a copper or two. No one ever let him take handfuls of coin.

'Who out there needs to feel the power of healing?' said Father Jeremiah. 'If you suffer, if you're afflicted, then come forward and you will be healed!'

'That sounds good,' said Crutch.

An old man hobbled up to the stage. Father Jeremiah helped him up the steps.

'What is it that afflicts you, my brother?'

The old man said something to Father Jeremiah Crutch couldn't hear. Then Father Jeremiah said, 'His shoulders give him pain, and he can't get his hands over his head. But today we're going to heal you, brother.'

A huge cheer went up from the pilgrims in the tent.

'Can you feel that?' said Father Jeremiah. 'That's the power of the people in here sending you their healing energy.'

The singers behind Father Jeremiah sang louder, pounding their feet on the stage in time. The pilgrims in the tent started clapping in time.

Father Jeremiah grabbed the hands of the old man and slowly lifted them up, high over his head.

'Pain be gone!' yelled Father Jeremiah.

The old man smiled and yelled, 'I'm healed!'

Father Jeremiah pushed the head of the old man, so he fell into the arms of two of Father Jeremiah's followers standing behind him. Then they lowered the old man to the floor of the stage.

'So he healed his arms but ruined his legs?' said Quicksilver.

'Looks like it,' said Sergeant Zander. 'I'm not sure how this healing thing works.'

More people walked, ran, hobbled, or were carried on stage. Father Jeremiah talked to them one at a time.

'How much is healing your hand worth to you, brother?' he said to one.

'Everything I've got,' said the man with a crippled hand.

The man couldn't work with that, thought Crutch. It would be worth a lot to him to get it healed.

'Give all you can,' said Father Jeremiah, 'and it will be given back to you multiplied.'

The man emptied his pockets into a wooden bucket one of Father Jeremiah's followers put in front of him, then Father Jeremiah pushed the man's head, and the man fell into the arms of two of Father Jeremiah's followers.

They carried him off the stage and out the back of the tent while two more followers took their place on the stage.

There was a long procession of people, all giving their money, then being pushed over by Father Jeremiah. When the people coming up to the stage were done, Father Jeremiah preached to the people in the tent again.

'Do we have any more of you out there who need a healing? Anyone sick, injured, or crippled?'

'Crutch is crippled,' said Boulder.

'Would you like me to heal your friend?' said Father Jeremiah.

'Yes,' said Boulder.

'Would you like me to heal his legs so he can walk freely?'

'Yes,' said Boulder. 'Yes please.'

'Then bring him up here!' said Father Jeremiah.

Chapter 14
How Much Can You Give?

Boulder picked Crutch up and carried him to the stage.

'How much is it worth to see your friend run free in Yavenland? How much can you give for your friend?' One of Father Jeremiah's followers pushed a bucket in front of Boulder.

Boulder wasn't sure what Father Jeremiah meant.

'How much coin do you have in your pockets?' whispered Father Jeremiah.

Boulder pulled out all the coins he'd taken from the bucket handed around earlier.

Father Jeremiah smiled and whispered, 'Put that in the bucket.'

Boulder did as he was told, then Father Jeremiah pushed Crutch's head. Crutch was ready for this. He wasn't going to let Father Jeremiah ruin his other leg, so he'd planted himself firmly on the stage with one foot and his walking stick.

Father Jeremiah pushed Crutch's head again, and Crutch was just as firmly planted the second time.

'I can only heal your legs if you let me push you over,' whispered Father Jeremiah.

'And it won't ruin my other leg?' said Crutch.

'No,' whispered Father Jeremiah. 'This is a healing.'

'Okay,' said Crutch.

Father Jeremiah pushed Crutch a third time, and this time Crutch fell into the arms of Father Jeremiah's followers behind him. They carried him over the stage and out the back of the tent, with

Boulder right behind him. The rest of the marines joined him a few seconds later.

Father Jeremiah's followers lowered him onto the ground and went back into the tent, past two burly lurking guards at the back entrance.

'Did it work?' said Sergeant Zander.

Crutch felt his leg. It didn't feel any different. He got to his feet and tried to put weight on it. Then he tried to walk on it and fell on his side.

'Didn't do a thing,' said Crutch.

'Are you sure?' said Quicksilver. 'We saw all those other people get healed.'

Crutch got to his feet again and tried his bad leg again.

'It's just as bad as it's always been,' said Crutch.

'Maybe he did something wrong,' said Longshot. 'We should go tell him to give it another go.'

They headed for the back entrance to the tent, and the two guards blocked their way.

'You don't go back in,' said the big one.

'You don't understand,' said Sergeant Zander. 'King Jeremiah in there tried to heal our friend Crutch, and he must have done something wrong because Crutch's leg isn't better. We just want him to take another shot at it.'

'You don't go back in,' said the big guard again.

'You know what,' said Sergeant Zander to the marines. 'This might be a good chance to use those pressure points you've been practicing.

'Okay,' said Boulder, and grabbed the big guard by the throat.

The other guard turned to punch Boulder, and as soon as he did, Longshot came around behind him and put him into a chokehold. Then Longshot pulled out his dagger and stuck it into the guard's head.

The big guard Boulder held by the neck pulled a dagger too, so Boulder leaned over, smashed the guard's head into the ground, then pulled him up and smashed his head into the ground again for good measure.

'How was that?' said Longshot.

'You're getting better,' said Sergeant Zander. 'But you're not supposed to kill them.'

'I knew I forgot something,' said Longshot.

'Sorry, Sergeant Zander,' said Boulder.

'Also, I told you not to bring weapons with you, Longshot. That includes daggers.'

'Sorry Sarge.'

'Who else is carrying a dagger?'

All the marines, including Crutch, looked down at the ground with guilt on their faces.

'Sorry Sarge.'

'Are you carrying a dagger, Sarge?'

'I might have a couple,' said Sergeant Zander. 'But that's not the point. Hide these bodies the best you can. Then we'll go in and have a little chat with King Jeremiah.'

'I think he calls himself Father Jeremiah,' said Crutch.

'So he's not a king?'

'I didn't say that,' said Crutch. 'He just doesn't call himself a king.'

'We'll have a chat about that too,' said Sergeant Zander.

When the marines came back into the tent and onto the stage, Father Jeremiah took one look at them and cringed back in fear.

'You shouldn't be in here. What happened to my guards?'

'They had a problem with their blood,' said Sergeant Zander.

'Their blood?'

'Not enough left in their bodies to keep themselves breathing,' said Sergeant Zander.

'We tried to use pressure points to keep them alive, but we're not very good at it,' said Longshot.

'Sorry,' said Boulder.

'What do you want?' said Father Jeremiah.

'Our friend Crutch here hasn't been healed. Look at his leg. It's the same as before you tried to heal him.'

'There's nothing I can do about that.'

'You could take another shot at healing him.'

'Okay,' said Father Jeremiah. 'I'll try.' Father Jeremiah walked up to Crutch, put his hand on Crutch's head, and yelled, 'Be healed!' He looked at Crutch, hopefully. 'Anything?'

Crutch felt his leg and tried to put some weight on it. 'Nothing,' he said.

'Try again,' said Sergeant Zander. 'This time, try a bit harder.'

Father Jeremiah motioned to his singers, and they started singing an uptempo song with gusto. Then Father Jeremiah whipped his hands around in the air, pushed forward on Crutch's forehead, and yelled at the top of his voice, 'Be healed!'

Crutch tried his leg. 'Still nothing.'

'Why are you holding out on us?' said Sergeant Zander.

Boulder moved to use the pulpit on the front of the stage.

'I'm not holding out on you, I promise,' said Father Jeremiah.

'Then why did you heal all those other people and not Crutch?' said Sergeant Zander.

Boulder picked up the pulpit and threw it. It landed five feet away with a crunch and smashed into a dozen pieces.

'You better start explaining, or Boulder's gonna break you into a million pieces like that pulpit of yours,' said Sergeant Zander as Boulder moved over to Father Jeremiah, towering over him.

'Crutch is my friend,' said Boulder, flexing his fists.

'I never healed anyone!' yelled Father Jeremiah. 'I never healed anyone. It's all just a pantomime to get people's money.'

Gasps came from the pilgrims in the crowd.

'So you can't heal Crutch?' said Sergeant Zander.

'I can't heal anyone,' said Father Jeremiah. 'Please don't hit me.'

'Are you the rightful king of Ironbay?' said Sergeant Zander.

'I'm not the king of anything, except for getting money out of gullible people.'

'Well, that's disappointing,' said Longshot.

'Do you want me to burn the tent down?' said Quicksilver. 'I've got some bluefire.'

'Why did you bring bluefire with you to a church service?'

'You never know when you might need it.'

'The problem is the preacher, not the tent,' said Sergeant Zander. 'No burning. Let's get out of here.'

Quicksilver looked at Sergeant Zander, disappointed.

'Sorry this didn't work out for you, Crutch,' said Longshot.

'Sorry Crutch,' said Boulder.

'It's okay,' said Crutch, more aware than ever that he limped and used a cane as he walked. 'I'm the same I was half an hour ago.'

For a few moments, Crutch had thought about what life might be like with two good legs. He thought about dancing with Abagail or walking freely without using a cane. But these were just fanciful ideas, like the kind of fairy tale mothers told their children.

Wave a magic wand, and everything will be okay. Crutch knew the world didn't work that way, and it never could work that way. He was a cripple, and he'd learned to live with it. Hoping for anything different was just a waste of his thoughts.

He'd already been lucky beyond anything he'd ever dreamed of when he met Abagail, and that was more than anything he ever could have hoped for. It was enough.

Chapter 15
Pressure Points

That night, Captain Sophia Kellar came to the Auld Faithful, asking to see the marines.

'What can we do to help you?' said Sergeant Zander as the marines stood with her on the docks.

'We had a report of two dead bodies at Father Jeremiah's tent. Also, we can't find Father Jeremiah anywhere,' said Sophia.

'We tried to use pressure points,' said Boulder.

'Pressure points?' said Sophia.

'You use them to disable an attacker without killing them,' said Sergeant Zander.

'So these two men attacked you?' said Sophia.

'They did,' said Sergeant Zander.

'And you used these pressure points on them?'

'We tried,' said Longshot, 'but we're not very good at it.'

'One man had a stab hole in the side of this head,' said Sophia.

'Sorry,' said Longshot.

'The other had his skull smashed in. That's a shit ton of pressure.'

'Sorry,' said Boulder.

'No great loss,' said Sophia. 'We got reports Father Jeremiah ripped off the people who went to his tents by taking money for fake healings. They got what was coming to them.'

'They did,' said Longshot, smiling. Sophia smiled back.

'So who wants to learn how to sail in the dark?' said Sophia.

The Auld Faithful had two longboats you could convert into a sailing dinghy. Longshot had to promise Cedric they wouldn't damage the boat sailing around in the harbour of Zuren on a moonless night.

As Crutch, Sergeant Zander, Longshot, and Sophia mounted the mast in the longboat, Sophia asked questions.

'Have you marines been together long?' said Sophia.

'Many years,' said Sergeant Zander. 'Crutch has been with us about three years.'

'Seen many campaigns?'

'Only a few we can tell you about,' said Sergeant Zander.

'Which was the most recent?' said Sophia.

'That would be the Kona track,' said Sergeant Zander.

Sophia looked at them like they were idiots. 'You fought at the Kona track?'

'Sergeant Zander led the forces there,' said Longshot. 'Until he got injured and Corporal Crutch took over.'

'By the gods. How much of an idiot do you think I am?' said Sophia. 'I might live in Yavenland, but I know the Kona track was fought by Ironborn reservists, not marines.'

'It's true,' said Longshot. 'We transported the reservists on the Auld Faithful to Port Vela.'

'The Auld Faithful? That old merchant ship you sailed into the harbour?' said Sophia.

'It's faster than it looks,' said Longshot.

'It would have to be,' said Sophia. 'If it went as slow as it looks, you'd be sunk at the bottom of the bay. So I suppose you trained these reservists to fight?'

'We trained them on the way to Port Vela,' said Longshot. 'Then Sergeant Zander taught them how to make traps while we climbed up the Kona track.'

Sophia looked at Longshot for a long moment, then she broke out laughing. 'That story is so ridiculously overblown, you must be compensating for a cock the size of a hamster.'

'No, I'm not,' said Longshot, flustered.

'So tell me,' said Sophia. 'How did you fight off three thousand Estovians?'

Crutch had enough of this. Many good men had died on that track, and he didn't think it should be a source of amusement for anyone.

'We set traps for them, burned them, and stood shoulder to shoulder and made them pay for every inch of the track with their blood,' said Crutch. 'Most of the reservists and Papageenans who fought with us are still back there on the track, dead, but somehow we survived it.'

Sophia looked at Crutch, shock on her face. Crutch realised he might have gone too far. Sophia was just trying to have some fun with them in her coarse way. He decided to change tack.

'At the end of it all,' said Crutch, 'we beat General Vasilev to death with our tiny hamster cocks.'

Sophia burst into laughter. 'You had me going there for a minute. Next, you'll be telling me you went to Teevilgrad and fought Emperor Solokov.'

'We did!' said Longshot.

'Stop it,' said Sophia, laughing even harder.

Sergeant Zander unfurled the sail on the longboat. 'Shall we sail?'

Longshot sat next to Sophia. Crutch couldn't make out much of his face in the dark, but before they extinguished their torch he wore a silly-looking smile.

'Sailing in the dark is simple enough,' said Sophia. 'First, you pick your target and the place you launch from.'

'How do you pick a launching place?' said Longshot.

'You need to get somewhere so you can sail to your target.'

'A ship,' said Longshot.

'Yes, so you can sail to the ship without having to tack. You need to sail in one direction the whole way so you can judge how far you've sailed.'

'So the real secret is knowing how fast your boat is going and how long it will take to get to your target?' said Crutch.

'Your friend here is clever,' said Sophia.

'He's one of the smartest people I've ever met,' said Longshot. 'Brave too. He won an Iron Cross.'

'An Iron Cross?'

'It's Ironbay's most important medal,' said Sergeant Zander. 'They only give them out for outstanding feats of bravery.'

'So he's a war hero,' said Sophia.

'Not so much,' said Crutch. 'The heroes are the men we left behind. The ones who gave everything.'

'Exactly what a true war hero would say,' said Sophia.

'Yavenland is neutral,' said Longshot. 'How do you know about war heroes?'

'We've been fighting two hundred years to stay neutral. We don't declare war, but it's the same. Always some arseholes wanting what you have.'

'So you kill them?' said Longshot.

'And make them wish they'd never picked a fight with us. Do you want to talk or do you want to sail?'

'Let's sail,' said Longshot.

'You take the tiller first, Longshot. Your friends can trim the sail. I assume you marines know how to trim a sail in the dark?'

'We can,' said Sergeant Zander.

'If you want to move quietly through the water, you can't let the sail luff,' said Sophia.

'How do you stop a ship's crew from seeing your sails in the dark?' said Sergeant Zander.

'We stain them black.'

'If they're black, how do you trim the sail in the dark? You wouldn't be able to see it.'

'You pay close attention to the direction of the wind,' said Sophia. 'And you train. I've heard you marines know a lot about training?'

'We do,' said Longshot. 'We train every day.'

'What do you train?'

'Killing mostly,' said Sergeant Zander.

'How many ways to kill are there?'

'You'd be surprised,' said Longshot. 'Sergeant Zander is always getting us to come up with something new we hadn't thought of before.'

'That sounds wonderful. Enough talking,' said Sophia. 'Unfurl those sails, and let's do some sailing.'

As the sails filled with wind, the longboat started moving, sliding through the water.

'You need to keep that tiller steady and pay attention to how strong the wind is and how fast you're moving.'

'So I guess where I am based on my speed?' said Longshot.

'To begin with. After you've done this for a while, you'll know where you are.'

'Nice,' said Longshot.

'How do you sabotage ships when you get to them?' said Crutch.

'That I won't tell you,' said Sophia. 'There are some things Yavenland needs to keep secret.'

'The sabotage we can work out ourselves,' said Sergeant Zander. I'm sure Quicksilver will have some ideas.'

A strong gust of wind came up, and the longboat heeled to one side.

'I'm not sure where we are now,' said Longshot. 'Do you want to take over?'

'Where would be the fun in that?' said Sophia, as the longboat heeled over even more in the wind.

Crutch went to let out the sails, but Sophia put her hand on his to stop him.

'If you let the sails luff you're no longer sailing quietly. Longshot needs to learn to control the boat without that help.'

'I've got no idea where I am,' said Longshot.

'That's what makes this hard,' said Sophia, half laughing.

'I think I see something on the port bow,' said Crutch. 'Something big.'

Longshot turned hard to starboard. The sudden change in direction, combined with the strong wind, pushed the boat over. Crutch tried to cling to the gunnels and lean over to stop the heel, but the boat capsized, throwing them all in the water.

'And now you learn to right the boat in the dark,' said Sophia laughing.

'That's not gonna be easy,' said Longshot.

'You should try doing it under enemy fire.'

Chapter 16
Black Death

He was dressed in black. Black pants, black hood, a black mask on his face, and soft black shoes. He crept over the rail of the Auld Faithful, placing each foot carefully, then crawled to the door of the captain's cabin, keeping his eyes on the guard on the deck, making sure he wasn't seen.

He tested the handle of the door, turning it slowly, careful not to make a sound. It was unlocked. He opened the door and crept inside. He didn't risk making a noise by closing the door. Captain Beaumont was inside the room, sleeping in his bed, with his back to the black-hooded man.

The black-hooded man slid across the room, one quiet step after another, then drew his dagger. He got to the edge of the captain's bed, and began to lean over so he could make the fatal cut.

'Move another inch, and it'll be the last thing you do,' said Sergeant Zander grabbing the dark-hooded man's dagger hand. Sergeant Zander put his own dagger at the black-hooded man's throat.

Crutch moved in from the assassin's side and took the dagger out of his hand.

Longshot went through his pockets. 'Couple of those poison darts here,' he said.

'What is going on?' said Cedric, sitting up in his bed in surprise.

'We were coming back from our sailing lesson and noticed someone sneaking aboard the Auld Faithful,' said Sergeant Zander. 'We followed him in here.'

'An assassin by the look of him,' said Longshot.

'Want to tell us what you're doing here?' said Sergeant Zander, tying the assassin's arms behind his back.

'I tell you nothing,' said the assassin.

'Estovian accent,' said Crutch. 'At least we know who sent him.'

'Why would the Estovians send someone to kill me?' said Cedric.

'That's a good question,' said Sergeant Zander. 'How would they even know who you were? Want to answer that for us Igor?'

'I tell you nothing,' said the assassin again.

'We'll see,' said Sergeant Zander.

They had the assassin tied to a chair. Boulder stood over him with Sergeant Zander at his side. Crutch stood in the corner of the room and watched. The last time they interrogated an Estovian, Crutch used trickery to get the information they wanted out of him. Sergeant Zander was hopeful they could try that again.

'Tell us why the Estovians want Captain Beaumont dead,' said Sergeant Zander.

'I tell you nothing,' said the assassin.

'Say that again, and Boulder here will punch you so hard your grandchildren will feel it,' said Sergeant Zander.

'I tell you nothing.'

Sergeant Zander nodded, and Boulder pulled back, swung, and punched the wall, smashing a hole through it.

'Sorry, Sarge, I missed,' said Boulder.

'That's the problem with Boulder,' said Sergeant Zander. 'He can punch hard, but his aim is terrible. Last time we interrogated someone, he missed and hit the guy in the nuts. It was like they exploded. Made a terrible mess.'

'You waste your time,' said the assassin. 'I say nothing.'

'We'll leave you for a minute to give you a chance to take a look at that hole in the wall and think about what it'll be like when Boulder punches you like that in the face.'

'I tell you nothing!' yelled the assassin as Boulder and Sergeant Zander left the room.

'Is terrible what they do to you,' said Crutch in his best Estovian accent. 'You brave man.'

'Don't waste your time,' said the assassin. 'I know you are Corporal Crutch.'

'That's disappointing,' said Crutch. 'You know we have to kill you then.'

'I know,' said the assassin.

If he hadn't just tried to kill Cedric, Crutch would almost feel sorry for him.

'All we want to know is why the Estovians want our captain dead,' said Crutch.

'You Ironworm are stupid,' said the assassin. 'Is Ironbay who want him dead, not Estovia.'

'Ironbay?' said Crutch. 'Why?'

'I tell you nothing more,' said the assassin. 'You stupid now. You stay stupid. I won't make you smart.'

Crutch tried getting more information out of the assassin. Sergeant Zander and Boulder tried threats and hit him a few times to loosen him up, but he wouldn't budge. They'd gotten all they could out of him.

They went to see Cedric in the captain's cabin.

'All we got out of him is that it's Ironbay who wants you dead,' said Sergeant Zander. 'We don't even know if that's true.'

'I tried to trick him into thinking I was Estovian, but he recognised me,' said Crutch.

'Do you think he'll talk if we interrogate him longer?' said Cedric.

'I can't see it,' said Sergeant Zander. 'I think it's time to end it.'

'We have another problem,' said Cedric. 'We could kill him, but then how do we dispose of his body?'

'What do you mean?' said Sergeant Zander.

'We're in Yavenland. We can't just throw the body overboard. The Yavenlanders don't take well to bodies found floating in their harbour.'

Crutch found that interesting. The city guard didn't care at all about bodies floating in the Ironbay harbour. Unless it was a noble.

'I'll get someone to help us,' said Longshot, and left the room.

Half an hour later, Longshot came back with Sophia and two soldiers.

Longshot introduced Sophia to Cedric in front of the assassin.

'Is this him?' said Sophia, looking at the Estovian.

'Yes,' said Cedric.

'Longshot tells me this Estovian tried to kill you in your sleep?' said Sophia.

'That's correct,' said Cedric.

'And you did nothing to provoke this?'

'I've never seen the man before he tried to cut my throat with a knife.'

Sophia turned to the Estovian. 'What do you have to say for yourself?'

'I tell you nothing,' said the Estovian.

'Are you sure,' said Sophia. 'This is your last chance.'

'Nothing,' said the Estovian.

'Very well,' said Sophia. She took a dagger out of her belt and cut the Estovian's throat, blood spilling down the chair onto the wooden planks below.

'Do you have a sack?' said Sophia.

Sergeant Zander went outside and returned with a sack. Sophia grabbed the Estovian by the hair, cut his head clean off with her dagger, and dropped it in the sack. She turned to one of her soldiers and gave him the sack.

'Take a shuttle to the Estovian warship at first light, give this to the captain, and tell him if he sends another assassin to Yavenland or engages in any act of aggression, it will be his head in the sack.'

'Yes, mam,' said the soldier.

'You can both go now,' said Sophia to her soldiers.

When they were gone, Sophia said, 'Sorry about the blood.' She wiped off her dagger on the headless assassin's black pants.

'You're so brutal,' said Longshot. 'I love that in a woman.

Chapter 17
Temple Of The Frog

The marines stood on the large steps at the entrance to the temple. Sitting around the walls on the large stone tiles inside the temple were men and women with their legs crossed, holding green tree frogs. In the centre of the temple was a large stone pond. Croaking echoed around the chamber.

A man in green robes holding a frog stood and made his way to them.

'Welcome; I am Quentus. Are you servants of the great frog?'

'We're on a pilgrimage,' said Crutch.

Quentus nodded. 'Then you may come and observe or leave as you choose. I hope you find what you are looking for.'

'I have many questions,' said Crutch. 'Too many for one sitting, but could I you ask one question before you return to your worship?'

'Of course. The great frog answers every question. But it is only the wise who can hear.'

'This might seem a little unusual, but is there anyone here who is your leader? Your king?'

'The great frog seeks no subjects and has no kings,' said Quentus. He sits, he jumps, he swims, he eats. Such is the wisdom of the great frog.'

'I like frogs,' said Boulder. 'They're friendly.' Quentus nodded and smiled at him.

'Thank you,' said Crutch. 'I will continue my pilgrimage.'

Quentus nodded, walked back to where he came from, and sat on a large stone tile with the frog sitting in his hand. After he sat, the frog jumped out of his hand across the temple tiles, up the stone wall of the pond, and into the water. Quentus smiled as if his god had bestowed a great secret on him.

'Next,' whispered Sergeant Zander.

They retreated from the temple back into the streets of Yavenland.

'I can't see the followers of the great frog trying to claim the throne in Ironbay,' said Sergeant Zander.

'Or the followers of the great possum,' said Longshot.

'What about the acolytes of the sea eagle?' said Quicksilver. 'They were into ruling everything from the sky.'

'Harder to say with them,' said Sergeant Zander. We'd have to go up to their temple on the mountain to be certain. They still don't sound like what we're looking for, though.'

'How many of these temples, and gods, and sects, and cults are there?' said Longshot.

'Hundreds,' said Crutch.

'At least your pilgrimage thing is making it easier to talk to them,' said Quicksilver.

'They have hundreds of years of people seeking wisdom and enlightenment,' said Crutch. 'The book I read talked about how a pilgrim can go freely in Yavenburg to most temples and places of worship to find what they seek.'

'At this rate, it might take us weeks to find this king,' said Longshot.

'You're right,' said Sergeant Zander. 'And all that time we'll be away from the Auld Faithful, leaving Cedric vulnerable to another attack. We need to find a way to speed the process up.'

'I might have an idea,' said Crutch.

Crutch stood on a wooden crate in the city square, with the marines standing behind him. He wasn't the only person with a wooden crate. At least half a dozen men and women stood on crates, preaching.

The pilgrims seeking enlightenment would walk from one preacher to the next, listening to see if that person held the wisdom they sought. Usually, they didn't. Then they'd wander on to the next preacher.

'Do you really think this will work?' said Sergeant Zander.

'Only one way to find out,' said Crutch. Crutch watched how the other preachers delivered their sermons. If he did it the same way they did, he might get a bigger audience.

'People of Yavenland!' yelled Crutch. He threw up his arms and was unable to stay balanced on the crate, falling backwards. Boulder caught him before he could fall to the cobblestones.

'Nice start,' said Boulder. 'Really loud.'

Boulder propped him back up on the crate.

'People of Yavenland,' yelled Crutch, starting again. 'I seek the king.'

The pilgrims in the crowd turned to him. So far, so good. Crutch powered on.

'I am no prophet. I just seek the true king so I can kneel at his feet and worship him.'

A pilgrim in purple robes said, 'I seek the true king too.'

Another said, 'We all want the true king.'

'So I ask you,' yelled Crutch. 'Who among you can lead me to the rightful king? Who knows this man?'

'You speak true,' said the Pilgrim. 'No one truly knows this man.'

'What other wisdom do you share, preacher?'

This wasn't going the way Crutch expected.

'I have no wisdom to share with you. I have no wisdom at all,' yelled Crutch. 'All I seek is the true king. The rightful king of Ironbay and all its territories. The king of my heart. That is my only desire.'

'Only a man with true wisdom would claim to have none,' said one pilgrim.

'Only a man on the true path would seek his king above all else,' said another.

A small crowd began to gather around Crutch.

'Is this working?' said Sergeant Zander. 'I can't tell.'

'I have no desire to preach. I have no prophecies or pronouncements to share. All I seek is an audience with my king.'

'I seek an audience with my king too,' said one pilgrim.

'The preacher shares wisdom beyond his years,' said another.

'He is the true prophet, born crippled but reborn for the hope of us all.'

More pilgrims began to crowd around.

'Can anyone tell me where the true king is?' yelled Crutch in frustration. 'Anyone?'

'No one knows where he is,' said one pilgrim.

'The preacher is telling us we must seek inside ourselves to find him,' said another.

'No, I'm not,' said Crutch. 'I just want to know where he is.'

'He has true humility.'

'Guide us, great wise one, in your true faith.'

'Lead us to the true king in our hearts.'

Crutch looked at the dozens of pilgrims in front of him, now bowing or kneeling. 'Oh, for pity's sake!'

Crutch and the marines headed back to the Auld Faithful for their evening meal. A dozen pilgrims tagged along behind.

'Is that what you planned?' said Sergeant Zander.

'Not exactly,' said Crutch.

'The prophet has no plans,' said one pilgrim.

'The man who seeks the true king needs no plans,' said another.

For the last four hours, the pilgrims hung on every word Crutch spoke. He was fairly certain that if he stopped to take a dump, they'd spend the next half hour seeking the meaning in his shit.

One of the pilgrims talked to Boulder.

'Do you have the wisdom of the prophet, great giant?'

Boulder looked at him. 'Who's the prophet?'

'The great one with the cane.'

'Crutch. He's my friend.'

'You are a friend to the prophet. You must be wise indeed. Do you seek the king?'

'Yes,' said Boulder. 'We sailed all the way from Ironbay.'

'So your heart desires the king?'

'Yes,' said Boulder. 'And cake. I like cake.'

'He likes cake?' said the pilgrim.

'There is hidden meaning in the giant's words,' said another pilgrim.

'A riddle,' said another.

Chapter 18
The Prince

When they got to the Auld Faithful, the pilgrims still followed.

'What are we going to do with them?' said Sergeant Zander. 'They can't come on board.'

'Let me try something,' said Crutch. Crutch walked in front of them and addressed his new followers.

'Now I must eat,' said Crutch. 'But you should start your search. Ask everyone you see if they know where the rightful king of Ironbay is. When you get an answer to this question, then share it with me. I will wait.'

'Another riddle,' said one pilgrim.

'Not a riddle,' said Crutch. 'Just a request.'

'We understand,' said the pilgrim.

The marines walked on board the Auld Faithful and pulled up the gangplank behind them. They didn't want the pilgrims to follow them.

'Why are there a dozen men in robes standing on the docks looking at my ship?' said Cedric.

'They're the new followers of Crutch,' said Sergeant Zander.

'Followers?' said Cedric.

'They seem to think I have the wisdom of the king to share,' said Crutch.

'So you found the man who's pretending to be king?' said Cedric.

'No,' said Sergeant Zander. 'But there's quite a large number of people who know we're looking now.'

'Well, that's something,' said Cedric.

'Unfortunately, they're standing on the docks waiting for Crutch to lead them to him,' said Sergeant Zander.

'I'm trying to decipher how that will help,' said Cedric.

'So am I,' said Crutch.

The marines went to the galley with Cedric to eat.

As they ate, they talked about the man claiming to be a king and who he might be.

'Do you think he's just a madman?' said Longshot.

'Plenty of those here in Yavenland,' said Sergeant Zander. 'The city's full of them.'

'Seems a long way to send us just to look for a madman, though,' said Crutch.

'Good point,' said Sergeant Zander. 'The navy and the palace aren't going to send us on a voyage this long unless they think there's something to the claims he's making.'

'So we might be looking for a man who has a genuine claim to the throne?' said Crutch.   'Most likely, so we can take him home to be hanged or thrown in prison,' said Sergeant Zander.

'But who do they think he could be?' said Crutch. 'I don't remember reading about any Ironborn princes.'

'There could be someone,' said Cedric.

'Really?'

'There's something about the siege of Crestona that's not in the history books,' said Cedric. Crutch, you must have wondered why the Ironborn fleet placed a small city like Crestona under siege instead of a major Estovian city like Teevilgrad?'

'I have,' said Crutch.

'When you put it that way, I'm curious too,' said Sergeant Zander.

'It's the details that historians miss,' said Cedric. 'The reason my fleet was at Crestona is because our spies told us Prince Alderon was there.'

'Prince Alderon?'

'The Ironborn prince. King Vargus had a younger cousin. A cousin who was next in line to be king.'

'Why isn't that in the history books?' said Crutch.

'You have to keep in mind that back then Ironbay had been at war with Estovia for many years. Princes of the king were targets. A new-born prince wasn't announced to the kingdom like they were once we were at peace.'

'So they kept the existence of the prince a secret?'

'Yes. Only the royal family knew he was alive,' said Cedric. 'And an Estovian spy, it would seem. Unfortunately, when he was a boy of five, he was out on the palace grounds playing with his best friend, a servant's son, when he was kidnapped.'

'And they took him to Crestona?'

'Both boys, it would seem. They don't know if the servant's son was involved, but the servant was tortured and executed, poor woman.'

'So when your fleet at the siege of Crestona was sabotaged and destroyed, what happened to the prince?'

'I honestly don't know. Keep in mind after the siege of Crestona, I wasn't given intelligence reports.'

'Working on a ship as a beastmaster,' said Sergeant Zander.

'Yes. Since they didn't ransom the prince back, you'd have to assume the Estovians executed him.'

'Or he escaped,' said Crutch.

'It seems unlikely a five-year-old boy would escape confinement and trained Estovian guards,' said Cedric.

'Not unless he had help,' said Crutch.

'So you think the man claiming to be the rightful king of Ironbay may actually be this Prince Alderon?'

'I don't know,' said Crutch. 'The age matches up. If only there was a reliable way to tell if he is the rightful heir.'

'There is something,' said Cedric.

'What's that?'

'There's a very specific way to identify the prince. Before I left for Crestona, the chief counsel at the palace explained it to me in detail. Then I was sworn to secrecy.'

'So if he's the prince, you can identify him?'

'Yes. I think so,' said Cedric.

'Even after all these years?'

'Yes,' said Cedric.

As they finished their meal, they heard one of the pilgrims calling from the docks.

'Could we speak with the great giant?' yelled the pilgrim. 'We only need a moment.'

'The great giant?' said Cedric.

'That would be Boulder,' said Crutch.

'Do you think these pilgrims are a threat?' said Cedric.

'They seem harmless enough,' said Sergeant Zander. 'We'll go with him. Come on, Boulder, let's go talk to the pilgrims.'

When they went on deck, three of the pilgrims were on the docks with cakes.

'We pondered over your words, oh wise giant, and we have brought you cake.'

Boulder smiled. 'I like cake.'

Longshot and Quicksilver slid the gangplank down, and Boulder went to get his cakes. The pilgrims seemed thrilled to give them to him. Crutch followed behind.

'Have any of you learned anything about where the rightful king of Ironbay is,' said Crutch.

'We have searched our hearts, but the king has eluded us.'

'Perhaps you could ask around in the city of Yavenland,' said Crutch.

'Another riddle,' said one pilgrim. 'He wants us to search deeper in our hearts for the king.'

'No, I want you to ask around in the taverns and shops,' said Crutch.

'We understand,' said one pilgrim.

Clearly, they didn't, because they weren't leaving to go into the city. The pilgrims just stood there on the docks waiting for more words of wisdom.

Chapter 19
The Prince's Mark

Sergeant Zander insisted that Cedric sleep in the marine quarters that night.

'It's the best way to keep you safe,' said Sergeant Zander.

'That assassin isn't the first to try to kill me,' said Cedric.

'We know you can look after yourself,' said Sergeant Zander, 'but it's hard to defend yourself when you're asleep.'

'Please,' said Crutch. 'It would make me feel a lot more comfortable. I don't think I could sleep at all, worrying about you up in the captain's cabin while I'm down here with the marines.'

'Very well,' said Cedric.

Boulder set up a hammock in the centre of the room for Cedric, and the marines slept around him. They took turns standing guard. Cedric posted two guards on the door and extra guards on deck and at the hatches, for good measure.

Before he fell asleep, Cedric asked Crutch for a word in private.

'If the worst should happen,' said Cedric, 'it would be wise for someone else to be able to identify Prince Alderon.'

'Nothing's going to happen to you,' said Crutch. 'Anyone who tries to hurt you will have to kill every one of us marines to get to you.'

'I don't doubt your loyalty for a second,' said Cedric. 'Nevertheless, I still think it's prudent that someone else can identify the prince accurately. It's a long way back to Ironbay if you have someone pretending to be the prince. And who knows how the palace would take that.'

'I get your point,' said Crutch.

'It's best I make any identification, but if I'm not here to do it, this is what you need to remember. Prince Alderon has a birthmark in the shape of a heart on his left butt cheek.'

'Okay Cedric. I'll remember. But I won't need to remember.'

'I hope you're right,' said Cedric.

The next day, six pilgrims stood on the docks.

'You're losing your followers,' said Sergeant Zander.

'That's a relief,' said Crutch.

'I like pilgrims,' said Boulder. 'They give me cake.'

'None of them have cake this morning, unfortunately,' said Crutch.

'That's okay,' said Boulder.

As they came down the gangplank, one of the pilgrims stepped forward.

'Good morning, oh great one with the cane. I am Eleezer.'

Crutch couldn't avoid him. He figured he had to talk to him.

'Good morning, Eleezer.'

'I have good news,' said Eleezer. 'I believe I have found the rightful king of Ironbay.'

Crutch sighed. 'Is he trapped deep in your heart or perhaps somewhere under your gall bladder?'

'No,' said Eleezer. 'He's hiding in the catacombs under the city.'

'Say that again,' said Crutch.

'The rightful king of Ironbay is hiding in the catacombs right here in Yavenland.'

'Do you know why he's hiding?' said Crutch.

'I don't. The fact he's in the catacombs is the only piece of information I could glean from hours of listening in to conversations in the bars and taverns.'

'Where are these catacombs?'

'I haven't been down there, oh great one, but I can show you the entrance.'

'Could you do that now?'

'Of course, but you must never go down there. The catacombs are filled with corpses and ghosts. The entrance was shut a hundred years ago, and whatever lurks in there must be foul indeed.'

'We better get our weapons,' said Sergeant Zander.

'I'll get the torches and some bluefire,' said Quicksilver.

'We can't carry our weapons in the open through the city,' said Sergeant Zander. 'The Yavenlanders get really sensitive about that here.'

'I have an idea,' said Crutch.

Ten minutes later, five of the pilgrims stood on the docks in their undergarments. The marines hid their weapons under the robes they'd taken from them.

The pilgrims smiled with joy.

'The great one with the cane wears my robe.'

'The great giant wears my robe even though it only comes down to his knees.'

'We have all found a little of the king in our hearts today, pilgrims.'

'Hopefully we can find him in the flesh,' said Sergeant Zander.

'We'll give your robes back once we reach the catacombs,' said Crutch.

'You can keep them forever, oh great one with the cane.'

'We only need them to walk through the city.'

Sergeant Zander made sure Cedric had two guards who stayed with him wherever he went. It wasn't perfect, but they all wanted Cedric to be safe while they were gone.

Eleezer led them through the side streets of the city with the pilgrims in their undergarments catching stares from the people of Yavenland as they passed. It didn't seem to bother the pilgrims at all.

'Our shame is also our joy,' said one pilgrim.

'Nakedness is a holy blessing to clothe the great one with the cane.'

After an hour's walk, they came to an older sector of the city where the temples were run down and the stones in the street were cracked. Crutch saw a statue at the front of a temple with its body broken off the top and lying across the entrance.

'What happened here?' said Crutch.

'These are the temples from the old times,' said Eleezer. 'They say a hundred years ago, a cult with dark magic forced themselves into power, and its mage was corrupted by the dark forces he tried to control. His Bloodshadow followers went crazy with an insatiable craving for human flesh and tried to devour the people of the city.'

'I know what that sounds like,' said Sergeant Zander.

'Yes,' said Crutch, thinking of the spirit keeper in Papageenar and the people he infected with the hunger.

'They say the stories of how the people of Yavenland fought the cult are inscribed on the tombs of the dead in the catacombs where they lie,' said Eleezer.

'Well, that's not creepy,' said Quicksilver.

'They also say Bloodshadows still live in the dark down there, trapped in the catacombs, feasting on the flesh of anyone who dares to enter.'

'It gets better and better,' said Longshot.

'This is the main entrance,' said Eleezer. 'You enter that crypt, and there's a barred gate that leads down into the catacombs.'

'Do you know anyone who's gone down there?' said Sergeant Zander.

'None who came back alive.'

'So are we going in there?' said Crutch.

'We are,' said Sergeant Zander.

'With a description like that, how could we do anything else?' said Longshot.

'Let's get these robes off before we go in,' said Sergeant Zander.

They took off the robes and gave them back to the pilgrims.

'I suggest you all go back to somewhere safe in the city,' said Sergeant Zander. 'This is no place for men who don't know how to fight.'

'But we should stay with the great one with the cane,' said one pilgrim.

'Yes,' said another, as if he desperately wanted to be convinced otherwise.

'You are brave men,' said Crutch. 'But this quest is something we must do alone.'

'Of course,' said one pilgrim.

'We will await your return.'

'In the city.'

That was a relief, thought Crutch. He really didn't want half a dozen pilgrims following him into deadly danger. He didn't want to be responsible for the safety or the death of anyone else. It would be the Kona Track in Papageenar all over again.

'I'm coming,' said Eleezer.

'Are you sure?' said Crutch.

'I'm sure. I can read the old language. That might be important for reading the inscriptions on the tombs.'

'That could be useful,' said Sergeant Zander.

'Do you know how to fight?' said Crutch.

'I'm a man of peace,' said Eleezer. 'But I am swift of foot.'

'So you can run?' said Crutch.

'Yes.'

'Better than nothing,' said Crutch. 'But not by much. I can't guarantee your protection.'

'I understand,' said Eleezer.

It was obvious Eleezer would come with them, and he couldn't be persuaded otherwise. Given the situation, Sergeant Zander did what Crutch couldn't bring himself to do.

'I admire your bravery, Eleezer. It will be an honour to have your help.'

'Good on you,' said Quicksilver.

'At the first sign of trouble, don't wait, don't think, just run,' said Crutch.

'I will,' said Eleezer.

Chapter 20
Only The Dead Pass Here

Quicksilver lit a torch, and they entered the crypt. At the back of the crypt, they found an iron gate, its bars rusted. Sergeant Zander looked at the lock.

'This lock looks weak,' he said. He pulled at it, and it fell off the gate. 'Quite weak, I think.' He opened the gate, and they moved through. Ahead was a long set of stairs going down into the darkness. The flame of the torch made the darkness even more foreboding, with strange shadows flickering on the stairs, the stone walls, and the ceiling.

They walked down the stairs slowly, every step echoing around them. After they'd gone down about a hundred feet, they came to level ground with a tunnel ahead of them. There was an arch over the tunnel with an inscription written above it in a language Crutch couldn't understand. It must be the old language Eleezer talked about.

'What does that inscription say?' said Crutch.

'Stop. Only the dead pass here,' said Eleezer. His voice echoed off the ceiling, making a deep, hollow sound that sent chills down Crutch's spine.

'Great,' said Longshot.

'At least we have our weapons,' said Quicksilver.

Crutch thought about the black beast that attacked him on the Auld Faithful, how it was made of mist, and a blade just went straight through it. If there were beasts in here like that, they were as good as dead.

'Come on,' said Sergeant Zander. 'The sooner we find the king, the sooner we get out of here.'

They moved on, Quicksilver's torch bringing light to the darkness, its flickering making huge, terrifying shadows of them on the walls.

They came into a larger room.

'What are they?' said Longshot.

'There's so many of them,' said Quicksilver.

Along the walls were bones and skulls. The bones and skulls of men long dead, stacked one on top of the other in piles that reached the ceiling.

'This is where the people of Zuren buried their dead,' said Eleezer. 'When the graveyards of the city were full, they brought the bodies down here to rot. Over time, there were so many of them, they stacked the bones in piles to make more room.'

'That's not creepy at all,' said Quicksilver, looking at a line of skulls staring back at him, eyeless.

'Keep going,' said Sergeant Zander.

They moved on, Crutch's hair standing on end, his ears training for any sound that might be out of place. He jumped at every large echo, then frowned at himself when he realised it was just someone's foot hitting the floor of the tunnel they were in.

Then there was a sound that definitely was not the marines or Eleezer. A rattling sound like rocks or bits of wood falling on the ground came from behind them.

'What is that?' said Longshot.

'Let's not find out,' said Sergeant Zander. 'Keep moving forward.'

They moved on till the tunnel ahead of them was partly caved in, a pile of rocks on the ground that had fused together over the years.

'We'll have to crawl through,' said Sergeant Zander. 'Smallest first. Then you can pull us through if we get stuck.'

Crutch crawled over the pile of rocks and rubble. He got through easily enough with his back just scraping against the ceiling, then he turned back and held the torch as Quicksilver crawled through. Longshot came next. It was a squeeze, but he got through.

Sergeant Zander took more work. Crutch and Longshot pulled at his arms, with pebbles and rocks falling from the ceiling above him as he came through. There was a new sound now, like someone walking with hollow footsteps. It echoed up from the tunnel behind them.

Crutch looked for the sound, and behind Boulder, he could see bones walking. Full skeletons of men, their bones weathered with the centuries, lumbering slowly towards them.

'Quick Boulder, crawl through,' said Sergeant Zander. He could see them too.

'What are those?' said Longshot.

Boulder squeezed into the small gap between the ceiling above him and the solid mass of rocks below him. He pushed in as far as he could, then stopped.

'I'm stuck,' he said.

The first walking skeleton was almost on him.

'Two men each arm,' said Sergeant Zander. 'Let's pull him through.'

Crutch and Longshot took one arm, Eleezer and Sergeant Zander took the other, crowded against each other in the tunnel.

'Pull!' yelled Sergeant Zander, and Crutch pulled with all his strength. Boulder moved towards them a few inches.

'It's got my foot,' said Boulder.

'Don't let it bite you,' said Crutch.

'Okay,' said Boulder, his face straining as he kicked out behind him with his leg. There was a clattering of bones in the tunnel behind him, then more footsteps.

'Pull!' yelled Sergeant Zander. Crutch clung on to Boulder's arms and pulled with every ounce of strength he had. Boulder moved forward a few more inches.

Crutch peered around the tiny gap at the side of Boulder and could see more of those skeletons flooding the tunnel behind Boulder, pushing against each other and over each other, trying to get to him.

'They're coming for him,' said Crutch. 'We have to get him out now.'

A skeleton fell forward onto Boulder's legs, its teeth gnashing and its bony hands clawing at him.

'Pull!' yelled Sergeant Zander. Crutch braced himself with his good leg and pulled, his arms burning with the effort.

Boulder's body finally moved, sliding over the rock mass with the skeleton still holding on to his legs. A huge rumbling sound came from above them, and the ceiling began to crumble, with small rocks coming down, then larger ones.

Crutch freed the blade from his walking cane and hacked at the right arm of the skeleton, breaking its bone. Sergeant Zander drew his sword out and hacked its left arm. Then Boulder was free.

More rocks fell. One hit Crutch on the head. He felt the spot with his hand, and his hand came away bloody.

'Run!' yelled Sergeant Zander.

The ceiling caved in above them as they ran, rocks large and small crashing and crumbling to the ground. Crutch ran with his cane, driving with his good leg, then with the cane, barely staying ahead of the falling rocks.

The tunnel behind them kept caving in. Crutch coughed, the dust in his eyes, in his mouth, and in his lungs. They came to a much larger chamber. Crutch glanced behind him and the cave in had stopped. The air was thick with swirling dust, the specks of dust lit by Quicksilver's torch.

'There goes our way out,' said Longshot.

'There's nothing for it now,' said Sergeant Zander. 'We go on and find another way out. Hopefully this king is in here somewhere.'

Chapter 21
Rats

The marines were so preoccupied with the collapsing tunnel behind them, they hadn't looked at the room they were in. Crutch looked around at the stone shelves on the walls, and he saw red eyes staring back at him from the shadows. Hundreds of pairs of red eyes.

'Sarge, we've got a problem,' said Quicksilver, lighting another torch and handing it to Crutch.

'What are they?' said Sergeant Zander.

'Rats,' said Crutch. 'Big rats.'

'I hate rats,' said Longshot.

Quicksilver lit another torch and gave it to Sergeant Zander.

Crutch really looked at these rats. They were at least three times the size of a regular rat, but there was something else about them that wasn't right. The rats snarled, their teeth gnashing and grinding together.

'They've got the hunger,' said Crutch.

'Use the torches,' said Quicksilver. 'Rats hate fire.'

'And whatever you do, don't let one bite you,' said Sergeant Zander. 'Keep moving.'

They moved through the chamber, the rats snarling on the shelves, backing off and scattering whenever the flame of a torch got close to them. Quicksilver led at the front, holding his torch out. Sergeant Zander, Boulder, and Longshot were in the middle, and Crutch went sideways at the back, torch in one hand and walking cane in the other.

Crutch never took his eyes off the rats behind them. The sound of them snarling got louder, and they got braver. One ran almost to his foot before Crutch lowered the torch close enough to smell its fur burning, then it ran back with a screech.

As they exited the room into another corridor, the rats kept their distance, but they weren't staying in the room.

'They're following us,' said Crutch.

'Can a rat give you the hunger?' said Longshot.

'I don't know,' said Crutch.

Another rat ran forward, snarling, and Crutch stabbed it with the blade of his walking cane and flung it off. A dozen rats immediately started ripping it to pieces and eating it, but the other rats still came after them, staying just outside the range of Crutch's torch. There were hundreds of them.

Quicksilver joined Crutch at the rear, so they were cramped together, both walking sideways holding their two torches out behind them.

'Burn them Quicksilver!' yelled Sergeant Zander.

'You sure, Sarge?' said Quicksilver.

'Do I have to ask you twice to burn something?' said Sergeant Zander.

'No, you don't,' said Quicksilver, pulling balls of bluefire out of the sack on his waist. 'Get ready to run. This will get wild.'

Quicksilver dropped three balls of bluefire into the centre of the rats. They scattered, but when the balls didn't do anything, the rats walked right over them. Then Quicksilver dropped another three balls of bluefire right at Crutch's feet.

'Three seconds,' said Quicksilver.

Crutch kept moving away from the rats, holding his torch as close to the balls of bluefire as he dared to stop the rats from moving out of their fire range.

Then they exploded in blue flame. Rats burning with blue fire went everywhere. Up the walls, back the way they came; some came straight at them, flames all over them screeching as they burned. Crutch stabbed at them as they came. He couldn't let any of them get past him or bite him.

'Make another wall of flame between the rats and us,' said Sergeant Zander.

'Will do Sarge,' said Quicksilver, throwing out another three bluefire balls near Crutch's feet. 'Three seconds, Crutch.'

Crutch moved back, stabbing the burning rats that came near him. Then the bluefire sputtered and burst into flames, making the heat more intense. The smoke in the tunnel made it hard to breathe.

'We need to get out of here before we run out of air,' said Crutch, stabbing a rat that tried to run on the ceiling of the tunnel.

'Keep moving,' said Sergeant Zander.

They walked down the tunnel, coughing with the smoke. Crutch sweated from the heat, and wondered what came next after living skeletons and rats with the hunger. Then he heard a loud snarling coming from the flames.

'What is that?' said Quicksilver.

Out of the flames stepped a rat as big as a dog, snarling and biting with the hunger, its eyes red with hate.

'Looks like mother's upset about what we did to her babies,' said Sergeant Zander.

'The flames aren't burning it,' said Crutch.

'Then we fight it,' said Sergeant Zander, drawing his sword and pushing past Quicksilver to the front line.

'Any ideas on how,' said Crutch. 'It only has to bite us once.'

'You keep its head busy,' said Sergeant Zander. 'I'll do the rest.'

The giant rat stood there, snarling for a few seconds, its red eyes burning, deciding who to attack first. Crutch knew for this to work, it had to be him. He jumped forward and thrust out with his walking cane.

Crutch didn't want to get in range of the giant rat's teeth and was a little too cautious. His cane barely scratched the rat's nose, but it was enough. The rat screeched and came straight at him, its mouth open, biting at him as he jumped back.

It was fast, much faster than he expected, and Crutch tripped as he went back, trying to avoid its teeth. The rat was on top of him, its weight pressing on his legs, then his stomach as it ran up his body, going straight for his throat.

He pulled a dagger from his belt and stabbed at its guts, but the rat's fur was hard as rock, and the dagger just bounced off. Crutch looked right into the rat's glowing red eyes and could see its mouth open, ready for that final bite, when Sergeant Zander's sword went straight through its left eye and out the other side of its head.

Sergeant Zander pulled back and thrust through its head again and again, making sure it was dead, then he kicked it off Crutch.

'Did it bite you?'

Crutch felt his body and felt his throat. 'No.'

'Good. Let's get out of here before another one of those comes after us.'

The smoke still billowed into the tunnel from the bluefire, so they moved faster to get ahead of it. After a couple of minutes, they came to a much larger chamber with some fresh air. Off the chamber were rooms, tombs of some kind, most likely. Crutch really didn't want to know what horrors lurked in there.

'Everyone check for bites,' said Sergeant Zander. 'We don't want any nasty surprises.'

Crutch didn't quite know what they would do if someone was bitten. The reality of the choice they'd have to make was too awful to think about. Killing an enemy or a rat with the hunger was bad enough. He didn't know if he could kill Boulder or Sergeant Zander if it came to that.

They were thorough, going over their own bodies, then checking each other. It looked like they'd been lucky. There were no bites from the rats.

Longshot took a quick look in the rooms leading off theirs. 'These rooms have corpses,' he said. 'And the two corridors go in different directions.'

Crutch looked in one of the rooms. There were stone shelves like the room with the rats, except on every one of these shelves was a corpse with skin drawn back on its face, its teeth showing, its flesh and clothing rotting. They stank with a horrible smell that made the bile rise in his throat.

'Let's get moving,' said Sergeant Zander. 'We don't wanna be around corpses in this place.'

CHAPTER 22
FEAR MEANS DEATH

They took the corridor to the left and walked a hundred yards before going down a long set of stairs into a larger room.

'Keep going,' said Sergeant Zander, pointing to the corridor at the other end of the room.

Quicksilver was almost to the corridor when a wall slid in front of him, blocking his way.

'What's going on?' said Quicksilver, banging on the wall with his fist. 'It's solid stone.'

Another wall slid closed behind them. Crutch felt it and pushed at it. It was solid stone too. They were trapped.

'This isn't good,' said Longshot.

Then they heard water. First a trickle, then it poured into the room from a series of small pipes in the stone ceiling. Crutch could smell it. It was salt water.

'Anyone have any ideas?' said Sergeant Zander as the water filling up the room reached their ankles.

Crutch searched the walls, walking along and hitting them with his hands. He found a small inscription near one of the corners.

'Eleezer, what does this say?'

'Fear means death. Patience means life.'

'What does that mean?' said Crutch.

'I have no idea.'

The water was already up to their waists.

'How much water do you think there is?' said Longshot. 'Will it fill up the room and drown us?'

'It's salt water,' said Crutch. 'How much water is in the ocean?'

'That's a cheerful thought,' said Longshot as the water reached their chests.

'If anyone has an idea, now's the time to talk,' said Sergeant Zander.

'We could all try to open the wall the way we came in,' said Crutch, the water now up to his neck.

Boulder, Sergeant Zander, and Crutch pulled at the wall that had slid across. They could get their fingers into a groove, but it was too heavy. They couldn't shift it. Sergeant Zander tried sliding his sword into the groove, but it only went in a couple of inches and wouldn't go further. He tried his dagger with the same result.

They had to tread water now with their heads just inches from the stone ceiling of the room, the pipes blasting salt water on them. The torch was out, and they were in darkness. Longshot and Quicksilver said they'd try opening the door on the other side of the room, but called back that they couldn't make it budge.

Crutch took in as many deep breaths of air as he could, then the water filled the room and he heard a clanking sound.

Crutch knew he had as much time as he could hold his breath, then he'd be dead. He had to think. Fear means death. Patience means life. What did that mean? And what was that clanking sound when the room filled?

He checked above him, but the ceiling was just solid rock and pipes. He swam down and felt the floor. It was just stone. His lungs burned, and cried out for air. More than anything, he just wanted to breathe, but there was no air to breathe, just lungs full of water if he tried, then death by drowning.

Crutch had one last thought. He swam back to the door they came in through, got his fingers in the groove, and pulled as hard as he could.

The door moved. Less than an inch, but it moved. His air was running out. Any second now, he'd pass out or breathe water, and it would be all over.

He pulled on the door as hard as he could, trying to slide it open. It moved again. Another inch. He could hear water spilling out of the crack in the door, but water must still be coming in through the roof because the water wasn't going down.

With his last breath, he pulled with everything he had left, and the door slid open. The water pushed him through the doorway, then it drained away, and he could breathe. He gasped in, desperate breaths filling his lungs.

Crutch heard the striking of a match, then as light filled the room, he could see Quicksilver had lit a torch.

The water was gone faster than it had come, and the pipes in the ceiling had stopped pumping out water. The marines were on their hands and knees in the room, coughing and sucking in air, with Quicksilver holding the torch in one hand, his other on the floor.

'How did you get that torch lit?' said Longshot.

'I always keep some in a waterproof sack,' said Quicksilver.

Eleezer turned to Crutch. 'You saved us,' he said.

'Thanks to you,' said Crutch. 'The inscription told us we had to wait for the room to fill with water, then slide the door open.'

'The room filling must have triggered some kind of lock to release,' said Longshot.

'Remind me to never go into any catacombs ever again,' said Quicksilver, coughing. 'This is not my idea of fun.'

'Let's get out of this room before it tries to kill us again,' said Sergeant Zander.

Longshot tried the door at the back of the room. 'This won't move,' he said.

Quicksilver and Boulder helped him, but the door wouldn't budge.

'Back the way we came then,' said Sergeant Zander. 'We can take the other corridor from the room with the corpses.'

They went up the steps and back through the corridor until they got to the main room. Crutch could feel the bile rise in his throat from the smell of the corpses in the tombs.

'Keep moving,' said Sergeant Zander. 'Down the other corridor.'

They went a hundred yards down the corridor into another large room with half a dozen rooms leading off it.

'More tombs,' said Longshot. 'More corpses in them.'

'They stink,' said Quicksilver.

'There's an altar in this room,' said Longshot.

Crutch and the marines looked in the room, where they saw a stone altar with metal wrist shackles and chains.

'A sacrificial altar,' said Quicksilver.

'Let's hope the cult that used it is long gone,' said Sergeant Zander.

'Not so much,' said Longshot, who was looking back the way they'd come.

Crutch looked and saw a man in red robes staring at them. The man started chanting and raised his hands. The ground around them trembled. The sound of movement then loud snarling came from the tombs around them.

Chapter 23
These Things Don't Die

'Time to leave,' said Sergeant Zander. 'Keep going down the next corridor.'

Crutch went last, with Eleezer just in front of him. He looked behind him, and he saw corpses alive and walking, coming after them, snarling and gnashing their teeth with the hunger.

'The corpses are following us,' said Crutch.

'Of course they are,' said Longshot. 'This place just keeps on giving.'

Sergeant Zander moved to the rear with Crutch.

'They don't look happy.'

'They've got the hunger,' said Crutch.

'So we have to get out of here without getting bit,' said Sergeant Zander.

'Let's hope there's an exit somewhere up ahead,' said Crutch.

'We're moving faster than they are,' said Sergeant Zander.

'Which is good until we come to a dead end, or a locked door, or something else that slows us down.'

'More piles of bones up ahead,' said Quicksilver.

'Are they moving?' said Sergeant Zander.

'No.'

'Keep going then.'

They went through a room with human bones in piles. Crutch saw legs, arms, and skulls. So many skulls. It didn't seem possible so many people could have died and been dragged down to make a bone pile like this. The bones were stacked from the stone floor all the way to the stone ceiling.

They went through the room fast. Crutch tried not to think about what it would be like if these bones started forming into living skeletons. He didn't have to wait long to find out.

As they passed the room into the next corridor carved from rock, Crutch heard the rattling of bones behind them. He looked back, and the first skeleton was on its feet, walking. Other bones pulled together from some foul, unseen force, then fell or rolled out of the heap, got to their feet, and followed, snarling, full of malice.

'We have company behind us,' said Crutch.

'Pick up the pace,' said Sergeant Zander, looking back. 'Let's get well ahead of them.'

They moved as fast as they dared down the corridor, not knowing what might lie ahead. Behind them, Crutch could hear the skeletons coming, their snarling, and the grinding of their teeth. To make so much sound, there must be dozens of them.

They came into a larger room, and there were three men waiting for them. Or at least they were men once. They all had fatal wounds. One had an open wound from a sword thrust into his chest. Another's head half hung off from a cut to the neck. The third man's guts dangled out of his stomach.

They'd been killed, but they were alive through some foul magic. They snarled and bit, and they held weapons. Two had swords, and the third had an axe.

Crutch looked behind him. They were still a distance away, but he could see them coming. Dozens of skeletons.

'We can't go back,' said Crutch.

'We have to fight them,' said Sergeant Zander. 'Cut their heads off and don't get bit.'

The room was big enough for the marines to make a line all five of them across with Eleezer behind them. Crutch was against the left wall next to Boulder as the half-dead men came.

The first man came, swinging his sword. He feinted left, then made his real swing right. Boulder was surprised and got his axe up to defend himself just in time. The second swordsman used a similar feint before attacking, with Sergeant Zander barely avoiding the cut of the sword.

'They're Komitav,' said Crutch. 'They fight like the Komitav.'

The marines had trained to fight against the Komitav in Teevilgrad. Once you understood the pattern of feints and attacks, you could fight against it, but it wasn't easy. Crutch never expected they'd be fighting dead men infected with the hunger who fought like the Komitav, but here it was.

Boulder swung his axe at the man in front of him, but the thing parried his blow easily. Crutch moved in with his cane, aiming for the thing's leg. If he could cripple a leg and get the thing on its knees, Boulder could cut its head off.

The thing was fast with his sword. It easily parried Crutch's thrust, then came up and parried Boulder's axe too. Then it moved forward with unnatural speed, aiming for Boulder's groin.

Crutch used all his strength to hit the sword. It was deflected down just enough to miss Boulder, who glanced down at the sword, dropped his axe, and grabbed the thing's sword arm with one hand, and pulled a dagger with the other, thrusting at the thing's head.

Crutch moved in and stabbed the thing in the side to distract it.

Boulder had to move close to stab with his dagger. Too close. It bit at him, moving its head forward, its teeth chomping and grinding, a wild look in its eyes.

'Don't let it bite you!' yelled Crutch.

Boulder moved back, and the thing moved right with him, biting at his face, and trying to push closer.

Crutch dropped his cane, pulled his dagger from his belt, grabbed the hair of the thing, and cut into its throat, its teeth inches from his hand. He kept right on cutting and sawing until the head came off.

Its body flopped to the ground, still moving, its hand reached for the sword on the ground.

'What is this?' said Crutch as Boulder picked up his axe and cut the limbs off the man.

Crutch threw the head down the corridor the way they'd come, its teeth still biting and grinding as it hit the floor and rolled away from them.

Sergeant Zander drove back the swordsman he was fighting, and Crutch picked up his cane, moved in, and stabbed at its leg. The thing moved its sword down to push away Crutch's cane, and Sergeant Zander thrust his sword straight through its eye.

The thing kept right on fighting, bringing its sword up, ready to run Sergeant Zander through. Sergeant Zander let go of his sword and dropped to his knees, making himself an easy target. The thing readied for a swing that would cut off Sergeant Zander's head, and Boulder's axe came from behind Sergeant Zander and took its head clean off with one swing.

'Nice work, Boulder,' said Sergeant Zander as the thing stumbled and its head fell to the ground behind it.

Crutch watched in alarm as it regained its footing and prepared for another strike with its sword. Crutch swung down on its sword arm with the blade in his cane and cut it off, the sword clattering on the stone floor of the room. Boulder cut off its other limb with his axe, then cut off both its legs for good measure, hacking with frightening intensity.

As Crutch looked over, Longshot and Quicksilver dismembered the limbs of the last man, its guts and pieces of its body scattered across the room.

'These things don't die,' said Longshot.

'I'd wager they don't burn either,' said Quicksilver. 'It's not natural.'

'We can talk about it later,' said Crutch, looking behind them. 'Run!'

The skeletons were almost on them, the grinding of teeth and snarling echoing down the corridor and into the room in a horrible, terrifying din. Eleezer looked behind them, then ran straight past everyone, slipping on the blood and guts of the men they'd just killed, getting up and going right on down the next corridor.

The marines ran after him with Crutch in the rear. One of the skeletons made it within a foot of Crutch, and he paused and swung his walking cane hard at its waist. Its bones smashed and scattered into pieces, and Crutch kept moving.

When he glanced back, the bones of the skeleton pulled back together, and in seconds, it was back on its feet, joining the other skeletons chasing them.

'They won't be killed,' said Crutch. 'We have to outrun them.'

Chapter 24
A Question

So they ran, Eleezer in front, fleeing in terror, and Crutch in the rear, using his cane. After two hundred yards, they came to another chamber with half a dozen tombs and another corridor on the far side. Crutch could see a corpse walking out of one of the tombs at the far end of the chamber.

'Stop!' yelled Crutch, but Eleezer kept running straight into the corpse. It snarled and bit at him as he tried to fight it off. As the marines came into the chamber, more corpses entered it. There were at least a dozen.

'Push them away and keep running!' yelled Sergeant Zander.

Boulder used the head of his axe and slammed one corpse so hard he drove it back into the tomb it came out of and knocked over two more corpses behind it. Crutch used the bottom of his cane to hit a corpse coming out of a tomb on the other side of the chamber, making it stumble backwards.

Eleezer screamed, pushed the corpse off him, and ran down into the corridor in front of him, with the marines following close behind. They kept running. Crutch's lungs burned with the effort of pushing off with his good leg, then with the cane over and over.

He looked behind him, and at least a dozen corpses followed, with the dozens of skeletons behind them. Their footsteps, their snarling, and the sound of their teeth grinding and snapping echoed in the catacombs, a constant reminder of the death that awaited them all if they tripped or slowed down.

Ahead, Crutch saw a long tunnel with a raised portcullis. Could they use it?

'If we lower the portcullis, it might close out the corpses and the skeletons,' said Crutch.

'Good thinking,' said Sergeant Zander.

As Crutch passed under the portcullis, he and the marines searched for the lever or the winch that would lower it.

'Where is it?' said Sergeant Zander as the corpses entered the tunnel.

'It has to be here somewhere,' said Longshot.

The corpses were just ten yards from the portcullis.

'There,' said Crutch, pointing up to the top of the wall, where a chain was driven, stopping the portcullis from dropping. Whatever winch or pulley system it used was clearly long gone. Someone had added the chain and spike later.

Boulder jumped and tried to hack at the chain with his axe, but he couldn't reach.

'Get me on your shoulders,' said Crutch.

The corpses were just three yards from the portcullis now.

Boulder knelt down, Crutch got on his shoulders, and Boulder stood and handed him the axe. The corpses were less than a yard from the portcullis. Crutch could see the skeletons coming up behind them. So many of them. Too many of them.

Crutch swung at the chain with the axe. The axe clanked against the chain, but the chain didn't break. One corpse was under the portcullis now.

Crutch swung again, and the chain broke. The portcullis slid down the spikes at the bottom of its iron bars, impaling the corpse underneath it. Its head in the tunnel snarled and bit, its arms reaching out, trying to grab at the marines.

Sergeant Zander stepped forward and cut the corpse's head from its body. The head kept snarling and biting as it rolled on its side. Sergeant Zander moved closer to the portcullis and created a frenzy of pushing, snarling, and biting from the corpses and the skeletons, now crowding in behind them.

'How long do you think those bars will hold?' said Longshot.

'I don't know,' said Sergeant Zander. 'And I don't intend to find out. Let's keep moving.'

'Wait,' said Eleezer, holding up his hand. 'I've been bitten.'

'Will he get the hunger?' said Quicksilver. 'Like that boy in Papageenar?'

'I don't know,' said Crutch.

'What's the hunger?' said Eleezer.

'Maybe we should cut his arm off like Waromi did,' said Longshot. 'To stop it spreading.'

Crutch didn't know if cutting off Eleezer's arm would help. It certainly didn't help Moris when he got bit in the jungle in Papageenar. Moris turned into one of those monsters chasing them now. The portcullis shook, the snarling of the corpses and skeletons was almost painful to listen to it was so loud.

'We can talk about it later,' said Sergeant Zander. 'Let's keep moving.'

They ran down the tunnel. Up ahead, they could see another raised portcullis. They were within two yards of it when it came crashing down.

'See if we can lift it,' said Sergeant Zander.

They each took a spot underneath the portcullis and lifted with everything they had, grunting and straining.

'It's no good,' said Longshot. 'It must be locked in place.'

Boulder tried bending the bars, but they were a much thicker, sturdier iron than the portcullis at the other end of the tunnel. They wouldn't bend. Boulder pounded at the bars where they joined the cross irons, but the joints were strong.

They were trapped, and it was just a matter of time before the corpses and skeletons broke through the portcullis behind them and devoured them all.

'There must be a winch,' said Sergeant Zander. 'They always have a winch.'

'The winch is here,' said a voice in the corridor. 'I may open it for you if you answer my questions.'

'Who are you?' said Sergeant Zander.

'If you don't know who I am, the winch for the other portcullis is here too. I can raise that just as easily.'

'You're the rightful king of Ironbay,' said Crutch.

'I could be. That depends on who you are,' said the voice.

'We were sent from Ironbay on our ship, the Auld Faithful, to retrieve you,' said Crutch. 'Orders from the palace.'

Crutch looked behind him. The portcullis shook from the force of the skeletons who'd piled on each other and pulled and pushed on it with their bony hands and feet.

'Can you prove you're from Ironbay?' said the voice.

'The main street is Kings Way,' said Crutch. 'It runs right past the Rosewood military cemetery, down through the town square, then on to the palace.'

'You could get that from a map,' said the voice. 'Tell me something only someone who lived in Ironbay would know.'

Crutch tried to think. If this was the prince, he wouldn't have been to Ironbay for over twenty years. What would a prince living in Ironbay twenty years ago know about the city? He remembered the bread cart that had been passed from father to son for at least two generations. Worth a shot.

'Mick's bread cart has the best pastries in the city,' said Crutch. 'But only on the first day of the week when they're cooked fresh. After that, they keep selling their old stock. By the end of the week, the pastries are stale, but they sell them like they've just been cooked.'

Crutch looked at the other portcullis with skeletons and corpses pushing against it, snarling and biting and prayed that would be enough.

Chapter 25
The King

There was the sound of a latch being unlocked, then the turning of a winch and the clattering of a chain as the portcullis came up. The marines and Eleezer walked through, then the portcullis slid down behind them.

There were two young men in their twenties there.

'I'm Prince Alderon, and this is my very loyal friend Damen. Best we get away from here. The dead get a little excited when they see anything living.'

Prince Alderon led them down a corridor to a thick wooden door. He took out a key and unlocked it. They went through, with Prince Alderon locking the door behind them.

'Can those things open doors?' said Sergeant Zander.

'No. The dead can't open doors, but they're not the only things down here. Damen was forced to kill three Estovians who came chasing us yesterday.'

'We came across those,' said Sergeant Zander. 'Not quite as dead as we'd like them to be when they attacked us. They're more dead now.'

'More dead,' said Damen, smiling. 'Nice one.'

Prince Alderon led them down another corridor to a door made of iron bars. He unlocked that, led them through, then locked it behind him.

'Wait,' said Longshot. 'Damen killed three komitav officers by himself?'

'I wanted to help, but Damen was insistent that I shouldn't risk my life.'

'Three komitav by yourself,' said Sergeant Zander. 'You must be a master with that sword?'

'They thought they could kill Prince Alderon,' said Damen. 'I showed them the error of their ways.'

'Are there more of those skeletons and corpses up ahead?' said Sergeant Zander.

'Not in this part of the catacombs,' said Prince Alderon. 'Or at least, there shouldn't be.'

'So we're safe here.'

'You're not safe anywhere in the catacombs, but we're about as safe as you can be down here,' said Prince Alderon as they moved through the corridors and chambers.

'Where are you leading us?' said Sergeant Zander.

'To the surface,' said Prince Alderon.

'You seem to know these catacombs well,' said Crutch.

'Damen and I have been coming down here since we were boys,' said Prince Alderon.

'You fought against those dead when you were boys?'

'There weren't as many of them back then,' said Prince Alderon. 'It seems there's a new high priest claiming the catacombs as his temple.'

'We saw him,' said Crutch.

'Really? That's not a good sign,' said the prince. 'I believe the high priest intends to free the dead and take control of Yavenland.'

'I'd like to show him a little freedom,' said Damen.

'Really?' said Prince Alderon.

'Yes. I'd free his head from his body if you'd just let me.'

'Damen is very enthusiastic about using swordplay to solve the world's problems,' said Prince Alderon. 'I keep hoping he'll embrace other strategies.'

'I'm happy to embrace another strategy,' said Damen. 'Separating his upper body from his lower body for example.'

'You'd make a good marine,' said Sergeant Zander.

'Please don't encourage him,' said Prince Alderon. 'He's difficult enough as it is.'

'I'm sorry,' said Damen. 'You know I'm not really that bloodthirsty. I just don't like men who kill innocents for their own gain.'

'We're with you there,' said Crutch.

'I forgot to ask if any of you have been bitten,' said Prince Alderon.

'Eleezer was bitten by one of the corpses,' said Crutch. 'Is there anything you can do for him?'

'I'm afraid not,' said Prince Alderon.

'So I'm going to turn into one of those things?' said Eleezer.

'Yes,' said Prince Alderon. 'Up ahead, there's a chamber with inscriptions in the old language that seem to talk about a cure, but Damen and I have been unable to decipher its full meaning.'

'Can I see it?' said Eleezer.

'I don't want to give you false hope,' said the prince.

'False hope is better than no hope,' said Eleezer.

They made their way through corridors until they came to a large chamber with inscriptions on the walls.

'This is it,' said Prince Alderon.

Eleezer began studying the inscriptions, speaking under his breath as he ran his fingers over the symbols carved in the stone wall.

Crutch turned to Prince Alderon. 'How long have you been in Yavenland?'

'Most of our lives. A wise old man, Lysander, helped us escape from Crestona in a wooden crate loaded onto a ship as cargo.'

'Inside a crate in the hold of a ship. That must have been difficult,' said Crutch. Crutch remembered what it was like mucking out the animal stalls in the Auld Faithful, how sea water would splash down from the hatches above you and water and muck would turn into a foul mud around your feet, mixed in with the animal shit and the piss.

'Honestly, I can't remember much from those days,' said Prince Alderon. 'We were very young. Damen's recollection might be better.'

'You were older than me, Alderon. I don't have memories of Crestona at all, or the voyage or Ironbay, beyond some vague thoughts of the palace grounds,' said Damen. 'My first real memories are of Yavenland and Lysander teaching us the ways of the world.'

'So Lysander helped you escape from the Estovians in Crestona and then raised you?' said Crutch.

'He did,' said Damen. 'He was a father to us.'

'And a hard taskmaster,' said Prince Alderon. 'He insisted we learn everything about Ironbay and its territories and told us stories of the city and its people. He also hired swordsmen to train Damen in fighting.'

Eleezer interrupted them. 'You should go on without me,' he said.

'Are you sure?' said Crutch.

'If I can decipher the words here, then maybe I have a chance,' said Eleezer. 'If I can't, the only help you can give me is a swift death. Either way, there's not much you can do for me.'

Crutch felt terrible about leading yet another good man to a horrible end. He didn't want to leave Eleezer here, most likely to die by himself, but he could see the logic in it. The longer they stayed in these catacombs, the greater the chance they'd be overwhelmed by the things that dwelt here.

'I hope you find the answers here,' said Crutch. 'Is there anything we can leave you?'

'Perhaps some food if you have any. All of a sudden, I have a ravenous hunger.'

The marines dug out some of their hard tack for Eleezer, left him a skin full of water, and left him behind, staring at that stone wall full of letters and symbols. Prince Alderon gave Eleezer a key.

'This is my spare key. If you find what you're looking for, you'll need this to get out of the gate,' said the prince.

They walked on, with Crutch staying next to the prince.

'There's something I don't understand,' said Crutch. 'You must have been here in Zuren for over twenty years without anyone knowing you were here. Why did Ironbay get word you were here now?'

'Because we spread the rumour that we were here,' said Prince Alderon.

'Why would you do that? Surely you know that your welcome in Ironbay might not be so friendly.'

'A couple of months ago, an Estovian assassin tried to kill us,' said Prince Alderon.

'He made the mistake of thinking I was asleep,' said Damen.

Assassins, thought Crutch. How many Estovian assassins were there in Zuren? He had a sudden urge to get back to the Auld Faithful and Cedric as soon as he could.

'I made the assumption that the Estovians wouldn't stop with one assassin,' since Prince Alderon.

'You were right, as usual,' said Damen.

'Yes. I already told you about the three Estovians who tried to kill us down here. I knew that Zuren and Yavenland were no longer safe for us. The isolation of Yavenland that had worked in our favour for so long was now our biggest liability.'

'We could hide in the jungle,' said Damen, 'but it's much the same as the catacombs. If they have enough men and they're determined, they'll find you.'

'And they do seem quite determined,' said Prince Alderon. 'They've had a warship anchored off Zuren for a week now.'

'The only advantage we have is that we're considered Yavenlanders,' said Damen. 'We can carry weapons openly in the streets of Zuren. The Estovians have to hide theirs.'

'So you're looking for a way to get off Yavenland safely,' said Crutch.

'Yes. And the best way I could think of was to let Ironbay know their rightful king is here.'

'But you saw this coming with one single assassin?' said Crutch.

'Lysander always said that Prince Alderon is brilliant when it comes to seeing the bigger picture,' said Damen. 'He was right.'

Crutch wondered about that. If this really was Prince Alderon, the rightful king, how happy would King Vargus be to let him take over the rule of Ironbay? If he was a pretender, then he'd be executed for treason.

Both paths likely led to death or the prince living the rest of his life in a dungeon somewhere under the palace in Ironbay. Was this his life now, leading men to their deaths in a variety of different horrible ways?

They came to a door made of iron bars. Beyond the door was a small, level stone landing, then a long set of stairs going up. Prince Alderon unlocked the door.

'This will take us up to the surface. Then we'll have quite the walk to get back to the docks at Zuren.'

After climbing the stairs, they came out into an old temple. The stone floor was cracked, the altar crumbling, part of the slab roof caved in.

'In the history books of Zuren, these temples were once filled with worshippers,' said Prince Alderon. 'Until the first high priest of the Order of the Tomb released an army of dead from the catacombs.'

'Why don't the people of Zuren destroy the catacombs?' said Sergeant Zander.

'They tried, but killing the dead is not a war you can win. Every soldier you lose adds to their army, and, as you've seen, the dead don't lie down so easily.'

'So they let the dead stay in the catacombs?'

'Yes. And the Yavenlanders hunt down the priests. It's an approach that has worked in the time we've been here. I'm told there hasn't been a serious rising of the dead for fifty years.'

After climbing the steps, they came out into the street, run down and broken temples around them. Crutch wondered how many people had been murdered here by some evil priest intent on claiming power for himself by spreading death and destruction before him.

As they walked down the cracked stone tiles of the street, past ruined temples with vines crawling up their broken walls, a sound came from ahead of them.

'Tell me that's not what I think it is,' said Sergeant Zander.

Feet. Crutch could hear feet. Hundreds of feet clacking on the stones of the street. And he could hear snarling and the grinding of teeth. They rounded a corner and they saw it. An army of skeletons and corpses marching for Zuren.

Chapter 26
The Priest's Power

'This is not good,' said Longshot.

'Is there any way to kill those skeletons?' said Sergeant Zander.

'Kill their priest,' said Damen. 'It's the priest's power that gives them life.'

The ground rumbled around them. Crutch had a terrible feeling of foreboding, like the life around him was being tortured and crushed.

'We need to get on a roof,' said Prince Alderon. 'There will be more of them.'

They found a stone temple and climbed up a couple of broken stone pillars to get to the roof, where they lay watching. Crutch looked out towards Zuren in shock. Skeletons and corpses streamed out of the buildings around them, all heading towards the city, snarling and gnashing their teeth.

The moans and growls of the skeletons were terrifying, coming from lungs and throats that were no longer there. Sound from beyond life itself, from somewhere in death.

Bells rang from far off in the city. From up on top of the temple, they could just see the edge of the city, the dead not there yet, but moving there in a horrifying mass of evil looking to consume and destroy every living thing it touched.

A cat took refuge on top of a broken stone pillar and hissed at the skeletons below it. The skeletons moved and pushed with such force, the pillar toppled. The cat landed between one group of skeletons and ran, but it had nowhere to go. The skeletons were all around it.

It ran up the back of one skeleton, then tried to run across their heads. A skeleton grabbed it with his bony hand while it hissed and scratched. The skeleton pulled the cat to its mouth, and tore it's body open with its teeth, then threw it on the stone street. The cat lay there lifeless, trampled by the moving mass of skeletons. After a couple of moments it got to its feet, hissing and snarling, its teeth grinding and snapping.

'Now you know why I don't like cats,' said Quicksilver.

'You don't like anything unless it's burning,' said Longshot.

'I say we get to the city and try to save some of the people,' said Damen.

'The bells are ringing,' said Prince Alderon. 'They already know what's happening.'

'But many of them will die,' said Damen.

'They'll all die if we don't kill the priest,' said Prince Alderon.

'If we get to the Auld Faithful, we can get away from the city,' said Quicksilver.

'If we can get to the Auld Faithful past that lot. Prince Alderon is right,' said Sergeant Zander. 'We find that priest, and we kill him. That's the only way we can get out of here.'

At the edge of the city, where the old temples began, Crutch could see soldiers evacuating pilgrims and civilians. Some helped or carried the elderly, some herded children from the temples where they studied.

The sight of living people turned the skeletons and corpses into a snarling, growling frenzy. The mass of them sped up. Crutch watched the people flee. Just keep running. Don't stop.

A female soldier ran into every temple, and every building. It was obvious she was determined not to leave anyone behind.

'That's Sophia,' said Longshot, getting to his feet.

'Stay right where you are,' said Sergeant Zander, grabbing Longshot by the shirt. 'There's no way you can get to her from here.'

Sergeant Zander was right. There were hundreds of skeletons and corpses between them and Sophia. Getting there was impossible.

Crutch saw Sophia with a young girl who pleaded with Sophia. Sophia ran back towards the mass of corpses and skeletons to a wooden building, then disappeared inside.

'What is she doing?' said Longshot.

Three corpses had lumbered their way along the street and were almost at the building when the door opened, and a small dog ran down the street to the young girl. Sophia came out and realised she was trapped between two corpses. She drew her sword and slashed at the first corpse, cutting through its guts.

'Its head,' said Crutch. 'Cut off its head.'

She pulled her sword out, then swung at the corpse again, taking its head clean off.

'Yes!' said Longshot.

But the time that took gave the third corpse a chance to move towards her. Sophia was still cornered, but it was worse. Skeletons came up behind the corpses. A few more seconds, and she'd be overwhelmed.

She had her sword up in front of one corpse, ready to swing, but the corpse moved forward, impaling its chest on her weapon. Its head was inches from her, snapping and biting.

The corpse on the other side of her moved closer too. She reached for the dagger at her belt, but not fast enough. Sophia used her elbow on the second corpse's chest to hold it off, but a few more inches and their snapping teeth would be on her.

The first corpse moved forward, its mouth open, and an arrow went straight through its head, pinning it to the wooden wall of the building. A second arrow pinned the shoulder of the second corpse to the wall on the other side of the doorway.

Longshot stood next to Crutch with his bow. Sophia looked up in the direction of the arrows, saw Longshot, saluted, then turned and ran. The skeletons were around her and behind her as she came to the wall of a building. The only way was up. Sophia climbed the wall, jumping on window frames and pulling herself up onto the roof.

She stopped briefly to look back, and the skeletons piled on top of each other in a pyramid, getting higher, coming for her The first of them was almost on the roof. She turned and ran, leaping from the roof she was on to the roof of the next building.

Crutch saw Sophia jump across the gap between two more buildings before she went out of sight.

'Just keep running,' said Longshot.

'What do you think the distance is between here and those corpses you shot?' said Sergeant Zander.

'Five hundred yards, give or take forty yards,' said Longshot.

'Nice work,' said Sergeant Zander.

'Thanks Sarge.'

Crutch wondered how many innocent pilgrims and Yavenlanders were now being torn apart by the dead down there and how many would soon be infected with the hunger. They needed to stop this march now before it got to the city.

'Can anyone see the priest?' said Sergeant Zander.

They all scanned the area around them. Crutch figured the high priest would be closest to where most of the skeletons were, so he looked harder wherever he saw the greatest number of them.

'There,' said Crutch, pointing at a mass of about fifty skeletons three hundred yards from them moving towards the city. 'He's in the middle of that lot.'

'Can you hit him from here, Longshot?' said Sergeant Zander.

'I can try.' Longshot took aim and let an arrow fly. It hit two skeletons in front of the priest, knocking them back, but didn't touch the priest. Longshot fired again, but by the time he'd loosed his arrow, more skeletons moved in front of the priest.

'I can't get a shot through all those skeletons.'

The priest turned, looked up, and pointed straight at them. Dozens of skeletons moved around the priest like a river around a stone, heading straight for where the marines were perched on the roof of the temple.

Crutch looked behind them. Skeletons and corpses were in the street that way, and they headed for their spot on the temple roof too.

'Keep firing,' said Sergeant Zander. 'We'll hold off the dead.'

Longshot took his time. He waited for an opening and let off another arrow, but the skeletons moved and closed up the space before he could get his shot off.

The first skeletons were at the base of the temple now. Longshot aimed and fired again. He skewered three skeletons in front of the priest with the same arrow, but the arrow didn't make it to the priest.

Crutch caught glimpses of the priest staring up at them, pointing at them, then he'd disappear behind skeletons and corpses. The skeletons climbed on top of each other, coming up towards the roof fast.

'Any time now,' said Sergeant Zander as he swung at the first skeleton to make it to the rooftop. The skeleton smashed into pieces that fell to stone tiles in the street, then the pieces pulled back together. The skeleton got to its feet and started climbing again. Quicksilver swung his sword at every skeleton that got within range, grunting as he swung, putting full force into smashing the bones as far as he could.

Damen joined Crutch, hitting skeletons coming up the other side, leaving just enough room for Longshot to fire in between them. Damen was a force of nature with his sword. The skeletons came fast, but Damen was faster, swinging hard and smashing the skeletons to pieces that flew in showers of shattered bones.

Crutch swung his cane hard at the legs of a skeleton that almost got behind him, and its upper body fell towards him as its legs broke. He pulled his cane up and swung at its head as it came, smashing it into shards of bone that scattered and fell over the side of the roof. He pushed the broken legs off before they could rejoin with the rest of its body.

Even with Damen driving the skeletons back, it was just a matter of time before they were overrun. There were too many skeletons for them to hold off and the skeletons weren't dying; just smashing then reforming, driven by some evil force.

Longshot waited, beads of sweat down his forehead, his arms taught, his breathing smooth. Crutch saw what he was waiting for. So many skeletons had headed for the temple they were on, if a few more moved, he'd have a clear shot. But they might be dead or bitten by then.

A huge mass of a dozen skeletons came at them, climbing over the others, snarling and biting, their hands reaching for them. Crutch and Damen moved back. There was no way to stop all of them.

CHAPTER 27
A GROUP EFFORT

Crutch saw the teeth of the skeletons coming at him, then Longshot let the arrow go, a perfect shot that got the high priest in the head. The skeletons made a high-pitched scream.

The skeleton, inches from Crutch, collapsed into a pile of bones. The skeletons around them, and stacked up in front of the temple fell, their bones clattering on the stones.

'That was way too close,' said Sergeant Zander.

Crutch looked at the streets closest to them, littered with bones and skulls. He could see three pilgrims in robes and the cat infected with the hunger, growling, and snarling. Then he looked over to the other side of the ruined temples and his heart dropped. Sergeant Zander saw it too.

'Why didn't all the skeletons fall?' said Sergeant Zander.

Crutch realised there could be only one reason. 'There's more than one priest.'

The skeletons were moving about two hundred yards to their right.

'Where is the priest?' said Sergeant Zander.

'He must be moving through the buildings to stop us shooting at him,' said Crutch.

'We need to get over there to educate him on the folly of killing innocents,' said Damen.

Crutch expected Prince Alderon to voice his objections or straight-out order Damen not to go anywhere near the high priest, but he just nodded.

They climbed and slid down from the roof of the temple on the bones of the skeletons that tried to kill them just a minute ago. One of the infected pilgrims came running at them, snarling, and Sergeant Zander swung and chopped its head clean off its shoulders, the head still snarling as it rolled across the stone tiles of the street.

Crutch headed for where the skeletons were thickest, keeping well behind the moving, growling, snarling mass. The priest had to be in there somewhere.

Another pilgrim came at him from his right, hands out, growling like a dog. Crutch used his cane in one hand and drove the blade into its chest, then pulled his dagger out with the other hand and hacked through its neck.

It took him four slicing, hacking passes to get the head off. The pilgrim bit at Crutch's hand every time it got close, but Crutch managed to avoid getting bitten. If they had to fight these things, it was just a matter of time before one of them or all of them did get infected.

The marines, Prince Alderon and Damen, closed around, beside, and behind Crutch, making a defensive wedge. That was good against ten or fifteen enemy soldiers, but it would do nothing against fifty skeletons swarming all over them and pushing them to the ground with their weight.

Crutch caught a glimpse of the priest up ahead, going out of one temple and through the open arch of another.

'He's that way,' said Crutch, pointing the way the priest went. They followed faster, but they were hindered by having to keep their distance from the horde of skeletons and corpses the priest led. When they entered the temple, the priest was already out the other side.

'I can't get a shot at him this way,' said Longshot.

'Can you burn him Quicksilver?'

'Same problem,' said Quicksilver. 'He's too far away to throw bluefire at him.'

'There's only a dozen skeletons behind him,' said Crutch. 'If we can push them out of the way, then we can get close enough.'

'And cut his heart out,' said Damen.

'Anyone have any other ideas?' said Sergeant Zander. 'Maybe a plan that doesn't involve certain death if we fail.'

Sergeant Zander was right. Getting that close meant if they didn't kill the priest, they'd immediately be pushed under dozens of skeletons and corpses and ripped to pieces. It was certain death if they failed.

'What if we get close enough to throw the bluefire at him?' said Quicksilver.

'That's a good idea,' said Sergeant Zander. 'But once we're that close, we face the same risk. And if the fire doesn't work, we've lost the element of surprise.'

Crutch couldn't think of another way. He hoped Sergeant Zander or someone would come up with something better, but they quickly realised killing the priest hand to hand was the only way.

Time was running out to save the people of Yavenland from this horde of skeletons. Crutch could see just a few more old temples left. The inhabited part of the city was up ahead.

'We go,' said Sergeant Zander. 'I'll be the head of the spear with Crutch behind me. Boulder and Damen, you go to the side next to Crutch and swing your weapons hard to get the dead away from us. The rest of you clean up what's left. Once we're in range of the priest, anyone who gets an attack should take it and make it count.'

They all nodded, and Sergeant Zander started moving fast. He reached the first of the skeletons behind the priest when the floor up ahead to their right started crumbling, rock falling, and stone tiles caving in to the ground underneath.

From out of the ground came more skeletons, spilling forth in a cloud of dust made by the falling stone mixed with the earth underneath.

'They're digging their way out of the catacombs,' said Prince Alderon.

'Keep going,' said Sergeant Zander. 'The only way to stop them is to kill the priest.'

They pushed forward. Sergeant Zander pushed two skeletons to his left that Boulder smashed to pieces with his axe, then Sergeant Zander pushed another two to his right that Damen smashed with a brutal swing of his sword. But they kept coming.

The priest raised his hands, and the earth rumbled and shook. Crutch struggled to keep his feet on the ground, the shaking was so strong. Crutch looked to his left behind him, and the skeletons that had turned to bones and skulls when they killed the first priest now pulled together, reforming into snarling, biting harbingers of death.

The skeletons were a couple of hundred yards away, but they were coming. Coming for the marines.

'Keep going!' yelled Sergeant Zander. 'We do this or we die!'

Sergeant Zander pushed hard, swinging his sword with one hand and pushing skeletons out to his sides with the other. Boulder and Damen swung hard, Boulder with his axe and Damen with his sword. As quick as they could swing and smash one skeleton, another was in front of them, and the skeletons they'd smashed reformed.

Sergeant Zander was just a few feet from the priest now with Crutch right behind. Sergeant Zander pushed the last skeleton away and raised his sword ready to plunge it into the priest's back when the priest turned toward Sergeant Zander smiling.

Sergeant Zander's eyes were locked with the priest. His sword stopped as if he were paralyzed. Then Sergeant Zander turned to Boulder and swung at him.

'Sergeant Zander. Stop!' yelled Boulder, grabbing the sergeant's sword arm.

Crutch moved forward towards the priest, who now looked straight at Crutch, smiling. Moving felt like walking through mud. Crutch had his dagger up, but it was like it wouldn't move.

Boulder let go of Sergeant Zander's arm and raised his axe, ready to swing at Crutch. Crutch saw the axe coming, and saw Sergeant Zander raise his sword, aiming to run it through Crutch's back. He saw the skeletons around them all closing in, their mouths wide, biting and growling.

Then he saw Damen out of the corner of his other eye, moving faster than everyone, hitting the priest's knee with his sword, and in an instant Crutch was free. He drove the dagger into the priest's chest with all his strength and saw the blood spurt out. He pulled out the dagger and thrust it home again and again as the priest fell back, still looking in Crutch's eyes, still smiling.

Crutch straddled the priest and stabbed him over and over. Crutch's arms, his face, his body, were covered in blood. He stabbed and kept on stabbing until Damen put a hand on his shoulder.

'He's dead, Crutch. We still have to deal with the infected.'

Crutch looked up. The skeletons were gone, turned to piles of bones. The corpses lay dead around them too. There were a handful of infected people and pilgrims.

Sergeant Zander and Boulder looked at each other, confused.

'It was the priest,' said Prince Alderon. 'He took over your minds. Tried to make you do what you'd never do yourselves.'

'That's an experience I never want again,' said Sergeant Zander. 'I'm so sorry, Boulder, Crutch.'

'That's okay,' said Boulder. 'It's not your fault.

'Are you okay, Crutch?' said Sergeant Zander. 'Were you bit?'

'I don't think so,' said Crutch, feeling all over himself. He must have looked a terrible sight, covered in the priest's blood.

'You fight well for a man with a cane,' said Damen, smiling.

'You're good with that sword,' said Crutch.

'Enough talking, said Sergeant Zander. 'Let's reform and deal with these infected.'

'That cat is mine,' said Quicksilver.

They quickly dealt with the few infected who remained. Damen was devastating with his sword, cutting into three infected before Sergeant Zander even got a chance to raise his weapon.

The cat proved elusive. It kept coming at them but jumped away fast whenever Quicksilver tried to swing at it with his sword. Eventually he got it by pretending he wasn't watching, then stabbing it through the top of its head when it came in close to bite him.

As they finished cleaning up the infected, they saw Sophia leading a group of Yavenlander soldiers.

'You killed the priest?' said Sophia, looking at Crutch.

'I got the second one,' said Crutch. 'Longshot got the first.'

Sophia looked at Longshot. 'I thought you were talking shit about your skill with a bow. That was you who saved me from the dead earlier, wasn't it?'

'Well, I don't like to boast,' said Longshot.

'After two shots like that to save my life, you can boast all you want.'

'If you insist. There was a crosswind that threw me off a little, but I accounted for that.'

Sophia walked straight up to Longshot, grabbed him by the back of the head and kissed him hard. 'That's to say thank you.'

'You can say thank you any time you want,' said Longshot.

Sophia kissed him again. 'That's thank you from the people of Yavenland.'

'The people of Yavenland are welcome,' said Longshot.

'Are we all getting thanked?' said Quicksilver. 'It was a group effort.'

Chapter 28
A Swineherd's Crotch

When the marines got to the Auld Faithful, it was night. Cedric waited on the deck, flanked by two guards.

'Is this the king?' said Cedric.

'This is Prince Alderon and his protector Damen,' said Sergeant Zander.

'It's a pleasure to meet you both and to have you aboard the Auld Faithful,' said Cedric.

'Thank you for your help,' said Prince Alderon. 'Your marines saved the city of Zuren from death today.'

'I've found they make a habit of doing things like that,' said Cedric.

'Prince Alderon is being hunted by Estovians,' said Sergeant Zander.

'It seems we have something in common then,' said Cedric. 'Would you be so kind as to accompany me to my cabin, Prince Alderon? There are some issues I'd like to discuss.'

The prince and Cedric went into the captain's cabin. After fifteen minutes, Prince Alderon came out and asked Damen to join them. After another minute, they all came out of the captain's cabin with Cedric looking worried.

'We leave at first light tomorrow,' said Cedric. 'Best not to give the Estovians any more chances to catch Prince Alderon.'

'Two more hammocks with us in the marine quarters then?' said Sergeant Zander.

'It might be crowded, but I think that would be wise,' said Cedric. 'Are you particular about your sleeping arrangements, Prince Alderon?'

'Damen and I will sleep anywhere,' said Prince Alderon.

'Do we have to leave tomorrow, captain?' said Longshot. 'I have some unfinished business here in Zuren.'

'You should finish it while you have the chance tonight,' said Cedric. 'With an Estovian warship so close, we can't take the chance that they send more assassins for us.'

Longshot's unfinished business arrived on the docks in front of the Auld Faithful after the crew had eaten their evening meal. He met Sophia on the docks.

'The city of Zuren would like to thank you Ironborn marines for stopping the high priest,' said Sophia.

'We leave tomorrow at first light,' said Longshot. 'I asked the captain if we could stay longer, but it's not possible.'

Sophia looked at Longshot. 'Then I guess it has to be tonight. I'll tell the city council. Can you all meet me here at the docks in an hour's time?'

'I'm not sure if we can,' said Longshot.

'Well, if you'd rather hang out here with your boyfriends on a ship that smells worse than a swineherd's crotch.'

'I meant, I'll have to check with the captain,' said Longshot.

Crutch, the marines, Prince Alderon, Damen, and Cedric all decided they'd go with Sophia into Zuren. Sergeant Zander didn't want to leave Cedric on the ship at night without the marines, and Cedric didn't want to leave the prince on the ship either.

Before they left, Longshot asked the marines for tips on how to impress Sophia.

'I flex my muscles every time I can,' said Sergeant Zander. 'The ladies love that.'

'Great idea,' said Longshot.

'You should bring her a gift,' said Quicksilver. 'Something that burns well.'

'A gift is a great idea,' said Sergeant Zander. 'The burning thing, not so much.'

'You should tell her about all the enemies you've killed,' said Quicksilver. 'Women love a strong man.'

'Good thinking,' said Longshot.

When Sophia met them on the docks, Longshot carried a leg of ham.

'This is for you,' he said to Sophia.

She looked at him like he'd lost his mind. 'An old leg of ham. Why would you think I'd want an old leg of ham?' said Sophia.

'It's a gift,' said Longshot. 'One time I shot a man with an arrow, and his eyeball came out the back of his head.'

'What does that have to do with the leg of ham?' said Sophia.

'Nothing,' said Longshot. 'Just don't want you to think I'm weak.'

'Yes,' said Sophia, looking at the ham then looking at Longshot like he'd taken leave of his senses. 'Shall we go?'

As Sophia turned, Quicksilver gave Longshot the thumbs up.

'It's working,' he whispered.

After a fifteen-minute walk, they entered a huge building made of stone blocks with a high vaulted ceiling.

'City hall,' said Sophia, holding the leg of lamb at a distance as if it might be carrying some kind of disease.

As they entered, a crowd of people started cheering and clapping. Crutch and the marines waved back. Sergeant Zander looked around, scanning the crowd. Too easy to hide an assassin in a crowd like this, thought Crutch, although after Sophia sent the head of the last assassin to the Estovians, it seemed unlikely they'd risk the full wrath of the city by trying the same thing again.

Sophia led them down a blue carpet with cheering Yavenlanders each side of them to a stage at the back of the hall where half a dozen dignitaries stood.

'This is the mayor of Zuren,' said Sophia.

'What is that you're carrying?' said the mayor.

'A leg of ham,' said Sophia. 'It's a gift for you from the Ironborn crew.'

'Thank you,' said the mayor, not sure what to do with the ham. 'We are indebted to you all. Sophia tells me you stopped an army of the dead.'

'It was a close thing,' said Sergeant Zander. 'You may want to improve your defences at the catacombs.'

'Sophia has been telling me exactly that for some time. I will have to take more of her advice in future. Perhaps less of her gifts.' The mayor handed the leg of ham to an assistant, who looked less than thrilled to take it.

'And hunt down every one of those priests of the Order of the Tomb,' said Sergeant Zander.

'Indeed,' said the mayor. 'Right now we have a special thanks for you all. We'd like to make you honorary citizens of Yavenland.'

'We'd be delighted to accept this honour,' said Cedric.

'Is there cake?' said Boulder. 'I like cake.'

'Yes,' said the mayor. 'We have cake.'

The ceremony was informal, and afterwards the marines mingled with the Yavenlanders, always staying close to Cedric and Prince Alderon. Longshot tried to flex his muscles every time Sophia looked in his direction, but the effect was comical, Longshot being tall and skinny. Sophia kept shaking her head, probably wondering what was wrong with him.

The mayor's wife talked to them briefly, thanking the marines for their help. Crutch's eyes were on her neck. She wore a stunning gold necklace with a heart on it.

'Where would I get a necklace like that?' said Crutch. 'My girlfriend in Ironbay would love it.'

'You can have this one,' said the mayor's wife, taking it off and giving it to Crutch.

'Really?' said Crutch.

'Of course. I have a jewellery box full of necklaces.'

'Thank you very much,' said Crutch.

Before they left, Sophia talked to Crutch.

'What is wrong with Longshot?'

'He's fond of you,' said Crutch. 'Us marines got together and gave him some advice on how to impress you. Not the best advice by the looks of it.'

Sophia broke out laughing. 'He is such an idiot.' She walked over to him, grabbed the back of his head, and kissed him hard.

'I guess we'll be leaving Longshot here then,' said Cedric.

Late that night, in the darkness of the catacombs, two men in red robes crept out of the darkness to the high priest Crutch had killed.

They picked up the body, one on each side, and carried it back to the catacombs, disappearing into the inky blackness of its depths.

Chapter 29

Quarry

The next morning, the ship's bell rang on the Auld Faithful. Longshot ran down the docks, making it just before the crew pulled up the gangplank.

'Glad you could join us,' said Cedric.

'Sorry captain. Got delayed.'

'Is that what you young people are calling it these days?' said Cedric.

Crutch watched Zuren as they pulled out of the harbour. Thankfully, his pilgrim followers hadn't returned. He guessed that their journey to the outside of the catacombs was enough to put them off following the 'great one with the cane.'

He did wonder what happened to Eleezer. Was he infected, or had he deciphered the inscriptions and found a cure to the hunger? He hoped he'd found that cure, but he knew it was far more likely Eleezer now haunted the catacombs under the old temples in Zuren, searching endlessly for prey to feed on.

Crutch wondered how many more men he'd lead to their deaths or an even worse fate like Eleezer.

As the Auld Faithful came into the open sea, Crutch could see the Estovian warship unfurling its sails in the distance and heading their way. Was it following them?

After a few more minutes of sailing, it became very obvious the Estovian warship was chasing them.

'Full sail,' said Cedric. 'Sound the bell. I want all hands on deck and armed.'

The marines joined Cedric on the bridge.

'Will they catch us?' said Sergeant Zander.

'We should be able to build a good lead on them after we get through the reef, at least until we have to slow for the next reef or tack for the wind,' said Cedric.

'So they're as fast as we are?' said Sergeant Zander.

'Our speeds are fairly evenly matched,' said Cedric. 'That means if we don't sail perfectly, the Estovians will catch us.'

'They're armed with ballistas, and we're not,' said Sergeant Zander. 'That wouldn't go well for us.'

Crutch thought about that. The Estovians could stay at ballista range and fire on them until they ran out of ballista bolts. By then, the deck and anyone on it would be dead or destroyed.

'They're heavier with a deeper draft,' said Cedric. 'We might take advantage of that.'

'Are there any islands near here with a river?' said Crutch.

'Only one,' said Cedric. 'With this wind, it will take us two days sailing to get there.'

'Can we stay ahead of them that long?' said Crutch.

'If we get creative, we might,' said Cedric. 'What did you have in mind?'

Crutch's idea could only work if they maintained a good lead on the Estovian warship. Even then, the plan would take perfect execution to pull off.

Cedric told them they'd have to take a different route than the way they got to Yavenland so they could get to an island. That route meant more reefs and hazards in the water.

'If the weather is good, we can navigate them,' said Cedric. 'If we get storms, then we'll be lucky to get through alive.'

The Estovian warship stayed on them. Any closer, and they'd be close enough to fire their ballistas. Cedric did everything he could think of to maximise their speed.

The warship stayed upwind of them in the standard chasing strategy. When the chasing ship came onto its quarry, it would create a wind shadow, making it easier to board. But Cedric had no intention of letting the Estovian warship get anywhere near that close.

When they were forced to navigate a set of shallow reefs, Cedric saw the opportunity.

'We can take advantage of their bearing,' said Cedric. He took the Auld Faithful on a long tack, sailing just yards from a reef. At the last possible moment, he tacked the ship, changing direction. The warship following couldn't make the same tack without hitting the reef. The Estovians had to sail around the reef, losing time, and that let the Auld Faithful get a lead.

They gained just a few hundred yards, but they needed every yard they could get.

'I think those Estovians are feeling way too comfortable chasing us,' said Crutch.

'Do you have an idea for making them a little less comfortable,' said Cedric.

'I do.'

Crutch and the marines made a raft out of wooden crates from the hold. Quicksilver added his own design to the top: a small holding basket. They got a boat anchor from one of the longboats and attached that to it, then they waited for an opportunity.

'That channel between the reefs up ahead looks like the kind of thing you're looking for,' said Cedric.

'That should be perfect,' said Crutch.

As they passed through the channel, Longshot threw the boat anchor and landed it on the reef. Quicksilver tied a sack into the basket on the raft, and the crew lowered it overboard, slow and steady, so when it got to the water, the raft was level.

The raft bobbed up and down in the channel, right in the path of the Estovian warship following them. As they came up to it, the Estovians pulled out long boathooks to push the raft out of the way.

'Should have gone off by now,' said Quicksilver.

Two Estovians had just started pushing the raft away when it exploded in blue flames. The flames ran up the boat hooks onto the deck. Part of the hull closest to the raft was on fire too, blue flames burning it.

The Estovian crew ran across the deck, throwing buckets of water over the flames and then wet sacks on top of any embers. They threw buckets down the side of the hull to douse the flames there.

'Nice work, men,' said Cedric.

'That should make them think twice about what might happen if they get too close,' said Sergeant Zander.

The next time they used a bluefire raft, the Estovians saw it and avoided taking the channel it was in, going around the whole reef instead. That helped the Auld Faithful get ten minutes ahead.

'One more of those, and we might lose her,' said Sergeant Zander.

'Maybe,' said Cedric. 'But the Estovians are clever. They'll be thinking up some way of dealing with the rafts.'

Cedric was right. The next time the Auld Faithful left a raft with bluefire in a channel, the Estovians fired on it with their ballistas as soon as it was in range. Bolt after bolt smashing the raft and the basket with the bluefire on it to pieces, the balls of bluefire sinking under the water.

By the time the Estovian warship got to the wrecked remains of the raft, the bluefire was harmless, burning underneath the water.

'It was fun while it lasted,' said Quicksilver.

'We're far enough ahead to try Crutch's plan,' said Cedric. 'The island is just a few hours sailing from here.'

Chapter 30
Up A River

Cedric took the Auld Faithful up the river as far as he dared. Too far, and they'd risk getting grounded. Not far enough, and the Estovian warship could follow and get close enough to fire on them.

Navigating up a river in the dark was challenging. Cedric had crew members with plumb lines on both sides of the bow checking the depth as the other deckhands held lanterns on sticks over the side so Cedric could see where he was sailing.

The Estovians followed to the mouth of the river and anchored there.

'They don't need to come any further than that,' said Cedric. 'They know we're trapped now.'

'Do you think they'll get off their ship and engage us on land?' said Crutch.

'They might,' said Cedric. 'But since that trick we pulled on them in the Yukalan Straits after we escaped Zanithburg, they're likely to be more cautious.'

'They don't know how many men we have or how well armed we are,' said Sergeant Zander. 'That should make them cautious too.'

'Time to see if you can make your plan work,' said Cedric. 'Douse all the lights.'

The crew put out all the lanterns. They were in the dark on a moonless night. They could see lanterns on the Estovian warship. After a few minutes, the Estovians put out their lanterns too.

'Just like you said Crutch,' said Sergeant Zander. 'With our lights out, they'll be worried we're gonna use the light on their ship against them in some way.'

The crew lowered a longboat over the side of the Auld Faithful. The Estovians would know they were up to something, but they wouldn't know what. The river had a current running out to the sea towards the Estovian warship.

'Why don't we just swim down there?' said Longshot.

'There's no way we could swim against that current,' said Sergeant Zander. 'We'd get to the ship, but then we'd be washed out to sea. And on the way past, we'd be sitting ducks for the Estovians.'

'I thought you'd want to use what you learned from Sophia,' said Crutch.

'I think he learned a lot more than sailing in the dark,' said Quicksilver.

Quicksilver, Sergeant Zander, and Longshot climbed into the longboat, raised the mast, and hoisted the sail they'd painted black. Then they waited.

Boulder and Crutch climbed down the hull with ropes attached to them. Crutch carried a huge shackle key. Once they were in the water, the rest of the marines set off in the longboat.

Crutch and Boulder drifted with the current towards the Estovian warship. Crutch had memorised where the anchor chain was and where the anchor would be on the river bed. When they got there, he pulled the rope to signal to the crew at the other end to stop letting them drift.

Crutch could barely hear the longboat pass them. If he didn't know it was there, he would have thought it was just a fish or something in the current. He knew Longshot would be at the tiller.

Crutch waited. The bell on the Estovian warship started ringing.

'Enemy boat in water!' yelled an Estovian on the deck.

Crutch and Boulder dove straight down for the anchor. Crutch found it and ran his hand down until he found the shackle that attached the anchor to the chain. He put on the huge shackle key, grabbed Boulder's hand, and guided him to it.

Boulder and Crutch strained at the shackle with all their strength, trying to turn it. With the full weight of the ship pulling against the current, they knew it would be under force and hard to move. That's why Crutch wanted Boulder with him.

They pulled as hard as they could, and it moved, but only a fraction of an inch. With his lungs burning, Crutch had to go up for air. Boulder went up with him. When he broke the surface of the water, lanterns were alight all over the Estovian warship.

Behind the ship, Crutch got a glimpse of the longboat, with its black sails visible in the lantern light. The Estovians fired on it with their ballistas. It was headed to the side of the river, but Crutch couldn't see anyone in it. Where were Longshot, Sergeant Zander and Quicksilver?

'Enemy in the water at bow,' yelled an Estovian.

Crutch and Boulder dove back down. They had to undo that shackle, and they had to do it now. Crutch found the shackle again, put on the shackle key, and he and Boulder pushed on it with everything they had. It turned, slow with the force of the ship pulling on the chain making it a struggle, but it turned.

A ballista bolt shot through the water inches from Crutch's ear and buried itself somewhere in the river bed behind him.

They kept turning. Crutch was out of breath, but he kept pulling on the shackle key, turning it. He felt down to the pin holding the shackle. One more turn should do it. Boulder and Crutch gave the shackle one last turn.

Crutch tapped Boulder on the shoulder, tugged his line twice, and they were pulled back towards the ship by the crew. Another ballista bolt hit the water in between Crutch and Boulder, narrowly missing them both.

Crutch looked back, and he could see two Estovians climbing down the anchor chain, one with a shackle key. Crutch prayed for a wave right now or anything that would knock that shackle loose from the anchor now that the pin was no longer screwed into the shackle.

The longboat was on the shore, barely visible in the lantern light from the Estovian ship. It was full of ballista bolts, with the Estovians raining down bolt after bolt on it. but he couldn't see Sergeant Zander, Longshot, or Quicksilver anywhere.

Another ballista bolt landed in the water just behind Crutch and Boulder. They were out of range. As the crew pulled them towards the Auld Faithful, Crutch saw a flame on the shore a hundred yards from the longboat. Then there was an arrow on fire, and Longshot, visible in the fire of the arrow, drawing back his bow.

Just as quickly, Longshot disappeared into darkness, and the arrow sailed to the stern of the Estovian ship, which exploded in blue fire. The force of the explosion shook the Estovian warship, and the anchor chain on the ship went loose as the shackle fell free from the anchor underwater. The ship immediately started drifting out of the river mouth into the ocean.

The crew on the Auld Faithful cheered at the flaming ship as Boulder and Crutch were hauled on board.

The Estovian ship raised its sails, but as the ship turned, Crutch could see their rudder at the stern was badly damaged and still burned with blue flames.

'Let's hope that damage is bad enough that they can't steer their ship at all,' said Crutch.

'They'll fix that, but hopefully that will give us enough time to get well away,' said Cedric. 'Light the lanterns, men.'

The crew lit the lanterns on the Auld Faithful. Crutch saw Quicksilver running up the bank of the river holding a torch with Sergeant Zander and Longshot close behind. They kept going until they were well upstream, jumped in the water and swam across, and came up the hull of the Auld Faithful on the climbing ropes.

The crew cheered them as they came aboard. Crutch looked out, and the Estovian warship was drifting further out to sea. In a few minutes, the Auld Faithful could clear her easily and head for Ironbay.

'Well done everyone,' said Cedric.

The crew patted Crutch and the marines on the back.

'You're all dead set legends.'

'Great plan, Crutch.'

'Great shot, Longshot.'

'That taught the bastards not to chase the Auld Faithful.'

'Unfurl the sails,' said Cedric. 'Let's head for Ironbay.'

Chapter 31
Captain Jack

Crutch and the crew expected storms and wild seas on this voyage, but so far the wind and the waves had been moderate. Cedric was grateful for it.

'I don't know if I have it in me to fight another storm like the one we came through on the way to Yavenland,'

There were still plenty of dangerous challenges. Cedric and the crew had to navigate uncharted reefs and huge rock formations. Because they had to change route to sabotage the Estovian warship chasing them, the route they took back was different from when they had come over the first time.

One morning, the lookout shouted, 'Reef ahead, captain.'

Crutch came on deck and could see a massive mountain of rock coming out of the water on the port side. In the distance, he could hear waves hitting the reef ahead.

'Any way around?' said Cedric.

'There's a channel next to that island of rock,' yelled the lookout.

'How wide?' said Cedric.

'At least sixty yards,' said the Lookout.

'The channel it is then,' said Cedric.

This was not a difficult passage for Cedric in calm weather like today. He steered the Auld Faithful with ease into the channel. Crutch watched the towering rock mountain coming out of the water on the port side, higher than the ship's mast, and the waves breaking on the reef on the starboard side.

They were halfway through when the lookout yelled, 'Enemy ship ahead!'

A deckhand rang the ship's bell, and the crew of the Auld Faithful swarmed on to the deck with weapons drawn.

The Estovian warship came around the mountain of rock in the water in a perfectly timed manoeuvre. There was no way the Auld Faithful could tack or get away. The crew's only choice was to surrender or fight.

Crutch looked at the warship, bristling with ballistas down each side, loaded with gunners ready to fire.

'Our only chance is to let them board, then fight them below deck where they can't fire their ballistas on us,' said Sergeant Zander.

'It's as good a plan as we're likely to get,' said Cedric. 'Take the men below. I'll stay up here.'

'I'll stay too,' said Crutch.

'You will not,' said Cedric. 'We need our best marines alive to win this fight.'

Crutch went below deck with the rest of the crew, and waited right next to the hatch closest to the bridge. A few deckhands stayed up top to man the lines. If the Estovian ship fired on the Auld Faithful, Cedric was dead.

In the clear weather, voices carried well across the water. He could hear everything that was said on deck.

'This is Captain Jack,' said a voice from the Estovian ship. 'If you resist, we'll kill your crew. There's no need to die today.'

'Captain Jack?' whispered Crutch. 'He's not an Estovian.'

'He's a pirate,' said Sergeant Zander. 'I didn't think he robbed Ironborn ships, though.'

'The Auld Faithful looks more Estovian than Ironborn right now,' said Crutch.

Crutch heard the grappling hooks thrown and could hear the two ships' hulls grinding together.

'You're not Estovian,' said Captain Jack from up top.

'No, we are not,' said Cedric. 'We're Ironborn to the core. Forged in steel.'

'Wait. This is the Auld Faithful.'

'It is,' said Cedric.

'Lower your weapons, men,' said Captain Jack. 'We're don't rob Ironborn ships.'

'Thank you,' said Cedric. 'I'm Captain Cedric Beaumont.'
'King of the pirates,' said Captain Jack.
'I find the label offensive. I've never engaged in piracy.'
'I apologise,' said Captain Jack.
'So my men and my cargo are safe?' said Cedric.
'They are,' said Captain Jack. 'May I come aboard?'
'Just you?' said Cedric.
'Just me.'
'You may,' said Cedric. 'Is it safe for me to bring my crew on deck?
'It is. You have my word as a gentleman.'
'All hands on deck,' said Cedric. 'Sheath your weapons.'

Crutch was the first through the hatch. When he came out, he could see the Estovian warship alongside. He saw their ballistas pointing down into the ocean and saw their crew with weapons sheathed.

Crutch moved behind Captain Jack. Fine words or not, he had his walking cane, and he could use it on this captain if he needed to.

'I served on the Auld Faithful several years ago,' said Captain Jack as the Auld Faithful's crew came on deck.

'Under Captain Wyld?' said Cedric.

'Have you met him?'

'We had the misfortune,' said Cedric. 'I bested him in a duel to take back command of this vessel.'

'It's a sad thing,' said Captain Jack. 'William Wyld was a fine captain once before he got on the jamaroot.'

'We only knew him as a tyrant,' said Cedric. 'He whipped our best marine, drugged and killed our captain, threw deck boys to the sharks, and killed crew members for the pleasure of it.'

'I've seen his dark side,' said Captain Jack. 'He pushed me off the deck into the ocean. I was lucky to survive. I still have fond memories of this ship, though.'

'We can't stand chatting all day,' said Cedric, looking at the reef and the rocks.

'Are you heading back to Ironbay?' said Captain Jack.

'We are.'

'I'm wondering if you might do me a favour. One of our crewmen was injured loading cargo in the ocean. There's nothing more our ship's doctor can do for him. He's Ironborn, and it might be some comfort to him if he could see his family before he dies. Would you be willing to take him back to Ironbay?'

'Of course,' said Cedric.

The injured deckhand was brought on board the Auld Faithful with two crew members holding him up, one on each side.

'His name is Kaydn,' said Captain Jack. 'He doesn't talk much. I think he was hit in the head by a barrel or crate when we loaded at sea.'

'We'll take good care of him and get him home,' said Cedric.

'Thank you,' said Captain Jack. 'It's a kindness I won't forget.'

Captain Jack left the Auld Faithful. His crew released the grappling hooks, and they sailed off.

'Take Kaydn below to the sick bay and have Doc take a look at him,' said Cedric as he turned the Auld Faithful to catch the wind.

Chapter 32
Damen

Damen joined the marines each morning for training. It was obvious to Crutch and the other marines that he was an exceptional fighter. He loved the different exercises Sergeant Zander set and was good at coming up with creative ways to kill opponents.

Instead of training on deck, one morning Sergeant Zander had them assemble in the corridor near the marines quarters.

'Today we'll talk about fighting in enclosed spaces,' said Sergeant Zander.

'I've done plenty of that in the catacombs,' said Damen.

'Yes, and you're very good at it, but it's different when you fight in a group of men against soldiers who've trained to fight in tight spaces.'

Crutch's memory went back to fighting the Komitav in the Komitav Operative building. They used spearmen and swordsmen together for deadly effect.

'First, you have to be aware of who's around you,' said Sergeant Zander. 'You don't want to take a backswing and cut open the marine behind you or beside you.'

'Especially important if that marine is me,' said Longshot.

'And you don't want to start a fire without having a way to escape before you die in the smoke or the flames yourself,' said Sergeant Zander.

'I don't know why everyone's looking at me,' said Quicksilver.

'You also want to think about cooperating. If you have a spear, or a pike, or even a sharp, pointy stick, you can stand behind the person in the lead and stab at your enemy's front line. One opponent can be predictable for your enemy, but when there's one opponent at the front and another behind with a spear, that makes everything unpredictable and dangerous. They avoid the sword and find a spear through their leg or their guts. They avoid the spear, and they get a sword to the chest or the head.'

'Nice!' said Damen.

'Unless you're on the receiving end,' said Crutch, remembering the komitav in Teevilgrad.

'Today we'll take turns. One person takes the lead with a blade, and another fights behind with a spear.'

Crutch spent some time talking to Damen alone. There was one conversation that stuck with him.

'The prince is not just the rightful king,' said Damen.

'What do you mean?'

'It's not something I talk about,' said Damen. 'If I tell you, can you keep it secret?'

'Of course,' said Crutch.

'When we were in the jungle in Yavenland, we were chased many times. But one time we were caught.'

'I find it hard to believe anyone could catch you,' said Crutch.

'They used a net trap and bashed our heads before we could get out. When we came to, they had us tied, ready to kill us in some kind of sacrifice.'

'That sounds like Yavenland.'

'They put Prince Alderon on some kind of stone altar there in the jungle, and a priest was about to thrust a dagger into his chest when the prince screamed, and I could feel it. It was like a surge of power coming from the trees around us.

'There was this wind that came from nowhere. Their priest dropped dead, and the rest of them fled. The trees around us had withered. When I finally got loose, I knew the prince had magic. Powerful magic.'

'I see why you keep that secret,' said Crutch.

If what Damen said was true, Prince Alderon had magic like the spirit keepers in Papageenar. The magic Crutch had seen on the

Kona track terrified him. Just being near someone who could use it made Crutch nervous.

Imagine if they made Prince Alderon king. What would it be like to have a king who could bring down magic to destroy anyone who displeased him?

All the marines liked Damen. He fit into their little killing squad perfectly. He had the skills and the mindset of a marine. It didn't surprise Crutch when Sergeant Zander gave Damen the offer as they ate their evening meal together in the galley.

'If you ever want to join the marines we have a place for you,' said Sergeant Zander.

'Thank you, but I belong by the side of Prince Alderon,' said Damen.

'Perhaps you shouldn't reject that offer so quickly,' said Prince Alderon.

'What do you mean?' said Damen.

'Being a king can be a staid affair. There are council meetings, visits with dignitaries, and other tasks that would bore you to tears. You've been a great protector for me all these years. More than any prince could ever ask for. But we both know you don't want to sit around at meetings all day.'

'I could join the king's guard,' said Damen.

'Of course you could, and you'd be a magnificent king's guard too, but you'd be happier in the thick of things using your sword as a marine.'

'It just doesn't feel right after all these years,' said Damen.

'But it is right,' said Prince Alderon. 'Serving with these marines, you'd get to use your talents, and you'd have some of the bravest, finest men I've ever seen who'll have your back.'

'I'll think on it,' said Damen.

'If you think on it, you'll see I'm right,' said Prince Alderon.

Chapter 33
Injured Sailor

The crew showed kindness to Kaydn, the injured sailor from Captain Jack's ship. He didn't speak much, but he'd smile sometimes, a weak smile that made Crutch feel sorry for him.

Injury or death was always close on a navy ship, and Crutch knew it could just as easily be him injured so badly he'd be unable to work the deck or communicate with the rest of the crew.

When the weather was good, the crew brought Kaydn up on deck and found a safe place for him to sit in the shade and enjoy the sea breeze. Every sailor loved the sea breeze. Just the smell of it was better than a tonic.

The one thing Crutch missed the most now when he was on land was that salty smell and the way the wind off the sea would blow across your skin, cooling your body and making you feel alive.

Kaydn sat there, smiling happily.

'I really don't know what's wrong with him,' Doc said when Crutch asked. 'They say he hit his head loading cargo, but I can't find an injury anywhere.'

'So you don't think he was hit?' said Crutch.

'I didn't say that. You can take a serious head injury, and all you can see on the outside is a bruise that heals up after a few days. Whatever it is, I can't find it.'

'Do you think he'll get better?' said Crutch.

'Very hard to say. The best you can do with a patient like this is hope. Maybe a doctor in Ironbay will have more answers.'

That night, Crutch woke to the sound of the ship's bell ringing. The marines, Cedric, Prince Alderon, and Damen stumbled out of their hammocks.

'What is it?' said Cedric to a deckhand racing past him in the corridor below deck.

'Three men found dead, Captain.'

They headed for the crew quarters. Doc was there, leaning over one of the bodies. The dead sailor's mouth was open, like he was screaming. All three bodies were the same.

'It's the shadow wraith again,' said Sergeant Zander.

'It has to be Kaydn,' said Crutch. 'We either kill him or throw him overboard. If we don't, there'll be more dead tomorrow.'

'Are you sure?' said Cedric.

'Last time, the thing that sucked the life out of our crew came out of the man we saved from the raft,' said Crutch. 'When I killed him the deaths stopped.'

'You can't be considering killing one of my patients,' said Doc. 'This is just sailor's superstition.'

'It's not superstition,' said Crutch. 'I saw the thing with my own eyes. It tried to kill me.'

'By sucking the life out of you?' said Doc. 'Does this not sound crazy to you, captain?'

'I've seen crazier things at sea,' said Cedric. 'And I trust Crutch. Are you certain Kaydn is the cause of this, Crutch?'

'I can't be completely certain,' said Crutch. 'But nothing else makes sense.'

'A black ghost sucking the life out of men doesn't make sense either,' said Doc.

'I have to agree,' said Prince Alderon. 'You'd be killing an innocent man for what sounds very much like superstitious nonsense.'

'Do you want to wake up tomorrow night with another three men dead?' said Crutch.

'No,' said Cedric. 'I don't. Make a raft for him and set Kaydn adrift.'

'I must protest,' said Doc.

'I add to that,' since Prince Alderon. 'We're all better than this.'

'Noted,' said Cedric. 'Sergeant Zander, get it done.'

'Yes captain.'

It took the marines a few minutes to nail a raft together from wooden planks they found in the cargo hold and take it up to the deck. When they were finished, the marines went to the sick bay to get Kaydn. Kaydn didn't struggle or try to fight them in any way, just walking along with them meekly as they led him to what would likely be his execution at sea.

There was really no way Kaydn could survive adrift on the ocean in a raft made of planks. He'd be lucky to last a day before he was washed off, and drowned, or eaten by sharks.

'It'd be kinder just to run him through,' said Sergeant Zander.

Sergeant Zander was right, but while they saw Kaydn as a threat, no one had the heart to kill him in cold blood. Easier to let the ocean do it for them.

They sat Kaydn on the raft and tied his thighs to it.

'I really must voice my objection to this,' said Prince Alderon. 'Surely there's another solution. You could throw him in the brig.'

'The thing that came out of the last man could pass through bars,' said Crutch. It killed one man while it was in the brig.'

'No one saw that,' said Doc. 'Can't you see this is wrong, Captain?'

'The safety of my crew comes ahead of what's wrong or right,' said Cedric.

'And if he's innocent and men keep dying?' said Prince Alderon.

'He wouldn't be the first innocent to die in the navy,' said Cedric. 'Not by a huge margin. I won't stand by idly and let my crew die.'

Crutch was surprised and relieved at Cedric's pragmatism. Either Cedric had total faith in Crutch's story or he was unwilling to take any chances at losing more crew to something they didn't understand. He lost three on the way to Yavenland, and now he'd lost three more.

'Please don't do this, Cedric,' said Doc. 'It will haunt you for years to come.'

'Of all the things I've done in command that haunt me, this will barely rate,' said Cedric. He turned to the crew. 'Haul him over the side.'

Prince Alderon jumped on top of Kaydn's body on the raft. 'No! You can't! We can't!'

'Get him off there,' said Cedric.

Damen pulled Prince Alderon off. As he did, Crutch could see Kaydn underneath. The man's face was no longer a smile. There was a fierce anger there as the raft was hauled up over the rail.

Then Kaydn's anger turned to something else. Something horrifying. Kaydn's mouth came open. He screamed, and something black came out of his mouth.

'Get that thing off my ship!' yelled Cedric.

The crew hauled the raft over the side so fast it tipped on its side. Kaydn slipped out of the ropes holding his thighs and fell head first into the water, sinking below the waves. The blackness that came out of him kept coming up from the water where he'd disappeared.

The black mist formed into a huge body vaguely in the shape of a man at its top, the base disappearing into the ocean off the ship. It folded itself around Prince Alderon, whose mouth was open like a scream, but no sound came out.

Damen drew his sword, stabbing at the mist, but the sword passed straight through. Crutch knew the only way to kill this thing was to kill the man it came out of, but Kaydn was sinking to the bottom of the ocean, and the ocean here was deep. They could never get to him.

Quicksilver pulled out a ball of bluefire.

'Don't throw that onto my ship,' said Cedric.

Quicksilver threw the ball of bluefire over the side, into where the black thing came out of the water. It burst into flames and lit the water as it went down but it had no effect on the black monster.

Damen tried to pull Prince Alderon away from the black thing, but he couldn't budge him. Crutch and Sergeant Zander joined them, but even with all three of them, it was like he was bound tight to a tree. Prince Alderon couldn't be moved.

Boulder swung an axe at the base of the thing coming over the rail, but the axe passed straight through it and stuck into the rail underneath.

Quicksilver lit a torch and thrust at the thing, then held it in the blackness of it, but it did nothing.

'Ideas? Anyone?' yelled Sergeant Zander.

Crutch couldn't think of anything. The only way he knew to kill it was to kill the person it came out of, and they'd thrown Kaydn over the side. Now he was at the bottom of the ocean, too deep to get to. They stood there helpless, watching this black thing suck the life from Prince Alderon.

What would it do after that? Would it kill them all, leaving them as empty husks of men on a ghost ship that drifted across the sea until it was found by another ship?

Damen screamed at the top of his lungs, 'No!'

Crutch heard the prince screaming with Damen as a wind began to whip and swirl around them. It grew into a howling tempest swirling around the Auld Faithful, with the black thing at its centre. Crutch was pushed to his knees with the sheer power of it and had to cover his ears. It sounded like the fabric of the air itself was ripping to pieces.

He looked up and saw the black thing ripped, torn, and scattered by the fierce wind. The shadow wraith made a high-pitched scream like a thousand fingernails scratched down a blackboard. The swirling tempest ripped and tore without relief at the shadow wraith until it exploded into a thousand pieces scattered across the deck and over the ocean. Then the pieces disappeared into the air like they'd never existed.

As quickly as it came, the wind stopped. Prince Alderon was on his back on the deck, Damen on his knees next to him, both gasping for air.

In the ocean around them, dead fish rose to the surface. Crutch could see hundreds of them tossed and floating on the waves on their sides, lifeless eyes staring at the sky.

'Are you alright?' said Damen.

Prince Alderon lay there. Still. Lifeless.

Doc joined Damen at the prince's side, putting his ear at the prince's mouth and checking his pulse. 'Get this man to the sick bay right now,' said Doc.

'Post a twenty-four-hour guard on the prince,' said Cedric. 'We don't need any more surprises.'

Chapter 34
Sure He'll Be Safe

The weather was good, and there was no more sign of Estovian warships. Crutch went to the sick bay, where Damen watched over Prince Alderon. Two crew armed with swords stood guard.

'I told you he had magic,' said Damen.

'I believed you,' said Crutch.

'Now everyone knows about it; do you think he'll be safe?' said Damen.

Crutch really didn't know what to think. He had no idea what kind of welcome the prince would get in Ironbay. His instincts told him it was unlikely to be warm and friendly. No king wants his throne to be usurped. None of that would help Damen now, so Crutch did what he was good at. He lied.

'I'm sure he'll be safe. Especially if he has you watching over him.'

'Thank you,' said Damen.

It was a full two days before Prince Alderon opened his eyes and spoke. When Crutch visited them, Damen laughed and joked with the prince, clearly relieved that he was okay.

'I owe you an apology,' said Prince Alderon when he saw Crutch. 'I should have trusted you and the captain.'

Crutch thought about that. Prince Alderon put his life in danger to protect someone he thought was innocent. What kind of place would Ironbay be if the king did that?

'You don't need to apologise for doing what you thought was right at the time,' said Crutch.

'That's kind of you to say, but I am apologising,' said Prince Alderon. 'After you helped us escape the catacombs and fight the priests, I should have had much more faith in you.'

'Thank you,' said Crutch. 'Trying to protect the innocent is not something I would ever hold against you.'

'Captain Beaumont was right when he said you're a truly remarkable young man,' said Prince Alderon.

After another day of rest, the prince was in good health and spirits.

Crutch looked forward to getting back to Ironbay. He looked forward to seeing Abagail's surprise when he gave her the necklace he got for her. Just seeing her after all this time apart would be wonderful.

Chapter 35
Ironbay's Gone Crazy

Crutch was on deck with the marines when Ironbay first came into view.

'Home,' said Sergeant Zander.

Their first view of the docks was a shock to Crutch. Soldiers stood guard everywhere, jostled by crowds of angry-looking civilians. As they came in to dock, six men from the king's guard waited for them, along with an official flanked by two soldiers.

Cedric met them on the ship's rail. The sergeant of the king's guard spoke first.

'You'd be Captain Cedric Beaumont?' he said.

'I am,' said Cedric.

'I'm Sergeant Rogmathon of the king's guard. We've come to escort your passenger to the palace.'

'He's ready for you,' said Cedric. 'I also have a letter here for the palace confirming his identity. Can you give him a couple of minutes to say his farewells?'

'We can,' said Sergeant Rogmathon.

Prince Alderon and Damen were deep in conversation.

'I should come with you,' said Damen.

'We've already discussed this,' said Prince Alderon. 'This is something I have to do alone. Right now, I have no authority and no power here. They won't let you in the palace with me.'

'It just feels wrong after all these years,' said Damen.

'I know,' said Prince Alderon. 'But for now, this is goodbye.'

Prince Alderon turned to the marines and Cedric. 'My thanks to all of you for getting us out of the catacombs. You are the finest group of fighters I've ever seen. And thank you, captain, for getting us to Ironbay alive.'

'You're welcome,' said Cedric with an air of sadness.

The king's guard escorted Prince Alderon through the crowds of civilians, then he was gone. A thin woman broke free from the soldiers who guarded the docks and got as far as the rail of the Auld Faithful.

'I have three children going hungry; please, can you spare some food. Just a yam or some hard tack. Please.'

Two soldiers grabbed her by the arms and dragged her off.

'We told you, you can't go to the ships,' said the soldier.

'But my children,' said the woman.

'We all have children,' said the guard. 'Follow the rules.'

The official spoke next.

'Captain Beaumont, I'm Inspector Herid from customs. By order of his majesty King Vargus, all cargo entering Ironbay is to be inspected and documented. All incoming foodstuffs are subject to possible seizure.'

'Siezure?' said Cedric. 'Why would you do that?'

'Problems with black marketeers,' said inspector Herid. 'The king is taking command of all food distribution to ensure the population of Ironbay is adequately fed.'

'I'm afraid we didn't bring any cargo with us. We were on a special mission to Yavenland for the palace. You saw the king's guard meet us.'

'I did,' said Inspector Herid. 'Nevertheless, I must inspect your cargo hold and your ship. Everything that enters Ironbay must be documented.'

'There's barely anything left after three weeks sailing,' said Cedric. 'Just some hard tack, dried fish, a few days worth of ham, and some watered down rum. We're desperately in need of resupply.'

'Show me,' said Inspector Herid. Cedric went below with the inspector.

'We go away for two months, and Ironbay's gone crazy,' said Sergeant Zander.

Cedric returned to the deck with Inspector Herid.

'Thank you for your cooperation,' said the inspector.

'Thank you,' said Cedric. 'As I said, our basic supplies are nearly gone.'

'After Teevilgrad, I almost expected him to ask for a bribe,' said Sergeant Zander as the inspector left with his two soldiers.

'Very unusual,' said Cedric. The inspector insisted on seeing the ship's log to confirm that we really did come from Yavenland.'

The inspector was barely gone when a messenger arrived from the navy office.

'Message for Captain Beaumont,' he said.

Cedric took the message and opened it.

'I'm to give the services of you marines over to Office 451,' said Cedric.

Crutch saw Jasper arriving on the other side of the soldiers at the docks.

'Better get your weapons, men,' said Sergeant Zander. 'We have some work to do. You're welcome to come with us, Damen.'

'Has to be better than sitting on this ship,' said Damen. 'After three weeks on the ocean, I've had enough of sailing.'

The soldiers moved the crowd of civilians aside so the marines could get through.

'So happy to see you're all okay,' said Jasper when they got to him.

'Good to see you too,' said Sergeant Zander. Their greeting was professional, but Crutch knew there was much more going on underneath.

'You have a new addition to your squad?' said Jasper.

'This is Damen. He was the protector of Prince Alderon. We offered him a spot in the marines.'

'It's a pleasure to meet you Damen,' said Jasper. 'You must have some special skills if Sergeant Zander invited you to join his marines.'

'Finest swordsman I've seen,' said Sergeant Zander. 'What do you need us for?'

'That's just one of the many things I like about you, Sergeant Zander. No preamble, just straight to business.'

'Best way to get the job done,' said Sergeant Zander.

'After Teevilgrad, it seems that Emperor Solokov has decided to return the favour. First, it was shipments of food going missing off the docks, then appearing on the black market at inflated prices.'

'So you think Solokov is buying up the food?' said Crutch.

'Yes, we do. When the food shortage became critical, King Vargus ordered all food documented and the purchase and resale of food coming into Ironbay regulated. But now many ships are entering the Ironbay harbour without their cargo.'

'Raided?' said Sergeant Zander.

'No. Our best guess is the captains are selling the cargo to someone and transferring it to smaller boats before getting to the harbour.'

'Clever,' said Crutch.

'King Vargus has threatened to throw captains in jail, but he has to tread carefully. He still needs those ships to bring in food.'

'So where is the food going?' said Crutch.

'My best student asks the right question. We aren't sure, but the best information we have is that someone is hiding food in the sewers. King Vargus has sent soldiers and the city guard down there, but they have no idea where to search.'

'If someone knows the sewers well, they could hide a year's worth of food in there, and the soldiers or the guard would never find it,' said Crutch.

'That's what we need you for,' said Jasper. 'Someone who knows the sewers and the people who live there.'

'So you want us to find the food?' said Sergeant Zander.

'We want you to find out who is buying and hiding the food. We know from our spies that Emperor Solokov is funding it. We need to know who he's working with.'

'To stop enough food to starve Ironbay would take a huge operation,' said Crutch. 'Can't just be one or two people.'

'Exactly,' said Jasper. 'You Crutch are the only person I could think of who is smart enough and knows the sewers well enough to find the players in this scheme.'

'We'll do what we can,' said Sergeant Zander.

'You need to do it fast,' said Jasper. 'If the food shortages continue, there'll be a total breakdown of civil order here in Ironbay. You can see what it's like already, just here on the docks.'

'We'll get started right now,' said Sergeant Zander.

'Do I need to tell you to let Crutch take the lead with this?' said Jasper.

'I don't know about that,' said Sergeant Zander. 'I was just getting the hang of this espionage thing.'

'As entertaining as it might be for Lord Boulderdash to make a reappearance, I think this will take a little more subtlety.'

'Well, if you insist,' said Sergeant Zander.

'I do,' said Jasper. 'We can discuss it in detail later tonight if you like.'

'I would like,' said Sergeant Zander.

'I'm Lord Boulderdash,' said Boulder.

Chapter 36
Ghost

After Jasper left, Crutch talked to Sergeant Zander.

'I need to start by talking to some street urchins,' said Crutch. 'They'll know what's going on in the sewers.'

'Good thinking,' said Sergeant Zander. 'Do you want us to come with you?'

'No. They won't talk to me if I arrive with a squad of marines, but there is something you can do here on the docks.'

Crutch left the marines after getting any hard tack they had on them. As he made his way into the city, the people he passed were thin, and many looked desperate. Normally, he'd see wagons with food driven down King's Way from the docks into the city. Today, he didn't see any.

He made his way straight to the town square. The first thing he noticed was the lack of food carts. No one was selling bread, or pastries, or fruit and vegetables.

The first street urchin he saw was a young boy, no older than nine, with a begging cup. The boy was painfully skinny. A few weeks with Ironbay short of food would leave most street urchins close to starving.

Crutch slowed his walk to a hobble and greeted the boy.

'Hard time to be begging,' said Crutch, pulling out a piece of hard tack and handing it to him.

The boy gave Crutch a weak smile and a thank, you and ate the hard tack in a couple of mouthfuls.

'What's your name?' said Crutch.

'They call me Midge.'

'Would you like some more?' said Crutch.

Midge nodded as Crutch knew he would, and Crutch handed him another piece of hard tack.

'I hear there's someone hiding food in the sewers,' said Crutch.

'Don't know nothing about that,' said Midge after he swallowed the hard tack.

'I wouldn't expect you to,' said Crutch. 'You obviously didn't have anything to do with it. Anyone can just look at you and see that.'

'That's right,' said Midge.

'But if you were to hear something that someone else is doing in the sewers with big crates of food, then there'd be a silver piece in it for you.'

'And some more hard tack?' said Midge. 'Even a silver piece won't buy much food these days.'

'I'll bring you more hard tack,' said Crutch. He gave the boy a copper piece and another piece of hard tack and went looking for more street urchins.

It occurred to Crutch that if a street urchin did find crates of food in the sewers, they wouldn't be on the street begging, they'd be hiding out with them somewhere so no one else could steal them. If the food was guarded, that might be a different story, though.

He walked a few blocks, looking for an older street urchin. Someone who'd been on the streets longer was likely to know more urchins and have a better idea of what was going on in the sewers.

He found an urchin about fourteen years old begging on a corner. The boy had a withered arm, and just like the other street urchin, Midge, he looked painfully skinny.

'Spare a copper or a scrap of food?' The street urchin didn't have to fake looking miserable and desperate. It was written all over him.

'I have some hard tack,' said Crutch, giving the boy one of the hard biscuits. 'What's your name?'

'The people what know me call me ghost,' said the urchin in between chewing and swallowing the hard tack.

'I'm Crutch. I begged on these streets just like you.'

'Corporal Crutch?' said Ghost. 'The iron cross winner?'

'That's me,' said Crutch, handing the urchin another piece of hard tack.

'I'm talkin' to a real live war hero,' said Ghost.

'Being a war hero's not all it's cracked up to be,' said Crutch, thinking of all the men he'd killed and all the men he'd led to their deaths.

'Least you get two meals a day,' said Ghost. 'Army and the navy won't hire me with this arm.' He flopped his useless right arm around. 'How did you get in with your leg?'

'It's a long story,' said Crutch. 'I got lucky. Do you know the other street urchins around here?'

'I know most of 'em,' said Ghost. 'We might not be friends, but we know each other.'

'I understand,' said Crutch. 'You can't trust anyone when you're living on the street or in the sewers.'

'Too right,' said Ghost. 'They'll stick ya in ya sleep if they think you've got a copper they can steal.'

Crutch's memories of scrabbling to survive on these very streets flooded back. The hopelessness, the desperation, and the danger from everything and everyone. He wished he could take every one of these street urchins off the street and give them a couple of good meals a day and a safe place to sleep at night.

'I have more hard tack and some coin for you and any street urchin who can give me information,' said Crutch.

'How much coin?' said Ghost.

'A silver piece for anyone who can tell me where to find what I'm looking for.'

'If it's the lost gold mine, there isn't one,' said Ghost.

Crutch laughed. Every street urchin in Ironbay had wasted their time looking for the lost gold mine that was supposed to be somewhere under the streets of Ironbay. There were still old mine shafts down there, but they were dangerous. You had to be desperate to go into them, and many who did got trapped in there forever and never came out.

'It's not gold I'm looking for,' said Crutch. 'I hear someone's hiding crates of food in the sewers.'

'If they are, they're not sharing it with us street urchins,' said Ghost.

'I can see that,' said Crutch, giving Ghost another piece of hard tack. 'Can you tell all the urchins you know I have hard tack and coppers for any kind of information that will help me find the people hiding this food and where it's being hidden in the sewers?' Crutch gave Ghost two coppers.

'I'll tell 'em,' said Ghost. 'I'll go down there myself to take a look.'

'Thank you,' said Crutch. 'I'll be back tomorrow.'

Chapter 37
The Heart

Now he'd got some street urchins searching for him, there was something else he wanted to do in the city. Someone he wanted to see.

When he reached the street outside the admiral's residence, Corporal Levi knocked on the door and called out, 'Miss Abagail. Corporal Crutch is here to see you.'

'Thank you, Corporal Levi,' said Crutch as he came up the steps in front of the entrance.

'Great to see you back safe, Corporal Crutch.'

Abagail burst through the front doors, her smile as wide as her arms.

'Crutch,' she said as she wrapped her arms around him. 'You're back. I missed you so much.'

'I missed you too,' said Crutch, feeling her body, thin underneath her dress.

'Father won't let me out of the house now. He says the streets are too dangerous.'

'Your father is right,' said Crutch.

'Do you know how long it will be until we get food again? I'm tired of yams and beans.'

'Soon I hope,' said Crutch.

'Everyone's hungry,' said Abagail. 'I share some of my food with Jenny and the other servants, but there just isn't enough to go around. We can still make pastries. That helps a little.'

Crutch knew what it was like to starve. All your thoughts are consumed with food and with getting food. It must be even worse for Abagail. When he was on the streets, Crutch could at least do something to get some food for himself. Abagail had to go along feeling helpless, relying on other people.

'I brought a gift for you from Yavenland,' said Crutch.

'Really,' said Abagail, smiling with that wonderfully crooked face.

'I had to fight off an army of the dead to get it,' said Crutch.

'I hope you're joking,' said Abagail.

Crutch pulled out the golden necklace with a heart on it. Abagail's ocean blue eyes went wide with amazement.

'My goodness. It's gorgeous. Real gold. It must have cost a fortune.'

'It was a reward from the wife of the mayor in Yavenland,' said Crutch. 'I told her I needed a gift for the prettiest girl in the whole of Ironbay, and she gave me this.'

'I love it,' said Abagail. 'Can I put it on?'

Crutch unclasped the necklace and reached around both sides of her neck to attach it. Abagail looked down at it, her eyes beaming.

'It's so beautiful.'

'Not as beautiful as you,' said Crutch.

Abagail looked up. Their eyes met, then their lips met. A long kiss that seemed to last forever and was still way too short for Crutch.

'Come inside,' said Abagail, leading Crutch by the hand. 'I have to show everyone. Can you come to dinner tonight?'

'I'd love to, but I can't. I have something I have to do with the marines.'

'Then you must come to dinner every night you're free,' said Abagail. 'Please say you will. It would mean a lot to me.'

'I will,' said Crutch.

Chapter 38
Don't Talk

Crutch and the marines used grappling hooks and ropes to climb down from the docks to the narrow ledge below it.

'This is one of a dozen spots you told us about where the sewers come out into the harbour,' whispered Sergeant Zander. 'When we checked them out today, this one looked the easiest to keep watch on without having to get into the water.'

'To get all the food they're taking into the sewers, they'd have to be using most of them,' whispered Crutch. 'One should be as good as another.'

'Why don't the city guard or the army do something about these?' whispered Sergeant Zander.

'There are strong iron gates that block off the sewers. They probably checked them and figured no one could get through.'

'Are they breaking them?' whispered Sergeant Zander.

'Not to get a boat through. They must have the keys.'

'To get the keys, whoever is running this must be in government or have friends in the government,' whispered Sergeant Zander.

'That's likely,' whispered Crutch.

Crutch heard something in the water and put his hand up to signal no more talking. The marines crushed up against the wall, concealed by the darkness of the night and the shadows. Crutch could hear the splash of oars as they left the water, the gentle swishing of someone rowing slow and silent as they could.

Then the boat came into view. Two men in a longboat carrying a bloated dead body on top of a canvas. They rowed into the sewers down to the iron gate. One of the men in the longboat put down his oars while the man at the tiller passed him a set of keys. The oarsman crawled to the bow of the boat and unlocked the gate.

They rowed through, then the tillerman locked the gate behind them. After a minute, they disappeared into the darkness.

'Clever,' whispered Crutch. 'Posing as corpsemen fishing bodies out of the harbour.'

'The canvas that body was on was more than high enough to conceal a pile of crates,' whispered Sergeant Zander.

'Come on,' 'whispered Crutch.

They crept down the stone side of the sewers designed for walking on, until they got to the iron gate. Crutch pulled at it, but it was rock solid. He slipped into the sewer water, checking for any holes or gaps in the bars underneath the sewerage. There were none.

'No way through here,' whispered Crutch.

'We could break the bars out of the stone,' whispered Damen.

'I like the way you think,' whispered Crutch, 'but then they'd know someone was on their trail, and they'd move their stash.'

'At least we know how they're getting the food in,' whispered Sergeant Zander.

'Some of it,' whispered Crutch. With the amount of food they stopped coming into Ironbay, Crutch knew they must be bringing it in other ways too.

When Crutch got to the city square the next day, Midge wasn't there. The mood in the square was strained. He saw emaciated people milling around. A bakery was open, but there was no bread on display. Customers were in a line to the bakery that went a hundred yards down the street.

Two city guardsmen stood watch at the entrance. People would go in and come out with a part loaf of bread that was no more than three or four slices. Crutch wondered if it was made with flour or if half of it was sawdust.

Crutch searched the alleys for Midge. Maybe he was hiding from someone. He went down one empty alley and saw what looked like a bundle of rags in the corner. When he got closer, he knew what it was. He'd seen dead bodies before.

Midge sat, hunched over, his eyes open, lifeless. Crutch looked closer and saw the copper he'd given Midge was stuffed in his mouth. On a piece of wood hung around the boy's neck was a small sign with the words 'Don't Talk' written in blood.

Crutch's guts churned. He never thought that whoever was behind taking control of Ironbay's food supply would kill an innocent street urchin. Whoever it was, they didn't like people looking around or asking around about them, and they would kill to send a message.

Crutch looked around the alley. One sewer grate, nothing else. If they went to the trouble of killing Midge to cover up their operation, it's unlikely they would dump his body anywhere that would make it easier for Crutch to find them.

This was a warning, but if they wanted Crutch to stop looking for them, they'd gone about it in the worst way possible. Crutch was more determined than ever to find the bilge scum who did this and to make them pay.

Crutch looked for the older street urchin, Ghost, near where he'd met him the day before when he saw him waving from an alley. As Crutch got closer, Ghost motioned for him to come behind some empty crates.

'Ya tryin' to get us killed?' said Ghost.

'It's not me doing any killing,' said Crutch. 'I'm the one trying to stop these bilge scum.'

'Either way, it ends up with street urchins dead,' said Ghost.

'If you know something, you should tell me,' said Crutch. 'Then I can get the people who killed Midge out of the sewers and into prison.'

'It's not just Midge,' said Ghost. 'They're killing any urchin they find in the sewers.'

Crutch felt a surge of anger at that. Without being able to escape to the sewers or hide in there, the street urchins had nowhere safe they could go.

'Now you know why I want to catch them,' said Crutch, reaching into his pocket and handing a piece of hard tack to Ghost.

'There's just one of you and hundreds of them,' said Ghost as he chewed on the hard tack.

'It's not just me. I've got the whole navy behind me.' A bit of an exaggeration, thought Crutch, but he needed to use whatever he could to get the information he needed.

'If I tell ya, how do I know it won't come back on me?' said Ghost.

'They'll never get it from me,' said Crutch, pulling a silver piece out of his pocket and showing it to Ghost.

'They call themselves the true royals,' said Ghost. 'I couldn't get close enough to see where they're hiding the food, but they've got plenty of it, and they got guards down there, so ya can't move anywhere without being seen.'

Crutch gave him the silver piece. 'The true royals?'

'Yes. Sounds like a stupid name to me. They got a gang in the sewers workin' for 'em too.'

'Thank you, Ghost.' Crutch gave him another piece of hard tack. 'You stay safe. If you get any more information, I'll pay for that too.'

'I'll keep an eye out, but bein' dead is a bit of a discouragement when it comes to seeking out the kind of information you're lookin' for.'

Chapter 39
Nancy Boys

Crutch knew they needed Jasper's help with this. Crutch didn't know who the true royals were. If they were nobility, he didn't have the type of contacts he would need to infiltrate them.

'Why does Jasper want to meet you in this part of the city?' said Crutch as he walked down Ortman Street with Sergeant Zander.

This was one part of the city Crutch always avoided in Ironbay. There was nothing wrong with the people who came here. They were generous enough. But there were bloodthirsty arseholes who got their fun by beating up anyone they found on the streets.

'Jasper wants to be seen with me here, so people assume we're that kind of couple,' said Sergeant Zander.

'A man and a man?' said Crutch.

'Exactly.'

'That's clever.' And it was. Be seen where men hang out to meet men, and no one would ever suspect Jasper was a woman.

'Jasper told me I wouldn't have to explain it to you; that you'd understand.'

'I do,' said Crutch. Must be hard having the whole crew thinking you're a nancy boy though.'

'It took some getting used to, but I'm okay with it now.'

Crutch saw Jasper up ahead, dressed as a portly man with a moustache, the same disguise she'd used the first time they met in Office 451.

'Hey Jasper,' said Sergeant Zander.

'Hey Zandy, Crutch.'

Jasper and Sergeant Zander didn't hug or touch. Crutch guessed pretending to be a nancy boy was hard enough for Sergeant Zander. Hugging a portly guy with a moustache would be asking for way too much.

'Thank you for meeting us,' said Crutch.

'That's my job,' said Jasper.

'What can you tell us about the true royals?'

'They're a group of nobles and landowners who believe King Vargus is a pretender to the throne. They think the rightful kind is still alive. Does that sound familiar to you?'

'You know it does,' said Sergeant Zander.

'Who do they think is the rightful king?' said Crutch.

'A prince who was kidnapped and taken to Crestona by the Estovians.'

'Well, they don't have to look far to find him,' said Sergeant Zander.

'It's still not common knowledge that you brought the prince back from Yavenland,' said Jasper. 'But I'd expect the true royals would know. They have money, influence, and friends in the prison and in the government.'

'That would explain where they got the keys to the sewer gates,' said Crutch.

'What else do you know about the true royals?' said Sergeant Zander.

'I pulled some strings and arranged a meeting,' said Jasper. 'It will mean disguising ourselves as nobles.'

'I've already had some practice at that,' said Sergeant Zander.

'I meant me and Crutch. Lord Zanderth and Lord Boulderdash won't cut it for this mission.'

'Lord Zanderth, the third, of the order of the red box,' said Sergeant Zander.

'Yes. So convincing,' said Jasper. 'Perhaps another time. This meeting will be dangerous. One slip up, and we'll be dead. My reports say the true royals are ruthless, and they have no problem hiding bodies.'

'What have we here?' said a voice from the shadows.

'Not again,' said Jasper.

Ten rough men stepped out of their hiding spots.

'Three nancy boys,' said the biggest with a sneer. 'What do we do with nancy boys, men?'

'Give 'em a beating.'

'Show 'em how to kiss the cobblestones.'

'Big improvement over what they spend most of their time kissing.'

'Now here's something I don't understand,' said Sergeant Zander. 'Why are you so obsessed with who someone else is kissing? What difference does it make to you?'

'You nancy boys are the reason there's no food in the city,' said the big man.

'How does that work?' said Sergeant Zander.

'It's obvious,' said the big man.

'Not really,' said Sergeant Zander. 'You'll have to explain it to me.'

There was a pause as the big man stood staring, trying to come up with an answer.

'It's the breakdown of society,' said the big man.

'You mean like people with clubs beating innocents?' said Sergeant Zander.

'Enough talking,' said the big man. 'Let's beat 'em boys, starting with the fat one.'

'I'll give you one warning,' said Sergeant Zander. 'You really don't want to do this.'

'Oh yes, we do. We're the nancy beaters. Get 'em boys.'

Sergeant Zander stepped in front of Jasper as they came. The first of the gang tried to punch him in the face, but before the blow could land, Sergeant Zander had driven a fist into his guts. He dropped face first to the street.

'Do you want some help?' said Crutch.

'That would spoil the fun,' said Sergeant Zander as three gang members attacked him at once.

He dodged a kick from the gang member in front of him by moving to his side, with Jasper stepping back to stay out of Sergeant Zander's way. The two gang members attacking from Sergeant Zander's sides didn't anticipate the sudden move back and hurtled towards each other. Sergeant Zander moved forward just enough to put a hand on each side of their heads, using their momentum to smack them together with a very satisfying crack.

'I can help too, Zandy,' said Jasper.

'It's quite alright, said Sergeant Zander as he grabbed the leg of the next gang member who tried to kick him and used it as a lever to fling the gang member backwards through the air, where he landed on his head with a thud. Sergeant Zander moved forward and kicked the guy hard in the crotch.

Jasper looked at Crutch and winced. 'That must have hurt.'

'You'd think with half of them down, they'd give up,' said Crutch. 'Especially after that.'

'The gangs who prey on Ortman street are not blessed with an abundance of brains,' said Jasper as they watched a gang member pull a knife on Sergeant Zander.

'A knife. That's never a good idea,' said Crutch.

The gang member stabbed at Sergeant Zander. Sergeant Zander let him get close enough, grabbed his dagger hand, and pushed it back until the gang member's wrist broke. Then Sergeant Zander kept going until the gang member's arm was ripped out of its socket.

'Fuck this,' said one of the nancy beaters as he turned and ran. Another turned and ran right with him.

'Only two of you left,' said Sergeant Zander. 'I'm guessing this didn't go the way you expected.'

The gang leader turned to run, but Sergeant Zander was on top of him, pinning him to the cobblestone street, pulling one arm up.

'My arm! Let go of my arm!'

'Now why would I do that?' said Sergeant Zander.

'I wasn't going to hurt you. Just let me go.'

'You said you were going to beat us, starting with my friend Jasper. I think you owe her… him, an apology,' said Sergeant Zander.

'I'm sorry. Just let go of my arm.'

'Not very convincing,' said Sergeant Zander. 'Were you convinced, Jasper?'

'Not really,' said Jasper.

'Oh god. Let go of my arm.'

'I asked you to apologise, not to talk about your arm,' said Sergeant Zander.

'I'm sorry,' said the gang leader, sobbing. 'I'm so sorry. Please.'

'Please what?' said Sergeant Zander.

'Please let go of my arm.'

'Now what did I tell you about making a genuine apology. You just keep talking about your arm. It's very confusing to Jasper. He's not sure what message he's hearing; are you Jasper?'

'It's one thing, then another thing,' said Jasper. 'It's like listening to two different people talking at once.'

'Two different people,' said Sergeant Zander. 'Now try sticking to a nice, heartfelt apology.'

'I'm sorry,' the gang leader sobbed. 'I'm so sorry. Please forgive me.'

'Now that is an apology,' said Jasper.

'Nice work,' said Sergeant Zander, and broke the gang leader's arm.

'You broke my arm!'

'I did. You tell all your mates Ortman Street is off-limits. If I hear of anyone giving beatings to innocent people going about their daily business, here or anywhere else, I am going to find them, and I won't be as kind to them as I was to you, you snivelling piece of shit.'

Sergeant Zander let the gang leader up, and he ran off, his arm dangling at his side.

'What chivalry,' said Jasper. 'Makes my heart warm.'

'You're getting soft, Sarge,' said Crutch. 'You didn't even touch one of them.'

'Yes, but to be fair, that guy didn't try to punch me. Or stab me.' Sergeant Zander kicked the gang member in the guts as he lay moaning on the street with a broken wrist and a dislocated arm.

'I'll see you tomorrow, then Crutch,' said Jasper. 'Do you have any of that face paint left?'

'I do.'

'Good. You can use the noble's clothes Sergeant Zander bought you and disguise yourself as an old man.'

Chapter 40
Lord Of Lies

It took Crutch an hour to get enough face paint on himself to look like an old man again. He put on the fancy noble clothes and headed for his meeting with Jasper. Jasper wanted to take a look at Crutch first before they went to their first meeting with the true royals.

'Very good,' said Jasper when Crutch came hobbling along the street with his cane.

'The walk gets longer every time I do it,' said Crutch, faking a gravelly voice.

'Nice,' said Jasper. 'You'll be Lord Crunden, a friend of mine from the territories with interests in shipping. You have several ships running food, supplies, and other goods to the other Ironborn territories. You're looking to expand into Ironbay because you heard there's a shortage of food in the city.'

'That's likely to get them fired up if they're trying to stop the supply of food into the city.'

'Exactly,' said Jasper. 'I'll be Lord Burnley. We're old friends from my time in the territories.'

'So who will we be meeting?' said Crutch.

'I'm guessing it will be an intermediary. They'll want to check us out before we meet anyone important.'

'How do we know they'll try to recruit us?'

'We don't,' said Jasper. 'But since they must already be getting a large number of ships to pass their cargo on to them, I'm guessing they're using money and persuasion rather than straight-out violence to get what they want.'

'So you think they'll make me an offer?' said Crutch.

'That's what I hope,' said Jasper. 'The alternative is a lot less enjoyable.'

'And what would the alternative be?'

'They kill us and dispose of the bodies,' said Jasper.

'That does sound less enjoyable when you put it like that.'

The coach driver helped Crutch climb down from the coach.

'Thank you, young man,' said Crutch in his gravelly voice. He gave the coach driver a silver piece.

'Thank you, my lord,' said the coach driver.

'We'll be looking for your help to get back if you could wait,' said Jasper.

'Certainly, Lord Burnley,' said the coach driver. 'I'll park the coach just outside the front gates and wait for you to emerge.'

'That would be perfect,' said Jasper.

Two servants opened the large wooden doors to the mansion, and a man in a red noble's suit came strutting out.

'I'm glad you could come, Lord Burnley,' said the man. 'You must be Lord Crunden.'

'Indeed, I am,' said Crutch. 'And you are?'

'Forgive my manners. I am Lord Jelric. Shall we go inside?'

Lord Jelric led them through the foyer of the mansion into a large sitting room.

'Please take a seat,' said Lord Jelric. 'Would you care for a drink?'

'I would,' said Crutch.

'We have honeysap rum,' said Lord Jelric.

'I don't know how you do it,' said Jasper. 'I'd love a rum.'

'Perhaps just some lolly water for me,' said Crutch, remembering what honeysap rum had done to his mind in Honeysap Grove. He needed his wits about him if he was to get out of this meeting alive.

'Lord Burnley tells me you're in shipping,' said Lord Jelric.

'Indeed,' said Crutch. 'It has been my passion for most of my life. Running ships and trading in the Ironborn territories.'

'You've never sent your ships to Ironbay?'

'No, strangely enough. I focused on trade routes with the least competition. While everyone else shipped food from major ports to

Ironbay, I took my ships to smaller ports that were underserved with goods that no one else was shipping. It's done well for me over the years.'

'Clever,' said Lord Jelric. 'But you're thinking of shipping to Ironbay now. Why the change?'

'It's come to my attention that there are opportunities here in Ironbay I may have overlooked,' said Crutch.

'Opportunities are my bread and butter,' said Lord Jelric. 'Perhaps I can be of service to you.'

'Perhaps,' said Crutch. 'It's been over twenty years since I've been in Ironbay. There are a few things I don't understand. Curiosities you might be able to explain to me.'

'Of course,' said Lord Jelric.

'The last time I was here, there was plenty of food. Now it seems the filthy commoners are fighting over it. When my ship docked, an inspector came and logged every crate and barrel of food on board.'

'King Vargus doesn't seem able to supply the city with food,' said Lord Jelric.

'Strange,' said Crutch. 'It shouldn't be too difficult to send more ships to Port Vela in Papageenar or one of the other territories with good working farms.'

'It does seem simple,' said Lord Jelric. 'Maybe the problem is beyond our current king.'

'And that's another thing I don't understand. The last time I was here in Ironbay, I don't even remember a Prince Vargus. Among the trusted nobility, we were told there was a Prince Alderon who was next in the line of succession.'

There was a long silence. Finally, Lord Jelric spoke.

'Perhaps it's best if we leave these topics for another time. I may have a friend who can shed more light on the topics that interest you.'

Crutch and Jasper exchanged pleasantries with Lord Jelric for a little while, then they made their exit. After they were in the carriage, Jasper explained that he had a home in the city that he used when he was Lord Burnley.

'Officially, you'll be staying there as Lord Crunden, the guest of Lord Burnley, while you're in Ironbay. You can't be seen arriving or leaving as Crutch, so you need to be very careful.'

'I understand,' said Crutch.

'I hope you do. The game we're playing now is dangerous,' said Jasper. 'If we make one mistake, the true royals will kill us both without a second's hesitation.'

'I'm familiar with being in this kind of danger,' said Crutch. 'Especially after Teevilgrad.'

'I know you are,' said Jasper. 'But we can never afford to get complacent. Good espionage is doing one thing at a time perfectly so you never, ever slip up. I'm putting a lot of trust in you, Crutch. It's my life at risk here too.'

Crutch thought about that. Jasper lived most of her life as someone else. Crutch didn't even know exactly why, beyond the fact that she didn't want the navy, government, and rulers of Ironbay to know who she really was.

The mental pressure on her to live that way without ever letting anyone see through her disguise must be immense. And now her life could depend on someone else doing the same thing.

'It's not something I'll take lightly,' said Crutch.

'Thank you,' said Jasper. 'Good work tonight. If I didn't know it was you, I would have sworn you were an old territorian noble whose passion was shipping and trade.'

'Was mentioning Prince Alderon too much?' said Crutch.

'Impossible to say,' said Jasper. 'Well have to see if they contact you again.'

Chapter 41
Heads Of Grain

Crutch didn't have to wait long. The next day, a message came for him inviting Lord Crunden to lunch at Lord Jelric's mansion.

'Looks like they're getting serious,' said Jasper. 'They want you by yourself so they can talk business. If you're lucky, you might even meet the leader of the true royals.'

'And if I'm not lucky?'

'Then there's a hole somewhere in your story, and they're isolating you so they can torture you and kill you.'

'That's comforting,' said Crutch.

'Not so much,' said Jasper. 'I doubt they'd leave any loose ends. I'd be next.'

Lord Jelric waited in the drive near the front doors as Crutch arrived at Lord Jelric's mansion.

'Welcome back,' said Lord Jelric as the coach driver helped Crutch down off the carriage.

'Thank you for inviting me,' said Crutch, speaking out of his throat so his voice sounded hoarse.

Lord Jelric led Crutch through the foyer and to a set of large doors flanked by two armed guards. Two more servants opened the door as they approached. Inside, Crutch could see a dining room with a large polished wooden dining table full of food.

There were yams, pineapples, bananas, and strange, wonderful-looking fruits Crutch had never even seen. There was fresh fish and a cooked pig with an apple in its mouth on a huge platter. At the head of the table stood another noble, a fat man in his fifties with an air of arrogance to him.

'We wanted you to see that some of us know how to bring food into Ironbay,' said Lord Jelric. 'This is Lord Rothchester. He's been anxious to meet you.'

'Anxious is a strong word,' said Lord Rothchester. 'I am rarely anxious about anything. Good management prevents most anxieties I find.'

'Indeed,' said Crutch. 'After a few days in Ironbay it's a pleasure to see so much food. It seems I'm with men who understand how to control the means of trade in a city.' Or how to steal food and leave a city to starve. Crutch felt anger boil in his guts.

He finally recognised the name. Lord Rothchester. Author of The Philosophy of Rothchester, a book Cedric had given him to read years ago. It was a book full on nonsense, written by a man born into wealth who'd never worked a day in his life. He thought that poor people's problems were totally self inflicted. He was an idiot.

'Food and controlling the means of trade is a topic we'd very much like to discuss with you,' said Lord Rothchester. 'Please sit. We can discuss while we eat.'

Lord Jelric led Crutch to a seat at Lord Rothchester's right.

'I have to admit I'm a fan of yours,' said Crutch as he hobbled to his place at the table and sat. 'I've read your book.'

'It was many years since I put quill to paper for that book,' said Lord Rotchester. 'Still I find some delight that you gleaned something worthwhile from it.'

'Such an important work,' said Crutch. *Such a load of vile nonsense.*

'Thank you,' said Lord Rothchester, taking his own seat to Crutch's right.

'This is quite the feast for three people,' said Crutch.

'We're the nobility,' said Lord Rothchester. 'We deserve the best. Filthy Ironbay commoners could never understand that.'

'Indeed,' said Crutch. If he thought he could get away with it, he'd like to take the knife in his hand and stab Lord Rothchester in the eye with it. Then the lord, would see what commoners understand.

'Lord Jelric tells me you're in shipping,' said Lord Rothchester.

'Indeed, I am. Shipping and trade. Food and other goods between the territories.'

'Do you travel around the territories yourself?' said Lord Rothchester.

'I'm afraid my old bones don't allow me to do that. I manage my operations from home mostly now.'

'And you're thinking of adding some routes to Ironbay?'

'Yes,' said Crutch. 'I look for opportunities, and Ironbay seems very short of food at present, although from what I can see here, there might be more to that.'

'Indeed. It seems our king has mismanaged supply lines here in Ironbay.'

Mismanaged, thought Crutch. The only mismanagement Crutch could see was to let these fat, greedy nobles live and suck off the hard-working people of Ironbay like parasites.

'And that's causing the food shortages?' said Crutch, as a servant offered him another slice of the cooked pig.

'It's complex, as you can understand, but most of the problems in Ironbay stem from King Vargus.'

'Really? I haven't ventured to Ironbay in two decades. I had no idea there were problems with the king's competency as a ruler.'

'It's more obvious when you live in the city,' said Lord Rothchester. 'Trade, taxes, the armed forces. They're all in shambles.'

'I see. When I was last in Ironbay, so many years ago, there was a Prince Alderon next in line to the throne. Do you know what became of him?'

'I can tell you,' said Lord Rothchester, 'but it's in the strictest of confidence.'

'Of course,' said Crutch.

'Prince Alderon was kidnapped by the Estovians. They held him in Crestona. Hence the siege of Crestona to retrieve him.'

'But we Ironborn lost the entire fleet at the siege of Crestona,' said Crutch.

'Your knowledge of history is good,' said Lord Rothchester.

'I am old enough to remember it well,' said Crutch. 'My bones might be weary, but my mind is as sharp as a tack. I assume the prince was executed by the Estovians after the siege?'

'We don't believe he was,' said Lord Rothchester.

'Really?'

'We have good information that he survived the siege and escaped.'

'Really?'

'And we have information that he is in Ironbay right now being held in the Black Tower.'

'In the prison. Outrageous!' said Crutch. 'This is no way to treat the rightful king of Ironbay. We must retrieve the prince at once!'

'I admire your passion,' said Lord Rothchester. 'But King Vargus would see any attempt to liberate the prince as treason.'

'Treason? It's Vargus who's committing treason, locking up the true king so he can hold on to power himself,' said Crutch. 'One thing I've learned in life is that you must be bold.'

'You're right, of course,' said Lord Rothchester. 'But I fear we don't have the resources to take King Vargus head-on. We need to use our wiles if we don't want to end up hanging from the gallows in the city square.'

'So you want to leave our true king wallowing in prison? It sounds like cowardice to me,' said Crutch.

'Not cowardice,' said Lord Rothchester. 'We need King Vargus to be weak to give us a chance to attack him successfully.'

'So your attack is coming?' said Crutch.

'Not just coming,' said Lord Rothchester. 'We're already striking at the heart of King Vargus and his rule by interrupting food supplies to Ironbay.'

'So you're behind the food shortages,' said Crutch. 'Clever. When do we rescue the prince?'

'Soon,' said Lord Rothchester. 'Very soon. First, we need to get the soldiers in the army onside so we can beat the king in a fight.'

'Good,' said Crutch. 'Use the fake king's own soldiers to take him down. Do you expect many deaths?'

'Only nobles loyal to King Vargus. And filthy commoners, of course, but commoners are like heads of grain.'

'Heads of grain?' said Crutch.

'Made to be cut down,' said Lord Rothchester, laughing.

'Oh how very clever,' said Crutch wishing he could ram his fist down Lord Rothchester's throat.

'Would you like some tea and cakes?' said Lord Rothchester.

'I would,' said Crutch. 'Are you worried about King Vargus uncovering your plans?'

'He's trying,' said Lord Rothchester. 'He tried to set street urchins to spy on us. As if a street urchin could outsmart a true lord.'

'Preposterous,' said Crutch. 'How did you handle it?'

'Just more heads of grain,' said Lord Rothchester. 'They hang a bit lower and smell a lot worse, but they're just as easy to cut down.'

After his lunch Crutch met with Jasper at the residence she used to pose as Lord Brumley.

'This is worrying,' said Jasper. 'For Lord Rothchester to admit to treason so quickly means their plans must be well advanced.'

'The true royals must believe the crown is within their grasp and soon,' said Crutch.

'Exactly,' said Jasper. 'Otherwise, they wouldn't risk their necks by speaking about it so openly.'

'It can't just be cutting the food supply,' said Crutch. 'Lord Rothchester talked about targeting the armed forces.'

'You can't seize the crown without getting the army and the navy on side,' said Jasper. 'Getting the palace guard on side would help too.'

'How are they going to do that?'

'That's the question,' said Jasper. 'We need to get an answer to that as quickly as we can. It seems we don't have much time.'

'They're keeping the food,' said Crutch.

'What's that?'

'The true royals could simply dump the food at sea or send it to another territory,' said Crutch. 'That would be much simpler and cause food shortages in Ironbay. They're smuggling the food into the sewers instead.'

'So they're using the food,' said Jasper.

'That means if we find out who is getting the food we'll also find out who's working with the true royals.'

Chapter 42
A Greedy Noble's Ambition

'If you took half the fleet around the island, then you could hit the flank of the enemy fleet and outnumber their ships three to one,' said Crutch. 'And they wouldn't be able to escape because they'd have to go through the other half of your fleet.'

'Remarkable,' said Admiral Hastings. 'I must say your grasp of naval tactics is exceptional.'

Crutch clutched Abagail's hand under the dinner table. He'd had dinner with the admiral, Abagail, and Lady Hastings twice now.

It was strained at first, but when Crutch came upon the idea of talking about naval engagements and strategy, Admiral Hastings had warmed to the conversation. They could spend a good half hour at dinner talking about a naval engagement of the past, the mistakes they made, and how the Ironbon navy or her enemies could have done better.

Crutch had spent years now reading naval history and practicing with tiny ships on a board with Cedric. He could see a naval battle in his head and picture the possibilities. To beat Cedric, he'd employed the same strategy Sergeant Zander had taught him. It's the attack you don't see coming. Be creative and do the unexpected.

Every time Crutch came up with another surprise attack or unexpected move to change the course of battle, Admiral Hastings would smile and shake his head in wonder.

'I'm glad none of the battles I fought had a fleet commander like you. Ironbay would all be ruled by Igor Solokov or some other tyrant from outside the territories.'

Crutch was certain this conversation bored Abagail and Lady Hastings to tears, but they were both thrilled that the admiral and Crutch finally got on so well together after they'd had so much animosity in the past.

That didn't mean Admiral Hastings was happy about his young daughter having a boyfriend who was a commoner, but at least there was no more open hostility.

'Well, that was thrilling,' said Lady Hastings. 'Seems you've beaten back those Estovian ships one more time and saved Ironbay and her territories again. I'd like to extend my personal gratitude for saving us all from the Estovian hordes. Would anyone like dessert?'

Dinner at the admiral's residence had been a sparse affair with a minimum of food on offer, but somehow Lady Hasting's servants had saved flour and sugar so they could make desserts.

'Yes, please,' said Crutch, and looked at Abagail, who smiled. At least he could entertain her by seeing how many pastries he could stuff in his mouth. That was an activity that scandalised Lady Hastings, but every time he did it, Abagail's eyes would light up, and she'd laugh that wonderful laugh that lit up a room and made Crutch's heart sing.

The servants were bringing in a large platter of something delicious when Crutch saw a shadow out of the corner of his eye that shouldn't be there.

'Are you expecting a visit from the army tonight?' said Crutch.

'I am not,' said Admiral Hastings.

The solider moved into the dining room fast, his dagger drawn, heading straight for the admiral, who had his back to him. Lady Hastings screamed.

Crutch already had his walking cane up with the blade out. He stood and pushed Admiral Hastings hard from the side to knock him out of his chair as Crutch brought up his cane and stabbed at the soldier's neck.

The soldier moved just fast enough that the blade of Crutch's cane grazed his neck instead of cutting it open. Admiral Hastings was now sprawled on the floor.

'Guards!' yelled the admiral.

The soldier stabbed at Crutch, but Crutch could reach further with his cane than the soldier could with his dagger. Crutch stepped back, the blade of the dagger slicing inches from his face. He plunged the blade of his cane into the chest of the soldier, pulled it out, and stabbed his chest again.

The soldier went down, but two more soldiers came into the room, this time with swords drawn.

'Guards!' yelled Admiral Hastings again as he struggled to his feet.

But Crutch knew the admiral's guards would already be dead. The true royals attempt to take the throne had begun, and their first move was to take out the leadership.

'Your guards are dead,' said Crutch as he moved between the admiral and the soldiers. 'We need to get Lady Hastings and Abagail out of here now.'

'Follow me,' said the admiral as he ran towards the rear door of the dining room.

The first soldier came at Crutch, slashing with his sword. Crutch parried with his walking cane and moved backwards, following the admiral. The soldier moved in again, stabbing at Crutch's chest. Crutch moved back, grabbed a chair, and toppled it towards the soldier's feet.

The soldier almost tripped but kept his balance. Crutch took hold of the tablecloth and ripped it off the table. Plates and spoons crashed around them. He tossed the tablecloth so it landed over both soldiers, blinding them.

Crutch moved forward, merciless and efficient. He stabbed through the tablecloth into the first soldier's head. The second soldier had just pulled the tablecloth off when Crutch stabbed him straight through the eye, drew back, and stabbed him in the throat.

Four more soldiers advanced into the dining room as Crutch turned and ran for the door after the admiral.

'There's four more soldiers behind us,' said Crutch when he reached the admiral. Abagail and Lady Hastings looked terrified.

'Are you alright?' said Abagail.

'You're covered in blood,' said Lady Hastings.

'Not my blood,' said Crutch. 'Stay calm and do what we tell you. We'll get you out of this safely.' Crutch knew it wasn't enough to get the admiral to safety. If the soldiers caught Abagail or Lady Hastings, they could use them as hostages and leverage against the admiral.

'There's a rear exit servants use for deliveries,' said the admiral. 'We can go out that way.'

Crutch had hung around that rear exit before. He'd gotten food scraps here at the admiral's residence when he was a street urchin. If they got out of the exit fast enough, there might be a way they could shake the soldiers chasing them.

'Run,' said Crutch. 'We need to get a lead on them.' He looked behind him. The four soldiers followed them. Steady and careful. Seeing three of their allies dead would make them cautious. But they were still coming.

Crutch couldn't fight four soldiers at once and expect to come out of it unharmed. One mistake, and he'd be dead or injured so badly that he'd be unable to protect Abagail, Lady Hastings, or the admiral.

They ran through a maze of rooms and got to the rear exit with the soldiers two or three rooms behind. When they came out into the alley behind the residence, Crutch saw empty crates.

'Give me a hand with this,' he said. 'Let's block the exit.'

Admiral Hastings and Crutch piled crates in front of the door, and Crutch smashed the door handle to make it harder to open. Now they were outside, Crutch could hear yelling and fighting in the distance. The true royals plan must be in full swing. Right now, innocent people were dying in Ironbay to fulfil some greedy noble's ambition.

'Follow me,' said Crutch. He headed for the hiding place he knew best. In the next alley, he found it. A sewer grate. He pulled the grate off. 'Climb down.'

'In there?' said Lady Hastings.

'It's our only chance,' said Crutch.

Lady Hastings was the first to climb down the ladder, with Abagail close behind. Crutch could hear footsteps coming closer. If they were seen now, this plan wouldn't work.

'It stinks down here,' said Lady Hastings. 'I got something on my shoe.'

'Stay quiet,' whispered Crutch as Admiral Hastings climbed down with Crutch close after him. Crutch slid the sewer grate back over just before he heard the soldiers running into the alley.

Crutch climbed down and motioned for Abagail, Lady Hastings, and the admiral to go further into the sewers. He put his finger over his lips. They could hear the soldiers above them.

'Did they go this way?'

'Can't see 'em.'

'Where will he run? We'll get him one way or the other.'

'Lord Rothchester wants the admiral dead tonight. Let's check the next street.'

Crutch and the admiral stayed silent until the voices faded away.

'Why would Lord Rothchester want me dead?' whispered the admiral.

'He's part of a group who call themselves the true royals,' whispered Crutch. 'They want to take the throne.'

'Traitors,' whispered the admiral. 'We need to get to the palace and warn the king.'

'From the sound of fighting in the streets, I suspect he already knows,' whispered Crutch.

'The palace should still be the safest place,' whispered the admiral.

Crutch thought about that. There were probably true royals in the palace too, but the one person who wasn't a true royal was the king. If he was still alive, the admiral was right. In the palace with the king would be the one place where they at least knew one person who wasn't a traitor. The guards and people loyal to the king would gather around him too.

'Alright,' whispered Crutch. 'I can get us close. Do you know a way in that doesn't involve trying to go through the front gates?'

'I do,' whispered the admiral. 'There's a passage through the side of the palace only a handful of people close to the king know.'

'Is it guarded?'

'Yes.'

'So we have to hope the guards are loyal to the king,' whispered Crutch.

'Do we have another choice?' whispered the admiral.

Crutch thought about it. They could head for the Auld Faithful, but it had probably already left the docks by now. It would be sitting in the harbour, away from any chaos in the city. They could go through the sewers to get to the docks, but there'd be no safe way to get all of them onto the ship.

He didn't like his chance of rowing a longboat out to the Auld Faithful with bowmen shooting at them from the docks. And there were ballistas on the docks too. If the true royals had control of them, they'd rip them to pieces with ballista bolts long before they even got close to the ship.

'We go to the palace,' whispered Crutch, leading them down the sewer tunnel.

'Wait,' whispered Admiral Hastings. 'They'll be trying to kill General Talbot too. We have to warn him.'

'How do we know General Talbot isn't a true royal?' whispered Crutch.

'Not a chance,' whispered the admiral. 'We're close friends. I'd know.'

'I hope you're right,' whispered Crutch.

'I'm right,' whispered the admiral. 'His residence is just two streets over from mine. It's on the way to the palace.'

Crutch knew where the general's residence was. He'd tried to scrounge food there when he was a street urchin. The servants were friendly. The guards were not.

'Okay, I'll go,' whispered Crutch. 'Keep following this tunnel straight. I'll catch up with you. Make sure no one's watching you from the street before you go under the sewer grates.'

'I'll come with you,' whispered the admiral.

'I'd feel much better if you looked after Abagail and Lady Hastings,' whispered Crutch. 'We can't let the true royals catch them.'

The admiral nodded his head. 'Alright Crutch. Thank you.'

Chapter 43
Your Guards Are Trying To Kill You

Crutch went through the sewers until he came to a sewer grate in an alley next to the general's residence. He checked the alley was clear before he slid the sewer grate off, climbed up, then slid the sewer grate back on.

He crept in the shadows. After each step with his good leg, he placed his walking cane on the ground silently, then repeated the process, constantly scanning around him for any sign of soldiers. When he got to the general's residence, there were no guards at the front entrance.

He knew from his days as a street urchin that there were usually at least two guards at the front doors. He crept up to the doors and checked them. They weren't locked. He eased open a door, slow and quiet.

Inside was dark. He crept through the entrance foyer, scanning around for any sign of trouble. Crutch expected to find the dead bodies of the two guards, but there were no bodies. Yet.

He moved deeper into the residence, looking for the bedrooms.

Crutch went down a long corridor, ears straining for any sound that was out of place. Crutch crept around a corner, then ducked back when he caught a glimpse of two men armed with swords.

Crutch pushed his walking cane into his belt and pulled out a dagger. Then he crept behind the two armed men. As he got closer, Crutch could see the men were in uniform. Ironborn army uniforms.

Crutch reached up to grab the mouth of one soldier, but he turned just before Crutch could get a grip on him. Ahead of him Crutch could see two soldiers entering a bedroom. In the bed was General Talbot.

The soldier in front of Crutch had pulled his own dagger as he turned. Crutch moved fast back and to his side and thrust his own dagger into the soldier's leg as he went. The soldier cried out, and the four soldiers turned towards them.

The soldier in front of him stabbed at Crutch's face. Crutch moved his head forward and to the side and bit into the soldier's wrist, biting down as hard as he could, blood filling his mouth.

Crutch stabbed again, this time at the guts of the soldier, and he struck. A knife to the guts wouldn't stop anyone fighting, so Crutch bit down harder with his teeth, pulled his dagger out, and stabbed it back into the soldier's chest. Once, twice, three times. Then the soldier went down.

Crutch looked up in time to see the second soldier swinging at him with a sword. Crutch dove to the ground, turned onto his back, and thrust a dagger up into the soldier's groin. As the soldier bent over in pain, Crutch pulled his dagger out and thrust it into the soldier's face.

The two soldiers came out of the general's bedroom, heading for Crutch. In the dark, Crutch couldn't tell if they'd already killed the general. He couldn't see any blood.

Crutch saw movement on the bed.

'What is going on?' yelled General Talbot. 'Guards!'

'Your guards are trying to kill you, general,' yelled Crutch as he pulled his walking cane from his belt. 'It's Corporal Crutch from the royal marines come to get you out of here safe.'

'Filthy rebels!' yelled General Talbot, coming out of his bed wearing his undergarments. 'Where is my sword?'

On the other side of the bed, someone moved. Lady Talbot.

The two soldiers coming out of the bedroom engaged Crutch, fighting together. One had a dagger, the other had a sword. The soldier with the sword tried to distract Crutch by swinging at him. Crutch parried the blow and immediately saw their plan.

The second soldier tried to get behind Crutch so he could stab him in the back. Crutch stopped that by backing against the wall of the corridor.

Defending against two trained soldiers at the same time with no way to escape was lethally dangerous. Just one wrong move, and you'd be dead or seriously injured. Even a minor injury would likely get you killed when your second opponent pressed a killing blow after the first one landed a minor blow.

Both soldiers were fast. The swordsman rained a series of thrusts and swings on Crutch. With nowhere to move to, the best Crutch could do was parry the sword with his walking cane. The other soldier prodded and stabbed at him from the other side. Crutch barely kept him off by threatening him with a dagger.

The soldier with the dagger moved in close, feinted a stab to Crutch's leg, then went up for his chest. Crutch moved fast, twisting to avoid the stab to his chest just in time, then pushed his own dagger into the soldier's throat. The soldier's eyes were wide with surprise as Crutch withdrew his dagger. Blood spurted from the wound and the soldier toppled to the floor.

Crutch turned back just in time to see the sword swing from the other soldier coming for his legs. He didn't have time to get his walking cane down to defend against it. He was about to lose his legs.

Then the tip of a sword appeared through the soldier's guts and the soldier fell forward. Crutch moved so the soldier's body missed him as he fell. The soldier's sword clattered to the floor, right next to Crutch's foot. Behind the soldier was Young Lord Talbot, fully dressed in military regalia, holding his sword covered in blood in front of him.

General Talbot came out of the bedroom carrying his sword.

'Good work, son,' said General Talbot.

'Hello Crutch,' said Young Lord Talbot happily, as if running through an attacker was all part of some kind of grand game.

'Thank you, Young Lord Talbot,' said Crutch. 'Do you sleep like that?'

'I heard swords and got dressed,' said Young Lord Talbot. 'Got to look your best when you go to battle, don't you, father?'

'Well yes,' said General Talbot, his bare feet and undergarments contrasting against the splendour of Young Lord Talbot's trousers and coat adorned in gold braid.

'We need to get out of here now,' said Crutch. 'All of us. There will be more of them.'

'Who are they?' said General Talbot as Crutch led them back towards the entrance to the residence.

'They call themselves the true royals,' said Crutch. 'They're trying to seize the throne.'

'Filthy scoundrels. Try to kill me in my sleep. I'll gut the lot of them.'

'Right now, we need to get out of here alive,' said Crutch. 'Admiral Hastings wants us to get to the palace.'

'Admiral Hastings,' said the general. 'Is he alright?'

'They tried to kill the admiral too. We got away. He's in the sewers now with Abagail and Lady Hastings.'

'Those filthy swine. There'll be a reckoning for this. Mark my words.'

They were at the front doors. Crutch put his finger to his lips, then opened one of the doors the finest crack so he could see out. He saw at least a dozen soldiers, all armed.

Crutch closed the door. 'Can't go out that way,' he whispered. 'Is there another way out of here?'

'There are two,' whispered General Talbot. 'The rear entrance and the basement.'

'Let's try the basement first. It'll be harder to see us in the shadows coming up the basement steps.'

'Good thinking,' whispered General Talbot.

General Talbot took them through the house and down into the basement.

'That door leads to the stairs,' he whispered.

Crutch crept to the door. He released the blade on his walking cane and opened the door the tiniest crack. As soon as he did, a soldier on the steps turned towards him, his mouth opening to speak. Crutch opened the door and plunged the blade of his walking cane through the soldier's mouth and into the back of his head.

The soldier collapsed on the stairs. Crutch grabbed his legs and dragged him inside, then closed the door, leaving a trail of blood behind him. Lady Talbot looked at the dead body, her mouth open in shock.

'What if he wasn't one of these true royals?' whispered General Talbot.

'Your residence was seized by them,' whispered Crutch. 'Anyone here is a true royal.'

The general nodded his head.

'Let me check to see if we can get out this way now,' whispered Crutch.

He crept back to the door, opened it a crack again, and looked out. He couldn't see anyone. He crept to the top of the stairs. The back alley was empty. He signalled for the general and his family to come.

General Talbot closed the door behind them. Good thinking. If someone came down this way, they wouldn't be sure if this was their escaped route.

Crutch led them out of the alley into the street, then down the next alley, where he knew there was a sewer cover big enough to climb through. The alley was full of empty crates and barrels. With so little food coming into Ironbay, the barrels and crates weren't being reused so they just stayed there.

Crutch began to slide off the sewer cover when he heard voices and footsteps coming from the street. He slid the cover back on and signalled for everyone to hide behind the crates. Crutch could see them. Four soldiers armed with swords.

Chapter 44
Chase To The Palace

'Does this alley go all the way through?' said one soldier.

'We'll take a look and see,' said another.

'Some of those nobles run fast.'

'They can do that when they see their family's throats cut,' said the first soldier, and laughed.

General Talbot lifted his sword and began to get up. Crutch grabbed his sword hand, pushed it down, and shook his head.

'The only good noble is a dead noble.'

'Except for Lord Rothchester. He gives us food and coin.'

'Another month with him paying us, and we'll all be rich.'

'It's a dead end,' said the first soldier.

'Can't see any noble coming down this alley anyway. Might get their feet dirty.'

'That's the truth,' said the first soldier as they turned and walked out of the alley.

'Should have let me gut the swine,' whispered General Talbot after they were gone.

'Then we'd all be dead,' whispered Crutch. 'Even if we got the best of those four, they'd sound the alarm for their mates, and this alley would be overrun with soldiers. Remember, they won't just kill us. They'll kill your wife and your son too.'

'Killing me might be a bit harder than they think,' whispered Young Lord Talbot.

'That's true,' whispered Crutch, 'but what about your mother? How do you think she'd go in a sword fight?'

Young Lord Talbot nodded. Crutch knew once Young Lord Talbot understood the strategy was to get everyone out alive, he'd also understand the weakness of their position. Strategically, the young lord was a genius.

'Let's get into the sewers where they can't see us,' whispered Crutch, breaking cover and sliding the sewer cover off again.

He kept a watch on the street as Lady Talbot, General Talbot, and Young Lord Talbot climbed down the ladder into the sewers. Crutch followed them and slid the sewer cover over.

'We need to move fast,' whispered Crutch. 'We want to catch up to the admiral so we can all go up into the palace together.

Crutch led the way, driving along with his cane and his good leg, only slowing to check the street above when they came to a sewer grate above them. The general and Lady Talbot kept pace with him, which was a relief.

Crutch knew Young Lord Talbot would keep up easily, but he was worried the general and Lady Talbot might not be able to. Maybe they carried less weight after a couple of months on meagre rations.

After five minutes, Crutch could see what he hoped was the admiral up ahead. As they got closer, he could see it was the admiral, Abagail, and Lady Hastings.

The admiral and the general shook hands while Lady Hastings and Lady Talbot hugged.

'Why did you stop?' whispered Crutch.

'You can't hear them now, but there's voices up ahead,' whispered the admiral.

Crutch hoped the true royals wouldn't be in this part of the sewers. That was a bad sign. The sewers close to the palace wouldn't be a good place to stash food and supplies. It was more likely there were soldiers up ahead preparing to storm the palace or attack in some other way.

'Did you see them?' whispered Crutch.

'No,' said the admiral. 'They didn't see us either.'

'Good,' said Crutch. 'We'll try to go around them to get to the side entrance of the palace.'

Crutch took the lead again, starting by going at right angles to the direction they'd been travelling. They went down the stone block sewers for about five hundred yards, moving slowly, with Crutch checking down every intersection before they turned left again.

He was happy it was dry season and it wasn't raining. At least they wouldn't have to worry about surges of sewerage submerging them in shit and piss. But if they ran into the soldiers who wanted to kill them, that would land them in a much bigger pile of shit.

Crutch knew these sewers well, but it had been a few years since he'd been down here. If he was right, heading the way they went now would get them to a street bedside the palace. They could peer through the grates on the street to get as close as possible to the side entrance the admiral told him about.

They were only about fifty yards from Crutch's goal when he heard the voices. They came from somewhere to his left. He put his hand up to get everyone to stop and crept to the next intersection. When he looked around the corner, he could see torches and thirty or forty soldiers at least two hundred yards away.

Crutch had travelled in these sewers so long, he could navigate them without a torch. The moonlight and street lights coming through the grates and his knowledge of exactly where he was were enough for him.

It was worth the chance to sneak past. If they went quietly and quickly, Crutch figured they wouldn't be seen. He went back to the group.

'We need to pass through this junction,' whispered Crutch. 'The grate we want to get to is just fifty yards ahead of us. I say we sneak through.'

'Sounds like a good enough plan,' said the admiral. The general nodded.

'Okay,' whispered Crutch. 'Go through the junction quick as you can while doing it quietly. If they see us, we run to that grate up there, straight up the ladder, and to the entrance at the side of the palace. Can you lead us to the entrance when we're on the street, admiral?'

'I can,' whispered admiral Hastings.

'Thank you,' whispered Crutch. 'Everyone understand what we're doing?'

They all nodded. Abagail looked terrified.

'You'll be okay, Abagail,' whispered Crutch and squeezed her hand. 'I won't let anything happen to you.'

Abagail squeezed his hand back.

Crutch glanced around the corner, squinting his eyes, trying to pick out if anyone looked their way. When he thought most of the soldiers' backs were turned, he waved them through.

Young Lord Talbot went first, swift and silent.

Lady Talbot and Lady Hastings went next. They were nervous, but they made it through. Crutch motioned for them all to keep moving up to the ladder underneath the sewer grate up ahead.

Admiral Hastings and General Talbot went next. They were half way across when Crutch heard a soldier shout.

'There's someone down there! I think it's the admiral!'

'Run!' yelled Crutch.

Young Lord Talbot was already climbing the ladder. He got to the top, slid off the sewer grate by himself, and started helping out his mother, Lady Hastings, and Abagail.

Crutch was right behind the admiral and the general, who ran fast. Six feet from the bottom of the ladder, the general slipped on the wet stone blocks underneath his bare feet and slid sideways into the sewer. He went in head first and came up covered in piss and shit.

Crutch grabbed his hand and helped to pull him back onto the walkway next to the sewer line. The admiral was already climbing when the general went up the ladder, dripping with sewerage. Crutch followed right behind, enduring the splashing and dripping on him.

When he got to the top, Crutch looked down the sewer the way they'd come and could see at least twenty soldiers coming around the corner of the junction. He expected there'd be more behind them.

Crutch came up on the street, and Admiral Hastings led their group towards an iron door a hundred yards away. Crutch looked to his left and saw hundreds of soldiers with weapons just a couple of hundred yards away, near the front of the palace.

As he fell in behind the admiral and the rest of their group, he saw the soldiers near the front of the palace start yelling and running towards them. The first of the soldiers who were in the sewers came up too.

'It's Admiral Hastings. Open the door!' yelled the admiral when he was fifty yards away.

A slot in the door slid open, and a guard peered out.

Crutch looked behind him. Soldiers poured down the street, screaming at the top of their lungs. At least twenty soldiers from out of the sewers headed for them, and still more climbed out.

'Open the bloody door!' yelled Admiral Hastings. 'What are you waiting for?'

'How do we know you're not part of the true royals?' said the palace guard.

'Look behind you, man,' yelled General Talbot. 'Do you think they'd be chasing us if we were their friends?'

Chapter 45
If We Can't Trust Him

As if to drive home the general's point, a spear clanged into the stone wall of the palace inches from him.

The first soldier reached Crutch, swinging his sword as the guard opened the door. Crutch ducked under the sword, stabbed the soldier in the guts, then moved back. General Talbot grabbed him by the shirt and pulled him inside. The door slammed shut, and the guard pulled heavy metal bars across, securing the door in place.

They were in a small room with another heavy iron door on the other side. The guard led them to the next door and unlocked it. Crutch could hear the soldiers pounding on the first door as they went through the second.

'We're safe for now,' said General Talbot as two palace guards led them through a tunnel in the palace. Above them were large holes in the stone roof. At each was a palace guard with a long spear. 'Is everyone okay?'

Abagail looked at Crutch with concern written on her face. 'You're covered in blood.'

Crutch felt himself over. 'I'm fine.'

'Thank goodness,' said Abagail.

'Are you okay?' said Crutch.

'I'm not hurt,' said Abagail.

'I'm so glad to hear that,' said Crutch, squeezing Abagail's hand.

'How did you know those sewers so well?' said Lady Hastings.

'I grew up there,' said Crutch.

'In the sewers?'

'Yes,' said Crutch. 'And on the streets.'

Crutch didn't see any point in pretending to be someone he wasn't. They may as well know where he came from. He'd saved the admiral, Abagail, and Lady Hastings twice now. If that wasn't good enough for them, then nothing ever would be.

Lady Hastings looked at Crutch as if she'd never really seen him before, but now it all made sense.

'That must have been horrible, but I'm glad you did,' she said, putting her hand on his arm. 'Thank you.'

Once they knew they were all unharmed, the guards led them deep into the palace. They came to a room with two guards in front of double doors.

'Only myself and Admiral Hastings can go in the war room,' said General Talbot.

'I would like Crutch to come with us,' said the Admiral.

'Yes. Good idea,' said the general. 'Young Lord Talbot, can you watch over Miss Abagail, Lady Hastings, and your mother for us?'

Young Lord Talbot looked at his father and puffed out his chest. 'I will guard them with my life, father.'

'I know you will.'

Crutch followed Admiral Hastings and General Talbot into the war room, past the two king's guards at the door. Inside were the king and four old men standing around a table. Next to the king was the chief counsel. Crutch recognised him from a picture he'd seen in a book from when the chief counsel was much younger.

'Glad you could join us, general,' said King Vargus. 'It seems quite a few of your soldiers would like to join the party too.'

'Not my doing your majesty,' said General Talbot.

'Guards. Please remove Corporal Crutch from the war room,' said the chief counsel. 'A mere commoner does not belong here.'

'You'll do nothing of the sort,' said General Talbot. 'If it wasn't for Corporal Crutch, I'd be dead along with my family.'

'So would I,' said Admiral Hastings. 'Corporal Crutch is here on my invitation.'

'As you wish,' said the chief counsel. 'Apparently we have no standards now. Anyone off the street is welcome in his majesty's war room. Come dressed in your undergarments covered in...what is that you're covered in General Talbot?'

'I fell while running for my life through the sewers,' said General Talbot.

'It smells like it,' said the chief counsel. 'Seems your appearance has gone to shit just like your army.'

'Enough,' said the king. 'I recognise Corporal Crutch. Iron cross winner. If we can't trust him, then we can't trust anyone. Did you see the situation outside, general?'

'I got a glimpse,' said General Talbot. 'Several hundred soldiers at the gates. More in the city. It seems Lord Rothchester is paying them to kill nobles who aren't part of his cause.'

Crutch watched the king's guard standing close to the chief counsel. Something was off about him. He couldn't tell what. Maybe he was just nervous that at any time he'd be the first line of defence as several hundred soldiers came to execute the king.

'The navy?' said the king.

'I can't say for certain,' said Admiral Hastings. 'But I expect most of our warships will now be anchored in the harbour out of range of the ballistas on the docks. That is the procedure for when the city faces a land attack.'

'You started this, you traitor!' yelled the king's guard, drawing a dagger and plunging into the back of the chief counsel.

Crutch used his walking cane to leap onto the table as the king's guard drew his dagger out of the kings counsel and lifted it up, ready to plunge down into the king. Crutch landed on the table, overbalanced, and started falling head first.

He released the blade on his cane as he fell, pushed it forward and caught the king's guard in the guts as he landed on top of him. Crutch bit into the king's guard's face, ripping his nose off.

Crutch drew his own dagger as the king's guard stabbed down at him. He twisted just enough so the knife grazed his shoulder instead of plunging into the top of his neck, then Crutch stabbed his dagger into the side of the king's guard's head.

'What is going on?' said King Vargus as Crutch looked up, straddling the body of the king's guard with the king's counsel dead next to him.

'Your guard was one of the true royals,' said Crutch.

'My own guard. This is an outrage,' said King Vargus. 'It seems I owe you my life corporal.'

'Just doing my duty as a royal marine to protect my king, your majesty,' said Crutch.

'At least there's one man here I can trust,' said King Vargus. 'Please close and lock the doors to the war room Admiral Hastings. Let's not make it easy for any more of my guards to try to kill me tonight.'

As the admiral locked the doors, Crutch thought the king was remarkably calm for a man who'd just survived an assassination attempt. He must be exceptionally brave or an exceptionally good actor.

'Should we remove the bodies?' said General Talbot.

'Leave them there,' said King Vargus. 'I don't want to take the risk of letting anyone else in this room. Does anyone have any ideas on how to deal with the soldiers at the palace gates?'

'If we could get word to them, we could have the marines and sailors on the warships come ashore and take back the city,' said Admiral Hastings.

'At what cost?' said King Vargus. Killing half my army and half of my navy to restore order would leave Ironbay as easy pickings for the Estovians.'

'I expect that's exactly what Emporer Solokov wants,' said General Talbot.

'Any other ideas?'

'We could try talking them into laying down their arms,' said General Talbot.

'How do you propose to do that?' said King Vargus.

'We appeal to their common decency as Ironborn men. Tell them they should lay down arms before they're forced to fight against the navy, Ironborn fighting Ironborn.'

'The soldiers at the gate have been poisoned against the nobility,' said Admiral Hastings. 'Paid to kill us in our sleep. They won't listen to you, general. They won't listen to any noble.'

'No. But they might listen to one of their own. Someone who led them to victory on the Kona Track.'

They all looked at Crutch. Then Crutch realised the position he was in. He had to think fast. Get this right, and he might save the lives of some good men. Get it wrong, and there would be more blood in the streets, and Ironbay would be so weak that Estovia could invade and rip what was left to pieces in days.

'I might be able to convince the soldiers to give up this coup, but it will take a few concessions, your majesty,' said Crutch.

'What kind of concessions?' said King Vargus.

'No executions or prison for the soldiers.'

'You want me to pardon them after they tried to kill me?' said the king.

'It's Lord Rothchester and his true royals who want to kill you, your majesty. The soldiers were just following orders and trying to feed their families.'

'Orders that amounted to treason,' said King Vargus.

'Execute all the nobles you'd like, but if you execute the soldiers or throw some of them in prison, they'll rise up against you again, your majesty. The only way you can keep the peace is to get the soldiers back onside.'

'And how do you propose to do that?' said the king.

'The food Lord Rothchester has stashed in the sewers. We have a good idea of where it is. With the soldiers' help, we can reclaim it.'

'And after you reclaim it?'

'We let the soldiers distribute the food to the people of Ironbay. To the commoners.'

'That should quell the unrest in the city,' said King Vargus.

'And it will help me convince them of the truth, your majesty.'

'The truth?'

'Lord Rothchester duped them into believing their king stockpiled food while they starved. In reality, it was Lord Rothchester using Estovian money to buy the food coming into Ironbay and stashing it in the sewers.'

'How is it Corporal Crutch here has a better grasp on the situation than my advisors?' said King Vargus.

'Corporal Crutch has been working undercover with Office 451 in the navy office,' said one of the men on the council.

'Please don't blame your advisors,' said Crutch. 'I just put the pieces of the puzzle together myself tonight, and we've been a little busy running for our lives. This is the first chance I've had to share it.'

Crutch knew he played a dangerous game here. He needed everyone in this room onside to save the lives of the soldiers at the gates of the palace. Getting the favour of the advisors and the king would help him avoid making enemies and increase the chances that no one else had to die for Lord Rothchester's folly.

'So the soldiers at the gates to my palace are conveniently blameless for this uprising?' said the king.

'Nearly all those soldiers are following orders, your majesty,' said Crutch. 'Apart from the three or four who are nobles and co-conspirators with Lord Rothchester.'

'Why is it your plan seems to involve the execution of so many nobles while I set all the commoners free?' said King Vargus.

'Because it's the nobles who are responsible for all of this,' said Crutch.

'I don't have much of a choice, do I?' said King Vargus.

'I can't see one, your majesty,' said Crutch. 'If we can't convince the soldiers to stand down, it's just a matter of time before they get into the palace and overrun your guards.'

'Are there any other concessions?' said King Vargus.

'Just one small request, your majesty. It's more personal in nature.'

Chapter 46
My Fellow Soldiers

Crutch had never seen the inside of the palace, and he'd never been inside the front gates. There were twenty palace guards, fully armed, looking nervous.

Just outside the gates, hundreds of soldiers yelled and pushed against the iron bars. Amongst the soldiers, he could see men he'd served with on the Kona Track. It looked like they were officers in the regular army now. Good men, brave men, with their lives in the balance because Lord Rothchester had sold them a dirty lie.

Crutch walked forward until they could see him.

'My fellow soldiers,' he yelled.

They kept right on yelling and pushing.

'My fellow soldiers,' yelled Crutch, this time louder.

The yelling died down, and murmurs came from the soldiers.

'It's Lieutenant Crutch.'

'He's trying to talk to us.'

'Quiet men.'

'My fellow soldiers,' said Crutch, quieter now as the soldiers fell into silence. 'I'm Corporal Crutch. I fought with some of you on the Kona Track.'

'That you did,' said one soldier.

'No one else could have got us back alive.'

'Others of you might know me as the iron cross winner,' said Crutch. 'One of the siege breakers. But more than anything, I'm a marine, just another boy from Ironbay like you, trying to make my way in this world, trying to get enough food to eat each day, and care for the people I love.'

'That's a lot harder when the king is stockpiling food in the palace,' said one soldier.

'Let us in there, and we'll make sure Ironbay gets fed,' said another soldier.

'I've just been inside the palace,' said Crutch. 'There is no food stockpiled in there.'

'Sorry if we don't believe you, Lieutenant Crutch. Let us in so we can take a look for ourselves.'

'I know how you all feel,' said Crutch. 'All your life, some lord, some noble, has been telling you what to do, giving you the scraps from their table while they get fat on your work. Hiding in their mansions while you fight their battles for them.'

'The only good noble's a dead noble.'

'Kill 'em all!'

That was the kind of talk that would get all these soldiers killed. Crutch continued.

'And when Lord Rothchester told you the king had all the food coming into Ironbay and stockpiled it for his noble friends, of course you believed him. But he was lying to you.

'Lord Rothchester bought up every crate of food he could coming into Ironbay and stashed them all in the sewers. Some of you guarded that food, so you know it's there.'

'He told us he bought that food to stop Ironbay from starving.'

'There it is again,' said Crutch. 'Another noble lying to you. All the food that went missing, it's all right there in the sewers. Did any of you wonder why only a cart or two would leave the sewers into the city?'

'That's true. Most of it's still there.'

'Lord Rothchester took out just enough food so he could have fancy banquets with his noble friends. He never gave any of it to commoners like you and me. It's Lord Rothchester who's been starving Ironbay.'

'That bastard.'

'That's not the worst of it,' said Crutch. 'Lord Rothchester took money from the Estovians to buy the food. That filthy lord is in bed with the Estovians. If he had his way, we'd all be bowing down to Emporer Solokov.'

'That lying sack of shit.'

'We'll rip him to pieces.'

The soldiers started yelling again. Crutch put his hands up.

'Men, please. Lord Rothchester will get his reckoning, but right now there's something much more important we need to do. There's a way we can set this all right, and we can get it done tonight. I say we get every wagon and every cart we can find, and we go down the sewers, get all the food down there, and give it all out to the people of Ironbay.'

A cheer went up from the soldiers.

'Who's with me?' yelled Crutch. 'Who wants to feed the people of Ironbay?'

Crutch walked at the head of several hundred soldiers. Some had sacks. Some had wagons, some being pulled by soldiers, some by horses. There were food carts and wheelbarrows. Anything that could carry food.

As they went, Crutch told them to put empty crates in the alleys onto the wagons so they could fill them with food. Spirits were high, and they made quite the noise as they talked and cheered, moving through the city.

Crutch saw civilians looking out their windows as they passed to see where the noise was coming from.

'What is going on?' yelled one old woman from a first-story building.

'Food. We're getting you food!' yelled a soldier.

'Food? Wait. I'm coming down.'

'Please stay inside,' yelled Crutch. 'We'll bring the food to you when we have it.'

The last thing they needed was a crush of starving people like Igor's kitchen at Teevilgrad.

'Tell everyone to stay inside and wait for us to bring the food to them,' said Crutch to the officers around him.

One of the soldiers told them where one stash of food was hidden. That was as good a place to start as any. He hoped the sheer force of numbers would be enough for any soldiers or hired thugs guarding the food to give up without a fight, but he knew there was a good chance more people would die tonight.

Crutch slid off the sewer grate and went down first, followed by dozens of soldiers. Captain Travis was right behind him. Crutch stopped ten yards from the first guards.

'You can't come in this way,' said one guard. 'There's nothin' down here but shit and piss.'

'Shit and piss and a big stash of food crates,' said Crutch.

'I'm not to let anyone through,' said the guard, the hands holding his sword shaking when he saw the number of soldiers coming down the sewers towards him.

'What's your name, soldier?' said Crutch.

'Robick.'

'Do you know who I am?' said Crutch.

'Everyone knows who you are. You're the iron cross winner.'

'That's right. Behind me are about a hundred soldiers, and there are another four hundred or so in the streets above us. We've all come here to get this food and to give it out to the starving people of Ironbay.'

'Give it out?'

'That's right, Robick. Now, when I saw you, I thought, here's a man who likes helping people and doesn't mind doing a little heavy lifting. What I'd like is for you to help us get the food I know is hidden just around the corner here, onto the wagons and carts we've got up in the street. And then help us give all that food out. Would you and your friends like to do that?'

'We would,' said Robick, looking nervously at the soldiers who kept coming down the sewer line.

'You could start by sheathing that sword,' said Crutch. 'And tell your good friends to do the same.'

'Of course,' said Robick, sliding his sword back into its sheath. 'Put away your weapons, men. We're giving this food away.'

'Indeed, we are,' said Crutch, patting Robick on the shoulder. 'One more thing. Could you tell us where the other stashes of food are down here in the sewers?'

'I can tell you two,' said Robick. 'Is that enough?'

'It's a start,' said Crutch. 'We have a lot of people to feed.'

The soldiers made a chain, taking food out of the crates in the sewers, then passing it along the chain and up through the open sewer grates. Crutch had the soldiers fill as many different carts, wagons, sacks, and wheelbarrows as they could before he sent them into the city to feed the people of Ironbay. He wanted to be sure the soldiers wouldn't be crushed by desperate, starving civilians.

'All you officers go ahead of the soldiers carrying food and tell people to stay inside,' said Crutch. 'Tell them you'll bring the food to them, and there's plenty more to come. Tell them everyone will get some food tonight and they need to be patient.'

The officers did the best they could, but after weeks of going hungry, people were desperate. Once word got out that there was food, people came out of their homes onto the streets. They begged and pushed, hoping to get anything to feed themselves and their children.

After the first few hours, the mood began to change. Crutch kept the food coming. Cart after cart, wagon after wagon. Women hugged and kissed the soldiers bringing the food.

When people who'd already eaten started getting more food delivered to them, celebrations broke out in the streets. Crutch watched people singing and dancing as they feasted on fruit, and vegetables, and ham.

For the people of Ironbay the famine was over.

Chapter 47
Teaching Monkeys To Dance

The next day, the city had calmed down enough that the navy ships felt safe to come back to the docks. Crutch had one more thing he wanted to do in the city before going back to the Auld Faithful.

He was walking near the city square when Ghost, the street urchin, waved him over.

'Found that man ye been lookin' for,' said Ghost.

'Where is he?' said Crutch.

'In the sewers under the leather warehouse. Ye know how to get there?'

'I do,' said Crutch. 'Have you got food?'

'I do, thanks to you,' said Ghost.

'Happy to hear that. Take this.' Crutch slipped a silver piece into his hand.

'Thank you,' said Ghost, smiling.

You knew you'd done some good when you made a street urchin smile.

Crutch headed for the leather warehouse. Getting underneath it was tricky. You had to go through a maze of turns and junctions in the sewers, but Crutch knew them well.

Once he was close, Crutch went down an alley, slid off the sewer grate, and climbed down. After a couple of minutes of walking on the slippery stone floor of the sewer walkway, he could see a light up ahead from one of the more open sections in the sewer that looked a little like rooms.

Candlelight. He crept forward and peered around the entrance. Lord Rothchester sat there by himself at a wooden desk with a candle on it, like he was sitting in an office.

'Come on in Corporal Crutch,' said Lord Rothchester. 'I've been expecting you.'

Crutch walked into the light.

'They tell me you were responsible for ending our rightful reclamation of the throne.'

'Your coup, you mean,' said Crutch.

'It's not a coup if the man on the throne is not the true king,' said Lord Rothchester.

'Why did your reclamation have to involve starving the innocent citizens of Ironbay?'

'Mere commoners,' said Lord Rothchester. 'Doesn't matter how many of them die; there's always more where they came from. They breed like the filthy rats in these sewers.'

'Must really stick in your craw then,' said Crutch. 'A filthy commoner like me messing up your plans.'

'It certainly does,' said Lord Rothchester. 'That's why I brought some friends of mine with me. They'll be dealing you some cold steel while I take a ship out of Ironbay. I'll be back with an army to finish the job I started. Boys!'

A dozen boys ranging in age from twelve to eighteen years, armed with knives, appeared out of the sewers running off from the chamber they were in. Crutch could see all the knives had black handles, some painted black, some black leather, some coated in charcoal from the fire.

Lord Rothchester looked surprised when Crutch laughed.

'Hello, Bram,' said Crutch.

'Hi Crutch. He fell for it just like you said he would.'

'What is this?' said Lord Rothchester, rising from the table.

'Bram and I have known each other for years,' said Crutch. 'We both grew up in these sewers. He's a filthy commoner just like me.'

'You betrayed me,' said Lord Rothchester, turning towards Bram. 'How dare you, you filth!'

Bram stepped forward and punched Lord Rothchester in the side of the guts.

'Better be a bit more careful what you say to Bram,' said Crutch. 'He might take it personally. I saw him kill a lot of men back on the Kona Track. Much better men than you.'

'Better men than me?' said Lord Rothchester, clutching his side and speaking between gasps. 'You don't know the first thing about loyalty or being a good man.'

Bram slammed his fist into the side of Lord Rochester's guts again. Harder this time.

Crutch moved in close, so his face was just inches from the lord.

'Bram knows more about loyalty than you ever will. He stood and fought shoulder to shoulder with me on the Kona Track while our mates died around us. All so fat toads like you could eat the food that comes from Papageenar.

'You're a coward and a traitor, Rothchester. Taking money from the Estovians to starve the people of Ironbay while you feast with your fat friends in your fancy mansions.'

'Just get it over with and kill me,' said Lord Rothchester. 'I can't abide any more of your lecturing.'

'We're not going to kill you,' said Crutch. 'We have a much better plan. Did you bring the sign we talked about, Bram?'

Bram smiled. 'I did.' One of the black knives handed Crutch a sign made of wood. The sign had a rope attached to it, so you could hang it around someone's neck.

'Nice work,' said Crutch. 'You even got the spelling right.'

'The black knives has its very own teacher now,' said Bram. 'We're all learning to read and write.'

'You can teach a monkey to dance,' said Lord Rothchester. 'That doesn't make it a man.'

Bram drew back his fist to punch the lord again, then thought better of it. 'Can me and the boys come with you? We've had to listen to this scumhole for weeks. It'll be nice to see this.'

'That would be delightful,' said Crutch, smiling. 'Shall we?'

They walked Lord Rothchester's through the sewers, got him up onto the street, then tied his hands behind his back and put the sign around his neck. The sign had the words 'The traitor who stole your food' painted on it in large red letters.

Bram's black knives went ahead of them and let everyone in the streets know who was coming. At first, people scowled and yelled at Lord Rothchester. He cringed as they hurled their insults.

Then people got more creative. Crutch kept a little distance from the lord, prodding him forward with his walking cane as people spat on him and threw rocks at him.

One woman disappeared into her small home and came out with a piss pot. Crutch ducked to the side as she threw the contents all over Lord Rothchester.

'Nice one,' said Bram.

'I love a good party,' said Crutch.

As much as Crutch would have liked to see it, they didn't let the people hit Lord Rothchester. Crutch knew once they got started on that there was no way the lord would get out of it alive, and Crutch really wanted him alive. At least long enough for what came next.

'I hope the king rips your guts out and cuts off your balls while you're still breathing,' yelled one woman who held a baby in her arms.

'They should burn you alive,' yelled another mother who had a little boy clinging to her leg.

It was frightening to see ordinary housewives so eager to see someone killed in the most horrible ways possible. It's awful what seeing her children starve can do to a woman.

They pushed on with Bram's black knives, telling people as they passed to stick to the rules.

'You can yell at him and throw things at him but you can't hit him or jump on him.'

'I can throw things at him?' said one woman.

'Well, yes, but...'

The woman disappeared inside and came out with a heavy iron pot. Before anyone could stop her, she flung it at Lord Rothchester with a strength that belied her small size. The pot hit the lord in the knee, and he fell to the cobblestones, groaning.

'How was that?' said the woman.

'No throwing pots!' yelled Crutch. 'Or frypans!'

A woman holding a heavy iron frying pan over her head lowered it, disappointed.

Bram grabbed Lord Rothchester by the collar and pulled him back up to his feet.

'Keep walking your lordship,' said Crutch, pushing him forward with his walking cane. 'Stop here, and there's no way we can keep this crowd from ripping you to pieces.'

It was a long walk to the palace gates for Lord Rothchester. Crutch and Bram enjoyed it though, chatting about all the ways he was helping the black knives learn how to read, write, and master real professions beyond robbery and theft.

Lord Rothchester was the worst for wear when he got there, covered in piss and shit, and limping on the knee that was injured by the iron pot.

'Could you take a message to the king?' said Crutch to the king's guard at the gate.

'What would you like me to tell him, Corporal Crutch?' said the guard.

'Inform his majesty that we've captured the leader of the true royals, one Lord Rothchester. Also, that I have a very modest request.'

'I'll tell him myself,' said the guard, and ran off.

'Well, this had been fun,' said Crutch. 'We should spend time together more often. Thank you for your help, Bram. I'll let the king know you and the black knives were responsible for hunting down and capturing Lord Rothchester.'

'Really?'

'Of course. You won't have to worry about being a deserter any more. I'll see if I can get you some funding for what you're doing with the black knives.'

'That'd be great,' said Bram. 'The money we got from this turd has already helped us hire a teacher and train up some of the boys.'

'Did you hear that, Lord Rothchester?' said Crutch, prodding at him with his walking cane. 'Your money has taught some of us monkeys to dance. A bit more from the king, and Bram here might work up his own troupe. Pity you won't be alive to see it.'

'Fuck you,' said Lord Rothchester.

'No fuck you,' said Crutch. 'The money you gave Bram here did more good in a few weeks than you've done with all your stinking gold sovereigns and fancy jewels in a lifetime.'

'You're still scum,' said Lord Rothchester.

'Scum who outwitted you and brought you to justice,' said Crutch.

Bram punched Lord Rothchester in the balls and spat in his face. 'That's for Midge and the other urchins you had killed. All the black knives will be there cheering at your execution, you piece of shit.'

'Nice touch,' said Crutch as Lord Rothchester dropped to his knees, writhing in pain.

'Everyone else in Ironbay had their chance,' said Bram. I didn't want to miss out.'

The guard returned to the gates. 'The king says he's most eager to meet Lord Rothchester. You can bring him straight up.' The guard unlocked a side door to let Crutch and Lord Rothchester through. Crutch nodded Bram goodbye, pulled Lord Rothchester to his feet and pushed him through the door.

'That sounds promising, doesn't it, Lord Rothchester?' said Crutch. 'The king is eager to meet you. I wonder if he'll have tea and cakes.'

Chapter 48
Black Tower

After dark, Cedric, Damen, Crutch, and Sergeant Zander quietly waited outside the gates of Ironbay prison. After a few minutes, Tugry appeared.

'Always nice to see the siege breakers again,' said Tugry.

'Nice to see you too,' said Sergeant Zander.

'You've got someone new with ya,' said Tugry as he unlocked the gates.

'He's a friend of Prince Alderon,' said Sergeant Zander. 'They grew up together.'

'Hard to have ya friends in prison,' said Tugry.

'Thank you for doing this,' said Damen as they all walked through the gates.

'It's the decent thing to do,' said Tugry. 'The king'll be upset if he finds out, but what's he gonna do. Throw me in prison?'

'Is the prince alright?' said Damen.

'He's in good spirits,' said Tugry. 'Tells us all stories and jokes with us. A very fine man he is.' They walked through a stone tiled courtyard, then around the walls of the prison.

'Got a bit of a climb ahead of us,' said Tugry. 'They've got your friend in the Black Tower.'

Crutch looked up. The tower went up a good thirty yards above them. Two guards stood on each side of an iron door at the base.

'Taking these men up for a quiet visit,' said Tugry. 'If you know what I mean?'

The guards nodded.

Tugry unlocked the iron door and heaved it open.

'These iron doors get heavier every year I get older,' said Tugry.

After they were inside, Tugry closed and locked the door behind them. Then they climbed up a set of stone stairs that wound around, and up.

'Stairs get longer too,' said Tugry, breathing hard. 'Haven't climbed this tower in years. Seems a lot higher than when I was a young guard.'

Eventually, they came out onto a landing made of stone blocks. There was a door made of iron bars, flanked by two more guards.

'Got some quiet visitors for the prince,' said Tugry to the guards.

'What visitors?' said one guard.

'Never saw anyone,' said the other.

'Good lads,' said Tugry, unlocking the door. 'See me later for some rum. Still got a barrel in me office.'

Tugry led them through to a single barred cell made of stone blocks with a barred window in the rear. There was a bed and a desk. Prince Alderon stood up and came to the bars of the cell when he saw them come in.

'Prince Alderon,' said Damen. 'Are you okay?'

'I'm good. They're looking after me well.'

'Are they feeding you?' said Damen. 'Food has been short in the city.'

'They have been feeding me well. You shouldn't be worrying yourself over me. I told you I'm fine.'

'That's a relief,' said Damen.

'What have you been up to?' said Prince Alderon.

'Working with the marines to find who was behind stealing the city's food supply.'

'Well, that sounds like a noble venture,' said the prince. 'I'm glad you marines are finding a good use for Damen's sword.'

'He's been a great help to us,' said Sergeant Zander.

'It's a foul thing,' said Damen. 'People went hungry all over the city. Corporal Crutch caught him today. I'd like to cut his heart out.'

'You might want to run that by the sergeant first,' said Prince Alderon. 'It's not just me and you now. You have to take commands from your sergeant and your corporal.'

'I will,' said Damen. 'Then I'll cut his hearts out.'

'Being a marine hasn't changed you then,' said Prince Alderon.

'Damen, could you leave me with Crutch and Captain Beaumont for a few minutes,' said Prince Alderon. 'There's something I need to discuss with them.'

Tugry took Sergeant Zander and Damen out onto the landing, where Sergeant Zander was promising Tugry a trip to the Ironhook tavern and as much rum as he could drink.

'They're going to hang me tomorrow,' whispered Prince Alderon.

'What?' whispered Crutch.

'Treason,' whispered the prince. 'Hanging is a good outcome. Better than many of the other alternatives for treason.'

'But you're the prince,' whispered Crutch. 'They can't hang you.'

'They say I'm a pretender,' whispered Prince Alderon.

'We can get you out of here,' whispered Crutch.

'You will not,' whispered Prince Alderon. 'That would just put you on the run, if you could even get out of the tower and the prison. We'd never survive.'

'The prince is right,' whispered Cedric. 'We'd be running from Ironbay and Estovia. There'd be no safe place for us.'

'We could go to Skull Cove,' whispered Crutch.

'Any plan that involves escaping to Skull Cove is no plan at all,' whispered Cedric. 'And after what happened the last time you were there, I doubt they'd be welcoming any of us.'

'I need you to make me a promise,' whispered Prince Alderon.

'Anything,' whispered Cedric.

'Promise me you won't let Damen attend my hanging. Whatever you have to do, he can't be there.'

'It's a small thing to ask,' whispered Cedric. 'I'll make sure it's done.'

'One more thing for you, Crutch,' said Prince Alderon. 'Keep Damen alive. Everything is not what you think. You'll understand one day.'

Chapter 49
Love Letter

That night, when the marines were together, Longshot asked Crutch for a favour.

'Could you write a letter to Sophia for me?'

'Why me?' said Crutch.

'You're the only person I know who has a way with words and can write,' said Longshot.

'I can give it a try,' said Crutch, 'but shouldn't you write this yourself?'

'No,' said Longshot. 'My writing's terrible. If I do it, Sophia will never want to see me again.'

'Sophia lives in Yavenland,' said Crutch. 'There's a good chance you'll never see her again, no matter what you write.'

'Don't say that. It's hard enough as it is.'

'I'm sorry, Longshot. Of course I'll help you write her a letter. Let me get a piece of charcoal to write with.'

'Thank you, Crutch.'

'What do you want to say?'

'Something about Sophia having big, ropey muscles,' said Longshot.

'Don't forget to mention how she's a ruthless killer,' said Sergeant Zander. 'That's a huge plus for any woman.'

'Thanks, Sarge,' said Longshot. 'Yeh, ruthless killer. Put that in. Maybe write about how she cut that Estovian's head off.'

'Perfect!' said Sergeant Zander. 'She'll love that.'

'I got something,' said Quicksilver. 'You gave us directions, but the only direction I needed was the ones to your heart.'

'That has to go in there. That's pure poetry, Quicksilver,' said Longshot.

'Thanks.'

'Anything you want to add, Boulder?' said Crutch.

'Say you love her,' said Boulder.

The marines were silent for a few seconds, then Longshot said, 'I guess we could put that in.'

'You don't think it'll make you look like a nancy boy?' said Quicksilver. Sergeant Zander started at him. 'Sorry Sarge.'

'Okay,' said Longshot. Put in, I love her, but don't make it soppy.'

Crutch scribbled for a minute, then said, 'I think I've got it. Let me read it out for you. Dear Sophia. You gave us directions pointing with your arms that have big, ropey muscles. But the only direction I needed was the ones to your heart. You're a ruthless killer. I remember how you cut that Estovian assassin's head off and sent it to the Estovians in a bloody sack. I love you.'

'That's perfect!' said Longshot.

'Nice one,' said Quicksilver.

'I reckon that would make any woman go weak at the knees,' said Sergeant Zander.

Chapter 50
A Hanging

Cedric, Crutch, and Sergeant Zander left Damen training on the deck of the Auld Faithful with Quicksilver, Longshot, and Boulder. Sergeant Zander told Damen it was so he could practice fighting three opponents at the same time, but the truth was Crutch and Cedric wanted to keep the promise they made to Prince Alderon.

As they walked down the docks, then down King's Way, the people they saw looked happier. No more people pushing at the docks, begging for food. Amazing what a few good meals can do to people's attitude and behaviour.

Hundreds of people walked in the same direction they were, towards the city square. When things go bad, everyone wants someone to blame, thought Crutch. Who they blame doesn't have to make sense, as long as they can yell, and cuss, and rage at someone.

The city square was already full of people when they got there.

'Nothing like a hanging to bring the people of Ironbay out,' said Cedric.

'They look angry,' said Sergeant Zander.

'A couple of months starving will do that,' said Crutch.

The king's herald walked onto the wooden platform the gallows stood on and unrolled a piece of parchment. The crowd fell silent.

'Hear you all this proclamation from his majesty King Vargus. The criminals to be hanged today were responsible for stealing the food supply of Ironbay, leaving the good people of

Ironbay to starve. They were also responsible for an attempted coup and the murder of innocents.'

The crowd booed and hissed as five men were walked onto the wooden platform with their hands tied behind their backs. Crutch recognised three: Prince Alderon, Lord Rothchester and Lord Jelric. The other two he didn't know, but from their bearing he guessed they were nobles too.

It looked like King Vargus had kept the promise he made to Crutch. Or at least if he planned on killing commoners, he wasn't doing it in public.

'On your left, you see their fake prince and pretender to the throne. All have been found guilty of murder, treason, and crimes against the people of Ironbay. They will be hanged until they are dead.'

A cheer went up from the crowd. Crutch's guts churned. He'd brought Prince Alderon all the way from Yavenland just so he could be paraded in front of an angry mob and executed for a crime he had absolutely no part in.

Lord Rothchester and Lord Jelric got what they deserved, but Prince Alderon was a good man who would have made a good king. He should be sitting on a throne making proclamations of his own, not having a noose put around his neck as the executioner did now.

When the last of the nooses were placed, the executioner and his assistants pulled their levers, and the five men dropped to their deaths. The crowd cheered. Crutch looked at Prince Alderon swinging at the end of his rope, his mouth open, his eyes lifeless.

Crutch felt something in him change, like something was broken and couldn't be fixed. He couldn't shake the feeling that this went way beyond leading an innocent man to his death. He'd become the kind of person who could do that, and then walk away without feeling anything.

'At least it was quick,' said Cedric. 'Shall we go?'

Crutch and Sergeant Zander nodded their heads. They felt like they owed Prince Alderon the courtesy of watching him hang, but they didn't need to wallow in it. They walked back along King's Way, away from the city square.

'I don't think they'll be trying to kill us any more,' said Cedric.

'Why's that?' said Sergeant Zander.

'I believe the king's chief counsel and I were the last two men left alive who could identify Prince Alderon. With the prince dead and the chief counsel dead, there's no reason to have me killed.'

'So you think killing you was related to the prince and the true royals?' said Crutch.

'I think the chief counsel was behind the kidnapping of Prince Alderon and collaborated with the Estovians.'

'And he ordered four ships to supply the enemy at the Siege of Crestona and to let Estovian ships through the line?' said Crutch.

'Yes.'

'So he was the reason you lost the fleet during the siege? That makes sense, but why would he do that?'

'Power,' said Cedric. 'The nobles loyal to King Vargus and the chief counsel have grown very rich with land grants and permits and every other favour a king might bestow on them.'

'That explains why the true royals wanted to seize the throne,' said Sergeant Zander.

'You're telling me I helped keep a king in power when he stole the throne?' said Crutch.

'That's possible,' said Cedric. 'But I think it's more likely King Vargus was unaware of the machinations of his chief counsel. King Vargus was crowned almost twenty-five years ago, after the Siege of Crestona. He was a young, naive man.'

'So the chief counsel was acting alone?' said Crutch.

'Not alone, but I suspect without the knowledge of Prince Vargus.'

'We should have just let the soldiers take over,' said Crutch. 'Then Prince Alderon would still be alive, and he could take the throne.'

'That would not have gone well,' said Cedric. 'And it's not what the prince wanted. There's a time for everything.'

'The prince wanted to die?' said Crutch.

'In a manner of speaking,' said Cedric. 'Our Prince Alderon may be one of the bravest, most selfless men I've ever met.'

'I still don't understand it,' said Crutch.

'One day you will,' said Cedric.

'Who's gonna tell Damen that Prince Alderon is dead?' said Sergeant Zander.

'That's my responsibility,' said Cedric.

CHAPTER 51
WHY AM I DIFFERENT?

Crutch, the marines Damen and Cedric were in full dress uniforms. Crutch really didn't want a second iron cross, but General Talbot insisted he be awarded one. To Crutch, it felt like he was being rewarded for sending Prince Alderon to his death.

Workers had dismantled the wooden supports for the nooses, but the presentation for the iron cross was held on the same platform they used to hang Prince Alderon and the true royals just a few days ago.

Crutch stood with the marines, Cedric and Damen, to the side of the platform near the stairs. He looked at those stairs that, for so many people, would be the last walk to their deaths. He wondered what went through Prince Alderon's mind as he made his last steps up to the wooden platform to be hanged.

There was a huge, happy crowd in the city square. With the true royals gone, food flowed freely into Ironbay off the ships and through the docks. Add that to the food Crutch had helped liberate and distribute to the people, and everyone was well fed for the first time in weeks.

'Welcome to this special medal presentation, citizens of Ironbay,' yelled the herald in his booming voice. 'For single handedly rescuing both the admiral and the general of Ironbay, for capturing the traitorous leader of the attempted coup of Ironbay, and for liberating the stolen food and returning it to the people of Ironbay…'

The crowd in the city square erupted in cheers. Getting food was clearly a big deal to them at present.

'For the first time in the history of Ironbay, double iron cross winner, your marine, your siege breaker, and hero of the Kona track, Corporal Crutch!'

'That's your cue,' said Cedric, smiling as the crowd in the city square went wild, clapping and cheering.

Crutch walked up those same stairs Prince Alderon had walked up, onto that same wooden platform. He forced a smile as he went and stood at attention, facing the same crowd who'd cheered the hanging of the prince.

General Talbot pinned the iron cross to his chest, adding to the iron cross and the iron star already there. 'Thank you, Corporal Crutch. Ironbay owes you a great debt, as do I.'

'Thank you, general,' said Crutch, feeling like the debts he'd accrued for his slaughter of innocents could never be repaid.

He looked out into the faces of the people in the city square, cheering and yelling. He wondered how he could be standing on this platform of execution and death feeling so full of guilt when they were so jubilant.

He caught the eye of Bram there with his black knives near the front of the crowd, cheering and clapping louder and harder than anyone. He wondered if they'd see him as their hero from the sewers if they knew he'd helped lead an innocent man to his death.

Most likely, like everyone else here, they wouldn't care. Having a belly full of food was their only real concern. Crutch remembered when that was all he cared about, when he dreamed of a day when he wouldn't have to worry about where to sleep at night or where his next meal came from.

Now that he had a hammock and all the food he wanted, why was his life filled with worries about the future and guilt for the things he'd done? Why couldn't he just be happy like everyone else in the city square? Why did he have to be different?

It was a relief for Crutch to get back to the Auld Faithful and away from all the people congratulating him. Cedric asked him to come into the captain's cabin.

'I received this written declaration from King Vargus while you were busy being lauded as the most decorated marine in history,' said Cedric.

'Really?' said Crutch. 'What does it say?'

'I think you know what it says.'

'Tell me anyway,' said Crutch.

'His Majesty King Vargus is pleased to inform you that your title as Lord Cedric Beaumont has been fully restored with full honours and privileges.'

'Congratulations, Lord Beaumont,' said Crutch.

'Furthermore any suggestions that Lord Cedric Beaumont was a pirate of any kind have been soundly refuted. Lord Beaumont should consider this letter complete vindication that he is a lifetime loyal, faithful subject of his majesty King Vargus.'

'Congratulations,' said Crutch. 'Your reputation is restored.'

'Thank you, Crutch. It means a lot that you thought of me when you were in the thick of it with the king in his war room.'

'I'd still be begging on the streets and living in the sewers of Ironbay if it wasn't for you giving me a chance,' said Crutch. 'I'll never forget it'

'Best decision of my life,' said Cedric. 'I am a little disappointed, though.'

'Why's that?' said Crutch.

'I was getting kind of used to being king of the pirates.'

'There's something else I need to talk to you about,' said Crutch.

'What's on your mind?' said Cedric.

'I'm not sure I can do this any more,' said Crutch.

'What do you mean?'

'We went all the way to Yavenland to bring back Prince Alderon just so he could be hanged,' said Crutch.

'It's a terrible business,' said Cedric, 'but it's not your fault.'

'It's not just that. I've been remembering things, like the way we burned down Quayside with all those innocent villagers. In Teevilgrad, we burned down the Komitav officers accommodation. There were innocent women and children in the building. We just watched it burn.'

'You can't let those things play on your mind,' said Cedric.

'That's the problem,' said Crutch. 'When we burned down Quayside, I felt sick about it for days. In Teevilgrad, I didn't feel anything for those innocent women and children. I'm afraid of who I'm becoming. What I'm becoming.'

'What are you saying?' said Cedric.

'I don't think I can be a marine any more.'

There was a long silence, then Cedric spoke.

'I can ask them to give you a job in the navy office. You've proven your mastery of logistics. I'm sure they can use another supply officer.'

'Really?' said Crutch. Crutch had thought he'd have to find a way to survive on the coin he'd hidden away.

'Of course,' said Cedric. 'You're their double iron cross winner. They'd put you anywhere to keep you in the service.'

Chapter 52
The Nicest Places

Crutch met Abagail at the admiral's residence. She waited for him outside the front doors with two guards Crutch didn't recognise. Abagail smiled, ran down the stairs to meet him on the street, and gave Crutch a huge hug.

'Where's Corporal Levi?' said Crutch.

'He was injured when the soldiers attacked our residence,' said Abagail. 'He's still recovering.'

Crutch hadn't thought about the guards. All things considered, Corporal Levi was lucky to be alive.

'Is it bad?'

'Father says he'll be fine in a few weeks,' said Abagail.

'So no corporal as a chaperone?' said Crutch.

'Father says you're a young man of honour, and you'll treat me with respect and never compromise my reputation.'

'He's right,' said Crutch.

'So what's this surprise? You know I love surprises,' Abagail said, stroking the heart necklace Crutch had given her when he got back from Yavenland.

'If I tell you, it won't be a surprise,' said Crutch. 'We have to walk a couple of blocks to see it.'

'I like walking with you,' said Abagail, putting her hand in his.

Crutch led her down the street a couple of blocks, then up a dark alley.

'We're not going down the sewers again, are we?' said Abagail. 'Once was enough.'

'No sewers,' said Crutch, laughing. 'And we're not going down. We're going up.'

Crutch came to a ladder at the rear of a two-story tavern that was popular with navy officers in training. Inside, Crutch could hear the type of drinking, swearing, and carousing you'd expect from navy crews.

'You take me to the nicest places,' said Abagail, as a man from inside the tavern described his last whore's genitals in graphic detail at a volume loud enough for anyone within a block to hear.

'It's quieter on the roof,' said Crutch. 'Shall we climb?'

'Anything to get away from that,' said Abagail, climbing up first with Crutch right behind her. Abagail had climbed many ladders on many buildings with Crutch since they first met. Now she made it look easy.

They reached the roof, and Crutch led Abagail to the other side.

'There it is,' said Crutch, pointing at the massive brick building with towering double doors on the other side of the street.

'You've shown me better views,' said Abagail.

'But this view is special,' said Crutch.

'Just looks like the navy office to me.'

'It's where I'll be working from now on.'

'What do you mean?'

'I've become the navy's newest supply officer. No more going to sea. No more fighting. I'll be working here just a couple of blocks from where you live.'

'Really?' said Abagail, smiling.

'Really,' said Crutch.

'I take it back,' said Abagail. 'This is the best view you've ever shown me. It's wonderful.'

'Not half as wonderful as you,' said Crutch.

Abagail smiled. 'There's something I wanted to ask you,' she said.

'Yes?'

'Can you teach me to fight?'

'You mean to defend yourself?' said Crutch.

'Yes. And to kill people if they try to attack me.'

'You want to learn how to kill people?'

'Yes,' said Abagail.

'Sergeant Zander and the other marines put you up to this, didn't they?' said Crutch. 'This is all their twisted idea of a practical joke.'

'No. I really want to learn to fight. I never want to feel helpless again.'

'Okay,' said Crutch. 'But not tonight. Tonight, let's look at the navy office and think of all the time we'll have together.'

Abagail kissed Crutch on the cheek. 'You may be the only person in the history of Ironbay who ever made the navy office sound romantic.'

Epilogue

Late that night, Damen went up on deck of the Auld Faithful alone to use the privy. On the ship, the privy was simply a seat on the rail. You sat on it, and your arse hung over the side of the ship. Any business you did would drop down into the water.

No one could see him in the dark, but as Damen pulled down his pants, there was a small heart-shaped birthmark on his left butt cheek.

Thank You
Please Read

As an author, I want to thank you from the bottom of my heart for reading my novel. Without you, the reader, there would be no novel. You make it possible for me to practice the craft I love.

If you enjoyed this novel please consider rating and reviewing it on Amazon. Leaving a review on Amazon is the single most powerful thing you can do for an author with their novels listed there. It helps the novels become more visible on the site which leads to more sales and downloads.

My genuine thanks again for reading this novel.
Andrew Cavanagh

Novels by Andrew Cavanagh available on Amazon include:
Ironborn: Book #1 in The Ironborn Saga
Our Blood Our Land: Book #2 in The Ironborn Saga
Igor's Kitchen: Book #3 in The Ironborn Saga
True Royals: Book #4 in The Ironborn Saga
With more to come.

Download Your FREE Novella:
Wyld Vengance: Prequel to The Ironborn Saga
is available FREE at andrewcavanagh.com

Printed in Dunstable, United Kingdom